Spy Girl

Once Upon a Crime

Carol Hedges

This one is for Martyn and Hannah.
Also many thanks to Lembit Opik, high flyer.

First published in the UK in 2007 by Usborne Publishing Ltd., Usborne House, 83-85 Saffron Hill, London EC1N 8RT, England. www.usborne.com

A CIP catalogue record for this book is available from the British Library.

JFMA JJASOND/15 01658/02 ISBN 9780746078334
Printed in Chippenham, Eastbourne, UK.

You don't look back along time,
but down through it, like water.
Sometimes this comes to the surface,
sometimes that, sometimes nothing.
Nothing goes away.
Margaret Atwood, *Cat's Eye*

The design and performance of each experimental
procedure involving human subjects should be
clearly formulated in an experimental protocol.
This protocol should be submitted for consideration,
comment, guidance and where appropriate, approval,
to a specially appointed ethical review committee,
which must be independent of the investigator,
the sponsor, or any kind of undue influence.
Helsinki Declaration

THE YOUNG FREE-RUNNER LEAPS BETWEEN THE TWO BUILDINGS. HE LANDS LIGHTLY, USING THE RAILINGS OF THE SECOND BUILDING TO STEADY HIMSELF. HE IS FOCUSING ON A POINT WITHIN, AS HE *always does when he is free-running across the rooftops of a city.*

Physical meditation.

There are so many noises and movements that can distract. And right now, right at this moment, it is absolutely vital that he is not distracted. He listens intently, crouching low on the railings, like a cat after a pigeon.

Then he straightens up, leaps off the railings and onto a narrow parapet, which he follows round to the back of the building. There, he climbs a fire escape, leading to the steep incline of the roof, which he scrambles up, using his hands and feet in perfect coordination. Spiderboy.

He feels the adrenaline buzzing. The sense of being invincible.

He is good at this; he is the best.

Now he stands atop the roof, feet perfectly balanced either side of the ridge, and looks around. Stretching ahead of him are other roofs. He sees Big Ben clearly outlined against the night sky, its hands wiping away the present. Minute by minute.

Life. Death. Only jumping-off points, he thinks. When he jumps, will there be angels waiting to catch him? Who knows. Steadying himself, he focuses once more on a point deep within.

The young free-runner takes a deep breath, and leaps into the unknown.

For a moment, nothing happens. It is as if the night is holding its breath. Then the sickening thud echoes round the empty street. His body lies sprawled on the pavement. It does not stir. It is a grotesque puppet finally cut free from its dancing strings.

For a beat, everything is utterly still. Time crawls, broken-backed.

Then the hands on Big Ben move, and the city seems to reclaim itself. A car horn sounds in the distance. Somewhere, a police siren wails. Music spills into the night from the window of a nearby apartment.

Life goes on. The future is already here.

JAZMIN DAWSON POINTED TO SOMETHING IN THE GLASS DISPLAY CASE. "SO, WHAT IS THIS EXACTLY?" SHE ASKED.

THE BOY BEHIND THE MARKET STALL GRINNED AT HER. HE looked like he'd just stepped out of the pages of some retro gothic horror novel. His hair was tiger-striped orange and black, and stood out from his head in long spikes. Dressed from head to toe in black, he had a lethal metal-spiked choker round his neck, and a wrist to elbow black leather cuff on his right arm. He had more rings in his eyebrows than a shower curtain rod, and his nails were painted black with tiny silver stars.

"That's a magnetic tongue stud," the boy said. "All the fun without the pain, yeah?" He opened the case, took out a silver stud and snapped it onto either side of his tongue. "Thee?" he said, sticking his tongue out at her so that she could appreciate the full effect. "Impreth your mateth and annoy your folkth!"

"Neat."

"Want one?"

"I'll definitely think about it."

"Sure." The boy unstudded his tongue. "You live round here?" he inquired.

"Nuh-uh." Jazmin shook her head. "Just visiting."

"Okay. Catch you later," the boy said, sensing that he was wasting his time and that he wasn't going to make a sale.

Jazmin moved away from the stall. She loved London's Camden Market on a Saturday morning. There were so many weird people to stare at, and so much to see. She retraced her steps, and returned to the stall selling incense sticks. A tongue stud, she thought dreamily as she threaded her way with difficulty through the brightly dressed crowd. She imagined the face of her rather strait-laced friend Zeb Stone if she turned up on Monday morning at the learning centre they both attended wearing a tongue stud. He would freak!

Briefly, Jazmin contemplated the mayhem she could unleash if she shelled out for one of the tongue studs. Then she sighed. Life was full of tempting challenges. Regretfully, this was one that she was going to have to knock back. Not that she'd mind freaking out Zeb for one minute, she thought, as she paid for a packet of vanilla incense sticks, but she didn't want her mum going angry on her.

Jazmin was proud of her mum, and the job she did. After all, it wasn't every teenager whose parent worked for the ISA, an international network dedicated to tracking down individuals and organizations that threatened global security. And it wasn't every daughter who got to help out occasionally, too. No wonder Jazmin wanted to become a crime-fighter when she grew up. That was probably why she had made up an aspirational alter ego to inspire her. Jaz Dawson was a kick-ass gorgeous super-spy heroine who wore cool designer outfits, a utility belt packed with state-of-the-art weaponry, and never wimped out on a case.

Making her way to the food area, Jazmin bought herself a large, freshly made apple-and-cinnamon doughnut, and a carton of grape juice. She found a place to sit and eat. It was only mid-morning, but shopping always made her hungry. She was halfway through her food when she saw the retro-goth guy from the jewellery stall making his way towards her table.

"Hi again," he said, setting down a bottle of mineral water and a plate of couscous and roasted vegetable filled pitta bread. "Mind if I join you?"

Secretly wishing she'd chosen something a bit more sophisticated to eat, Jazmin hastily brushed sugar from her upper lip. "Go for it," she said.

"Name's Tony," the boy said. He pointed upwards to his head. "After the hair."

"Excuse me?"

"Tony the Tiger. Used to advertise kids' cereals back in the old days. Vintage joke." The boy settled into his seat.

He dug into his jacket pocket, produced a packet of cigarette papers and a tin, and proceeded to manufacture a small, skinny roll-up.

"Want one?" he said, offering it to her.

"Nuh-uh, thanks. I don't smoke."

The boy lit the end of his roll-up. "Good for you. Neither do I," he said.

Ah. Another joke, Jazmin thought to herself. She smiled politely.

"And your name is...?" the boy inquired, puffing smoke out of the corner of his mouth.

"Jazmin."

"As in the blossom?"

"Something like that."

The boy took a couple more drags, then pinched out the roll-up, and began to eat his lunch.

"I like your hair," he remarked as he ate. "It's great – sort of wild and free."

Hell-*o*? Jazmin's jaw practically hit the floor. She loathed her untameable hair. It was long and curly. Some mornings when she woke up, her hair looked like it had been arranged overnight by a hurricane with treacle on its fingers. It was so unfair. In her opinion she had been born with the Hair from Hell. Nobody had *ever* paid her a compliment about it before now. Despite his scary appearance, she found herself warming towards the boy. She eyed him with renewed interest.

"Ever thought of colouring it?" Tony asked casually.

"What – like yours?" Jazmin teased.

"Woah – that'd be crazy. The colour'd really suit you, though." The boy stared at her, head on one side. "Y'know, red hair'd look good too. You should think about it."

"Thanks, I will."

The boy continued eating. Jazmin cast about for something genius to say.

"So, did you sell many tongue studs this morning?" she inquired.

"A few," the boy told her. "Mainly people like to buy the more usual stuff." He pointed to his ears, which like his eyebrows, were also heavily pierced and silver-ringed.

"If you ever want to get your ears pierced," he remarked, "I know a good place to go."

"Right." Jazmin winced. She'd had her ears pierced last year when she was thirteen. The memory of the ear infection and the weeks of pain that followed still returned to haunt her every now and then.

"Or if you want a tattoo," the boy went on. He pushed back the left sleeve of his battered leather jacket to reveal his forearm. There were a couple of Chinese symbols tattooed on the inside, close to his wrist. "They mean Prosperity and Good Luck," he remarked. "At least that's what the tattoo guy said. Of course, they might mean Sweet and Sour Pork and Special Fried Rice for all I know." He grinned. His smile was infectious and Jazmin found herself smiling back. She'd never talked to a goth before. This one was really nice. It all went to show you shouldn't stereotype people, and be judgy.

The boy finished off his pitta and drank his water. He wiped his mouth on the back of his hand. "Well, Jazmin, gotta run. Customers to serve and all that." He rose to his feet, smiling. "Hey, it's been great talking to you. Will I see you again sometime?"

Jazmin looked up at him. At his orange and black hair, multiple body piercings and black clothes. This boy was like nobody she'd ever hung out with before. She held a quick, silent debate with herself. On the one hand, she reminded herself, she was a bit crayon-breaky around boys. On the other hand, maybe her luck was just about to change: new year, new opportunity. She'd already made several important resolutions about changing her lifestyle, getting fitter, making the world a better place, and becoming more girl powery. And hey, she had a pile of black cast-offs from her rich cousin Clea. She also had a pair of eight-eye black Docs. This could be the perfect time to give goth a go.

She gave Tony a little finger-wave. "Maybe I'll stop by next week. Who knows?" she said, cutting him an "air-of-mystery" smile.

FBI AGENT CHRIS MBEKI WAS CERTAIN THAT HE WAS BEING FOLLOWED. HE DUCKED INTO A SHOP DOORWAY, WAITED A COUPLE OF MINUTES, THEN SHOT HIS HEAD OUT AND STARED DOWN THE street. Nobody. He continued walking. Whoever it was, they were good at this, he thought. He was pretty sure he'd been followed yesterday evening, too.

He went on walking steadily, stopping every few seconds to listen intently for footsteps, or to look behind him. Eventually, he stopped at the door of the small, steamy café he'd recently discovered. It did what the menu board called "Traditional all-day English breakfasts". Mbeki preferred the delights of his usual New York corner deli with its bagels-and-coffee-to-go, but if this was what the Brits traditionally ate, he was up for it.

Entering the café, he nodded a friendly greeting to the guy behind the counter, and sat down at his usual table. Back to the wall, eyes on the door. Watching for a shape, a shadow or a silhouette. Better than constantly looking behind you. The trouble with looking behind you was there was always a "behind you" where you weren't looking.

Mbeki picked up one of the free newspapers, glancing at the front page stories. Some more young people had died over the past weekend. Again for no apparent reason. There were the usual posed photographs of the youngsters in their school uniforms, smiling brightly for the camera. Police statements saying they were treating the deaths as suicide. Bewildered comments from parents, who had noticed absolutely nothing unusual in their behaviour in the days or weeks before they died. Mbeki sighed. He read through the article until the counter guy appeared, carrying a thick white china plate and a blue striped mug.

"Here you are, sir, one lovely fry-up, cuppa tea with milk," the man said, placing the mug and the plate of glistening food in front of him. "Oh, and someone found this note on the mat: 'For the man in the blue shirt and jeans at the far table' – that'd be you, right?"

Mbeki turned the note over, read the superscription. He glanced around. Yes, he was the only customer wearing those items of clothing. Puzzled, he unfolded the piece of paper. Inside, a single line of writing read: *"The condemned man ate a hearty breakfast."* Hope you enjoy yours.

He breathed in sharply. When he'd left the States, he had told his New York boss airily that he'd have this assignment wrapped up in a couple of days. No big deal. Unfortunately that was not the case. In grim silence, he picked up his fork, and began eating.

OH GEEZ, I DO SO HATE MONDAY MORNINGS, JAZMIN THOUGHT TO HERSELF. SHE PEERED MOROSELY AT HER REFLECTION IN THE BATHROOM MIRROR AND SIGHED. IT WAS GOING TO TAKE A LOT MORE than a wave of a magic wand and a few sprinkles of pixie dust to turn her into a glam spy-babe. Narrowing her eyes she did a quick spot count. Unh – the spot goblin had definitely paid another visit in the night. The Himalayan mountain range on her chin was still making its presence felt – even though she'd covered it with Blitzo!, the latest and greatest complexion enhancer, as advertised in all the fashion mags, and costing a whole week's allowance. Huh!

Jazmin ran her fingers through her damp, snarly hair. Freaksome. She dressed, then went downstairs to make herself some breakfast. In the kitchen, she discovered her mum sitting at the table, nursing a mug of black coffee. She was still wearing her red tartan dressing gown and slippers. No make-up. Jazmin regarded her anxiously.

"Hey, are you sick?" she asked.

Her mum shook her head. "They're redecorating the office," she said, with a long-suffering expression. "Everybody's hot-desking for a couple of days. I was going to go in this morning, but I decided it was easier to work from home."

"Whoa, maybe I could do that," Jazmin suggested brightly. She hated the learning centre.

Her mum smiled thinly. "Nice try," she said.

Jazmin got some orange juice, then slapped peanut butter on a thick wedge of white toast. She took a big bite. "What are you working on? Anything interesting?" she asked, sliding into the seat opposite.

Assia eye-rolled. "I wish. No, it's just boring admin stuff," she said.

Jazmin's top lip curled in sympathetic disgust.

"Quite," her mum said. "Sadly, that's how it goes, hon. Most jobs are 30% fun, 70% paperwork."

Jazmin finished breakfast, and went to get her stuff ready for class. When she ran her own crime-fighting agency, she thought, stuffing a couple of half-finished assignments into her bag, she'd make damn sure the 70% paperwork was done by other people, leaving her free to do the world-saveage.

As soon as Jazmin had gone, Assia showered, put on sweats and a baggy jumper, then headed for her laptop. She worked diligently throughout the morning. She wrote up all her notes on the Arkady case, and made a start on sorting her file of useful contacts into logical order. She even began reading through some of the cold-case reports downloaded from her boss's database that she'd promised to sort out for him. She also drank numerous cups of strong coffee, and tried to ignore the inner Assia screaming her head off.

Meanwhile on the other side of the city, Hally Skinner, Assia's deputy, stared out of the office window. She was feeling awkward and lost. This was not her desk, nor her office. This was not the view she was accustomed to. Even the pigeons on the window sill looked subtly different. Hally did a face-scrunch. She switched on her laptop ready for another day. A shadow suddenly fell across her desk.

"Hey, lady, care to share your workspace?"

Hally looked up sharply. Then her features softened. Chris Mbeki was standing by her desk, smiling down at her in a friendly way. He was carrying his silver powerbook in one hand, and a cardboard tray in the other. "See – I have coffee and muffins," he murmured persuasively, sliding the tray onto Hally's desk.

Hally blushed, shook her head in mock disapproval. "Hey, man – do you want to make me break my diet?" she said, moving her stuff to one corner of the desk to make room for him.

Mbeki had only started working in the ISA building a fortnight ago. He was *hot*! The gossip around the water cooler was that he was single, and renting a small loft apartment in one of the new glass and steel high-rise community spaces in Rotherhithe. The water cooler gossip also said he worked as an undercover FBI agent. He was here on official business, but the reason he was currently using the ISA as a base for his investigation was because the head of the ISA rented his boss's East Hampton summer house. It was a quid pro quo thing. Which figured. The head of the ISA had a contact list to die for. Of course, Mbeki was not a permanent fixture. But right now, Hally wasn't worried about that.

Mbeki eased himself into a second swivel chair, and Hally suddenly felt that maybe life wasn't so bad after all. She sat up a little straighter, and sucked in her stomach. "So," she remarked conversationally, "how's things?"

"Things are just great," he told her equably. He peered at his screen, then picked up a pencil lying on the desk and absent-mindedly stirred his latte.

"Hey, I'm sure they have spoons someplace!" Hally laughed.

Mbeki glanced swiftly left and right. He leaned towards Hally. "Out here, sister, on the vast plains of this wild uncharted office, you have to learn to adapt," he murmured, his dark eyes sparkling with humour. Hally felt bits of her insides going into freefall. He really was gorgeous. And if she played her cards right, she'd have him all to herself for the whole day. Maybe the whole week. Yum. Hally smiled at her computer screen, her mind busy scheming.

BACK AT THE LEARNING CENTRE, JAZMIN WAS TRANSFERRING BETWEEN FACULTY BUILDINGS, ACCOMPANIED AS USUAL BY HER GOOD FRIEND AND SELF-APPOINTED LIFE COACH ZEB STONE.

"That was an interesting class about the Council of Trent, wasn't it?" Zeb remarked as they walked along the corridor.

"Mmm," Jazmin agreed. She was into history like fish

were into bicycles. She'd spent most of the lesson staring out of the window, letting the causes of the Renaissance happen to other people. She had more important stuff to focus on. Like trying to connect with her inner-goth.

"I'd never realized the Spanish Inquisition was so important," Zeb observed.

"Uh-huh," Jazmin nodded, wondering how Zeb managed to be so mind-numbingly enthusiastic about everything. Sure, there were things she enthused about: reading crime fiction, eating cake, working on her future career as a secret agent and crime-fighter. But the Council of Trent? Stroll on.

"You *did* copy the homework down, didn't you?" Zeb inquired cautiously.

"Yeah, yeah, of course I did. Don't stress," Jazmin lied.

Zeb cast her a doubt-ridden look. "Good," he said. "Because you remember your New Year's resolution is to hand in all assignments on time this term?"

"Yeah, yeah," Jazmin repeated, waving her hand airily. She had made many New Year's resolutions. Few of them had lasted further than the first week of January.

There was a pause. Then, "So, do you think I should dye my hair a different colour?" she asked.

Taken aback by the out-of-the-blueness of the topic, Zeb blinked. "Uh, well, er," he stuttered awkwardly. "What sort of a different colour?"

"I was thinking maybe red."

Zeb peered at Jazmin's hair. "What's wrong with the colour it is now?"

"It's brown. Boring, uninteresting, mousy brown. Time for a change, don't you think?"

"Right," Zeb floundered on helplessly, mapless in girl territory. "Err...maybe. Why?"

Jazmin eye-rolled. Zeb Stone might be at the very top of the academic food chain, but in matters of style, fashion, in fact *anything* female, he was so far out of his depths that the fish had lights on the ends of their noses. "Because it's good to try new things," she said patiently.

"Sometimes it's just as good to leave well alone."

They walked the rest of the way to the science block in silence.

"You know what? I think your hair looks perfectly all right as it is," Zeb said.

Jazmin groaned. "Hey, just forget it, okay?" she told him wearily. "I'm sorry I asked."

THE MAN STOOD IN A DOORWAY WATCHING THE ISA BUILDING. IT WAS LATE AFTERNOON, A CHILL WIND BLEW AND IT WAS RAINING. HE TURNED UP HIS COAT COLLAR AND WAITED. STAFF WERE quitting the building and hurrying along the pavement, keeping their heads down against the wind and rain. The man remained where he was until his chosen victim appeared on the steps opposite. Then he began to walk in the same direction. He stayed on the other side of the street, dipping skilfully in and out of the home-going workers who were all heading in the direction of the train station.

You like following people, he told himself. *You like getting that feeling of power, don't you? Carrying out these little experiments. Preparation, method, results.* His eyes glittered. *A climate of fear is not a good place to live in, as the quarry will soon find out.*

The man crossed the road and went on following, just keeping enough distance not to be noticed. Chris Mbeki entered the station, crossed the forecourt and stepped onto the travelator leading to the commuter express. The man swiftly moved in closer, so close that he could have reached out and laid a hand on Mbeki's unsuspecting shoulder. But he did not touch him. That was for later. *You always ration your treats, that way they last longer, remember?* He smiled, feeling the adrenaline circulating through him, bright as mercury. *You will watch the unsuspecting animal move closer and closer to the trap. Because soon it will blunder in, and then the jaws of the trap...will...slam...shut!*

He curled his fingers tightly into the palms of his hands.

JAZMIN LET HERSELF INTO THE APARTMENT. SHE DROPPED HER COAT AND BAG ON THE FLOOR, AND WENT STRAIGHT TO THE KITCHEN, WHERE SHE FIXED HERSELF A MARMALADE AND cream cheese sandwich on white, snagged a carton of apple juice, and returned to the hallway to pick up her bag.

The door to the living room was closed – a sure sign that her mum was working, and did not want to be disturbed right now. Jazmin carried the plate of food and her bag up to her room, where she dumped the day's homework on top of the pile of previously set homework. Good intentions were all very well in their way, but you wouldn't want to run your life by them, that was her philosophy. Besides, she was hoping that any day now the Homework Fairy might start paying house calls.

Jazmin loved her room. The walls were painted deep blue, a colour that always made her feel as if she was sitting by the ocean on a calm summer's day. In her room, she was surrounded by all her favourite things: her collection of crime fiction, her scented candles and seashells. The little china house from Prague, her posters of fractals. In the window hung her dreamcatcher, a small wooden circle, leather-bound, with a plastic thread spider's web and at its heart, like the spider itself, a small green bead. It was a Christmas present from Zeb.

The dreamcatcher was supposed to trap the bad dreams in its web, letting the good dreams through. It was an excellent present, Jazmin decided. It showed that underneath it all, Zeb was a thoughtful and sensitive person, which was why she was prepared to put up with him getting discipliny and frowny over things like homework and missed deadlines. He couldn't check up on her now, though, because she'd deliberately switched off her micro. Heh, heh. Jazmin lay back on her bed contentedly. She took a big bite out of her sandwich. Food and the absence of textual harassment. Who could ask for more?

After supper, Jazmin and her mum spent some "Quality Family Time" in the living room. Quality Family Time meant her mum asking inquisitiony questions about school and homework deadlines, and Jazmin giving vague and evasive answers. Tonight, however, before her mum could start applying the verbal thumbscrews, Jazmin spotted a small cream-coloured card on the coffee table. She pounced on it, waving it in the air.

"What's this?" she demanded. "It wasn't here when I left the apartment this morning."

Assia looked up. "Oh, that. Yes. It's an invitation; it came in the post today. I meant to tell you about it earlier."

Jazmin scrutinized the card. It wasn't just an invitation, she thought, it was a Darn Impressive invitation. The card was thick and glossy. It had gold edging, glittery as syrup, and there was a lot of posh runny writing that was hard to read, but looked very important.

"*Nerissa Cole and Cesare Frascati cordially invite you to join them in celebrating their commitment ceremony,*" she read aloud slowly. "Sounds interesting. Who are Nerissa Cole and Cesare Frascati?"

"Nerissa Cole is somebody I went to school with," Assia

told her. "You remember: a whole bunch of us got back in touch recently through one of those reuniting websites. We went out for a meal in Covent Garden."

Jazmin remembered. Personally, in a future life she'd rather stick pins in her eyes than ever meet up with anybody from her learning centre. But hey, why be judgy? "Was she a best friend?" she asked, interested.

"No," Assia replied shortly, "I don't recall us ever being close."

"Uh-huh, I see. What's a 'commitment ceremony'?"

Her mum shrugged. "I'm guessing it's a non-religious way of getting married. But whatever it is, we're both invited to it."

"*I'm* invited?" Jazmin's eyes widened in surprise. Most adult parties had a cut-off point, rather like the height restrictions on the best funfair rides. Below sixteen, you weren't generally welcome, in case you threw food, fought, got drunk or were sick on the furniture. Jazmin often wondered why adults regarded these things as so socially unacceptable. They happened at practically every good teenage party she went to. It was no big deal.

"It's okay – I'm sure Nerissa will understand if you don't want to go," Assia said hastily. She had vivid memories of dragging a reluctant and sulky Jazmin to and from various formal social functions in the past because she couldn't find a babysitter. It had never worked out. Her daughter could scowl for England.

Jazmin checked the address. "Whoa – your friend must be loaded," she remarked.

"She certainly seems to have done well for herself, doesn't she?" Assia said drily.

"What does she do?"

"She runs a private clinic," Assia told her. "Although I also recollect her telling us at the dinner that her new partner was the head of some Italian bank."

Jazmin studied the invite again. At the end of the day, a party was a party, she reasoned to herself. There were bound to be other people her age there. Also, it would provide her with the perfect excuse to blow some of her Christmas money on something new to wear. "Well, okay. If you really want me to, I guess I'll come," she said slowly, feigning reluctance.

"If you're sure," Assia said cautiously. She held out her hand for the card. "I'll reply tonight, and tell them to expect us both," she said.

NEXT DAY, JAZMIN DECIDED TO LUNCH OUT. SHE WAS SICK OF THE CANTEEN FOOD, WHICH IN HER OPINION COULD EASILY FEATURE IN ONE OF THOSE "HOW TO" MAGAZINE ARTICLES. (AS IN: HOW TO Develop an Eating Disorder in Five Easy Steps.) There was good eaty stuff in the mall. And she could check out clothes at the same time too.

Passing through the double doors of the learning centre,

Jazmin stood on the top step and breathed in deeply. She had spent the last hour studying some poem about daffodils. The poet had been very fond of them. After all that, it felt good to reconnect with the real world. She started walking. Maybe she wouldn't come back after lunch. It was only Girls' Phys. Ed. this afternoon. Which, translated, meant being tongue-lashed around a windswept field by a female fascist with a high ponytail, a whistle and a power complex. Jazmin shuddered. She didn't do team sports. She was a solo operative. She lurked in the shadows, waiting for the right moment.

As she walked, Jazmin envisaged herself crouched in the lee of a tree, her slim lycra-clad figure taut, eyes steely and focused. Jaz Dawson, crime-fighter and glam spy-babe. Her fingers were clenched around her small, black, snub-barrelled Beretta .32, the covert user's weapon of choice (carried for defensive purposes only). Anyway, she'd forgotten her games kit, so there was absolutely no point whatsoever in coming back after lunch.

Reaching the mall, Jazmin entered her favourite snack place. She selected a ham and Swiss cheese on rye with rocket, a muesli bar, and a bottle of organic apple juice. The aspiring crime-fighter's lunch of choice. While she ate, she reviewed her plans for the afternoon. Unfortunately it looked like she was going to have to reschedule her clothes hunt: most of the shops were still holding end-of-season sales. She was *so* not going to waste her money on something nobody had fancied buying in the first place.

Jazmin sipped her juice. Of course, there *was* always Camden Market, she reminded herself. She could go back there on Saturday. Lots of interesting stalls selling vintage and retro stuff. She was *bound* to find something good there. And oh – maybe she'd run into that boy again. Jazmin thought back to their first encounter. Her lips curved. She was sure there had been some sparkage.

Lunch over, Jazmin decided to wander round for a bit longer. There was no point going home for a couple of hours. Her mum was still working there and her mental radar was tuned to the exact time the school day ended. She strolled round the mall until she found herself passing by a newly opened hairdressing salon. It had a big notice in the window: *Perming, colouring, and cutting. Models always wanted.* She paused. Read the notice through carefully a second time. Stood in thoughtful contemplation. Reread the notice. Stared through the window for a couple of minutes.

Then she opened the door and went in.

Five minutes later, Jazmin was seated on a black swivel chair in front of a spotlit mirror. Swathed in a bright mauve floral gown, she was studying colour charts, while a young trainee hairdresser stood by, waiting for her to make up her mind.

This was kismet, Jazmin smiled happily. It was meant to be.

MEANWHILE, ASSIA WAS ENDURING HER SECOND DAY WORKING AWAY FROM HER OFFICE. FIRST THING, SHE'D RUNG HALLY TO SEE WHETHER ANYTHING IMPORTANT HAD HAPPENED, AND WHETHER IT was worth going in. Hally had been most emphatic that nothing had happened, and there were no work spaces free. She'd checked, she said. Thoroughly. Although, she assured Assia, she'd let her know as soon as somewhere became available. Still, she added consolingly, there was nothing to be done here that Assia couldn't do at home, was there? And hey, at least Assia wasn't having a tough day out there on the mean streets.

A tough day? Assia thought grimly. Her day had passed tough at 9 a.m. when she had resigned herself to more report reading and caffeine consuming. By midday, she found herself pacing the floor, and feeling the walls closing in on her. She hated the lack of action. Nothing was happening except paperwork. She really needed to be assigned to something exciting. Something that got her away from the endless files, and returned her to the "mean streets" once more. As her daughter would say: she was feeling all messed and out-of-the-loopy.

BACK AT THE MALL, JAZMIN'S HAIR MAKEOVER WAS WELL UNDER WAY. "SO," THE TRAINEE HAIRDRESSER ASKED BRIGHTLY, AS SHE ASSEMBLED HER EQUIPMENT, "YOU GOING SOMEWHERE special then?"

"Er, yeah, kind of," Jazmin replied vaguely. She didn't want to overshare with a complete stranger.

"That's nice then." The trainee poured hot water into a bowl of green-tea-smelling powder. "This is top quality Turkish henna," she said, stirring vigorously. "Really strong."

"Excellent." Jazmin stared at the gloopy mixture in some dismay. It resembled spinach purée. She had a sudden spasm of doubt. Was she doing the right thing? Was she going to end up looking like a green-haired alien?

The girl sectioned off Jazmin's hair with clips. Then she took a flat brush and began to paint the henna mixture along the roots. "Haven't you got nice hair?" she commented cheerfully as she slapped brushfuls of gloop onto Jazmin's head. "Have you ever had it coloured before?"

"No," Jazmin whispered. She was trying very hard to sit extremely still. She did not want a faceful of henna.

"That's nice then," the girl repeated, painting vigorously. She scraped out the bowl, applied the last bit of henna to Jazmin's hairline, then wrapped her head in some plasticky stuff and led her to a dryer. "Forty-five minutes," she said, lowering the hood and setting the timer. She dumped a pile of fashion mags onto Jazmin's lap. "Coffee?" she inquired. Jazmin mouthed a "no" in reply. "Okay," the girl said, "be with you in a bit, then." And she mooched over to one of the basins, where she began washing another client's hair.

Left to herself, Jazmin began idly flicking through the pages of a magazine. She stared at the photos of stick-thin models wearing clothes that cost the equivalent of the annual food budget of a small Third World country. But she was not really concentrating. Her mind was racing ahead, envisaging the wonderfully transformed Her shortly to emerge, like a beautiful glossy butterfly, from under the dryer. She was picturing the admiring looks on people's faces.

No more fading into the background, she decided. From now on, she was strictly a Foreground Girl. She was also thinking about the retro-goth boy she'd met at Camden Market. He was going to be amazed when she turned up with her newly coloured hair. Maybe he would ask her out. Jazmin's mouth curved into a smile. This had been *such* a great idea. She checked the time. Not much longer now. Oooh, she was going to look so *good*! She could hardly wait.

TWO HOURS AFTER SHE'D CROSSED THE THRESHOLD OF THE SALON, JAZMIN'S MAKEOVER HAD FINALLY REACHED ITS CLIMACTIC CONCLUSION. THE TRAINEE HAIRDRESSER BENT HER FORWARDS IN THE chair, did some energetic backcombing, worked some wax through her hair, then spun her round to face the mirror. "*Ta-daa!*" she exclaimed. "Great, innit? What do you think?"

There was a long pause.

Jazmin stared into the mirror. For a few seconds, she was confused. Where had she gone? Then she spotted a small, familiar face peering out anxiously from a vast halo of the brightest, reddest hair she had ever seen outside a circus ring. *Omigod*, she screamed silently to herself. *O-mi-god!!*

For some obscure reason, Jazmin suddenly recalled the time when her Religion and Ethics class had studied the Bible story of Moses and the burning bush. She couldn't answer for Moses, but right now she knew exactly how the bush felt. She stared open-mouthed, and with a rapidly mounting sense of horror, at her flaming reflection in the glass.

"Whoa – I said that henna was really strong," the girl gabbled on happily. "Your friends aren't going to recognize you tomorrow, are they?"

Friends? Jazmin thought frantically. She could just see the expression on people's faces when she turned up at the school gate looking like a walking traffic light. Everyone was going to die laughing.

The trainee untied the overall. "Right, I guess you'll want to be getting off home now," she suggested. But Jazmin still continued sitting in front of the mirror, mute and frozen with shock.

Home? Omigod. What on earth was her mum going to say? She was going to totally blow. For a couple of seconds longer, she sat and stared at the freak in the mirror. Then she got up, silently collected her stuff, and stumbled out of the salon.

Jazmin walked home as fast as she could. She kept her head down, and deliberately did not make eye contact with anybody. Finally, after what seemed like the longest journey ever, she reached her apartment block. She sprinted straight up the stairs to the third floor. Opening the front door, she tiptoed gingerly along the hallway. If she could only make it to her bedroom before her mum saw her. But as usual, the tide was out on Luck Beach.

"Jazmin?" her mum called out brightly. "Is that you?" She opened the living-room door, then froze, staring open-mouthed at Jazmin's hair.

Silence fell.

It continued falling for a long time.

Okay, get the litter tray, here come the kittens. Jazmin stood and waited for the maternal wrath to descend. When the wrath failed to materialize, she decided to get in first herself. "So I dyed my hair, right? Hey, it's no big," she declared, trying to fake a nonchalance she wasn't feeling.

Her mum's face was a study in expressionlessness.

"Practically every girl in my class dyes their hair. All the time," Jazmin continued, waving a dismissive hand.

Still no response.

"Actually, for your information, it's been hennaed, which is a natural product, and comes from plants, and is very good for the hair," she ploughed on.

Her mum went on looking at her thoughtfully.

"Look, it's *my* hair, okay," Jazmin finished up defiantly. Her mother's lack of reaction was beginning to scare her more than her hair had done.

Her mum subjected her to some more thoughtful contemplation. She shrugged. Then she nodded. "Yes. I guess it is," she said crisply.

"Huh?"

Her mum did a palms-up. "What do you want me to do? Punish you? You're too old to be confined to your room."

No, no I'm not, Jazmin pleaded inwardly. *Punish me: send me to my room – please! At least until the red fades a bit.*

Her mother shook her head slowly from side to side. Her mouth twitched. If she hadn't known better, Jazmin could have sworn her mum was trying not to laugh. Then, without saying another word, she turned and went back into the living room, closing the door firmly behind her.

Sheesh, Jazmin reflected, as she made her way gloomily upstairs. Would you believe it! Sometimes she just couldn't catch a break.

NEXT MORNING, JAZMIN GOT UP EARLY. A TWICE WEEKLY RUN WAS ONE OF HER NEW YEAR RESOLUTIONS AND, FOR ONCE, SHE WAS DETERMINED TO KEEP IT. IF SHE DIDN'T, THE TOPS OF HER LEGS might have to apply for separate postcodes. She dragged on her tracksuit, then went to examine her hair in the bathroom mirror. To her relief, it had flattened down considerably overnight. Maybe it was her imagination, but the colour seemed a tad less vibrantly *RED,* although overall it still looked pretty freaky.

Jazmin did some lacklustre pre-run warm-ups in the hall. Her body felt as if it was parked sideways in a parallel universe. She wondered whether some of the henna had leaked into her brain while she slept. She checked the time, then hit the street.

There was one major advantage to winter running: because it was so cold, you tended to go faster to get it over with. Jazmin puffed her way round the block, her breath coming out in little foggy clouds.

Run, Freak-girl, run.

Usually when she ran, nobody noticed her. Today, however, it was totally different. Every few metres of the run was accompanied by a staccato of car horns. Some drivers even leaned out of their windows to shout encouragement. Muffled up against the cold, Jazmin couldn't quite make out what they were saying, but the words "Go ginga!" seemed to occur with a certain regularity. Unh!

BACK AT THE APARTMENT, ASSIA STOOD AT THE KITCHEN WINDOW LOOKING OUT AT THE GLOOMY SKY. ANOTHER GREY DAY. THE POET GOT IT WRONG, SHE PONDERED RUEFULLY, IT WAS JANUARY, NOT April, that was the cruellest month. She poured oatmeal into a bowl, set a place at the table. She knew from the past few weeks that Jazmin liked a hot breakfast after her morning run.

Assia visualized her daughter pounding along the neighbourhood streets. She pursed her lips. What was she like! Dying her hair bright red was just the latest in a line of unpredictable events. Assia stared into the middle distance, thinking back to Jazmin's childhood. She recalled when Jazmin had decided to dig her way to China. She was eight years old at the time. She shovelled away in the garden for a whole week. Miraculously, Assia had just managed to scoop her out of the hole before the whole thing collapsed on top of her.

Then, when Jazmin was ten, she'd managed to get herself locked in the library overnight. She'd gone AWOL more times than Assia could count. She'd spent much of last summer dressed as a clown. Never a dull moment. The question was, as it had always been: should she admire her daughter's free spirit or punish her? She heard the front door slam, the sound of Jazmin's footsteps running quickly upstairs to the bathroom. She picked up the bowl of oatmeal and placed it in the microwave. Maybe she'd give herself a break for once, she decided. Outsource the responsibility. Jazmin was going to get teased unmercifully at school today. That would be punishment enough.

'THERE'S SOMETHING DIFFERENT ABOUT YOU TODAY, ISN'T THERE?" ZEB STONE VENTURED CAUTIOUSLY. HE AND JAZMIN WERE WALKING TO THE LEARNING CENTRE TOGETHER. THEY'D BEEN WALKING FOR ten minutes. Zeb kept shooting her the odd curious glance as they went. Now he turned to face her. He stared hard, frowning in fixed concentration. From under her beanie, Jazmin stared silently back, refusing to help him out. All at once, Zeb's face cleared as the bright sun of enlightenment dawned on his mental horizon. "Got it! You're wearing a hat."

"Genius observation," Jazmin said tartly.

Zeb's eyes narrowed. "And you've done something to your hair, haven't you?"

"Whoa – there's no fooling you."

Zeb stabbed a finger at her head. "It's not brown any more."

"No, really? Isn't it?"

They walked a bit more.

"Umm...what exactly have you done?" Zeb ventured cautiously.

Jazmin eye-rolled. "Duh. I've had it hennaed."

"Right."

There was a pause. More walking was accomplished.

"Interesting colour," Zeb said pensively. "What would you call it?"

Jazmin sighed with exaggerated patience. "Hey, I'd call it RED, okay."

"It looks Titian to me."

"Bless you."

Zeb's lips twitched. "That's 'Titian' as in the red colour used by the Venetian painter Tiziano Vecellio in the sixteenth century," he informed her gravely.

"Oh." Jazmin had the grace to look embarrassed. How on earth did he know all this clever stuff?

"It's very...different," Zeb said, picking his words carefully.

"Yeah, well, I'm making a statement."

"Your hair certainly is."

Jazmin tossed her head. "Hey, this is the new me. Get used to it," she said, as she swept grandly through the school gate, trying to act like she was sashaying down the red carpet at some big Hollywood gala. She smiled and finger-waved at the gate-girls. Reality is 80% illusion, 20% facade, she informed them silently. You'd better believe it!

THE FLORIST AT "LILIES OF THE FIELD" FLEXED HIS CHILLED FINGERS, AND GLANCED QUICKLY AT HIS TO-DO LIST FOR TODAY. WEDDING AT 3.15: *TWELVE YELLOW AND WHITE ROSEBUD buttonholes, three bridesmaids' posies, bride's bouquet and crown,* he read. No problem. There were also the usual hand-tied bouquets to prepare for the customers who bought flowers from him during the day. By the door, an early morning delivery of long flat boxes waited to be opened and sorted.

Deciding to unpack the boxed blooms first, the florist filled buckets with water from the sink at the back of the shop. He had just sorted the first box of egg-yolk-yellow daffs and candy-pink tulips when his phone rang. Wiping wet hands on his apron, he went to answer it.

"Lilies of the Field – Shawn here, how may I *help* you?" he intoned, reaching for pad and pencil as he spoke. Then he listened to the instructions he was given. As he listened, he frowned, made a few notes.

Mmmm, the florist thought to himself after the caller had rung off. *Well*. You certainly got asked to do all sorts in this job. He pursed his lips. Still, the customer was always king, he reminded himself. That was his philosophy. He shrugged, and went to finish unpacking his boxes.

MUCH LATER THAT AFTERNOON, JAZMIN WAS SITTING IN HER BEDROOM NOT DOING HER HOMEWORK WHILE WORKING HER WAY STEADILY THROUGH A PACKET OF CHOCOLATE BISCUITS. SHE WAS breaking the biscuits into pieces before eating them to allow some of the calories to fall out. Outside the window, some birds were being blown backwards by the strong wind. She began thinking about how the day had gone. To her great surprise, it had gone exceedingly well. All things considered. And it was all thanks to her new red hair. Funny how a good idea, which had become a bad idea, had morphed back into being a good idea again.

All day, girls Jazmin'd barely spoken to before had come up and complimented her. She'd actually overheard a couple of boys utter the word "babe" as she passed. Nobody had ever called her a "babe" before. Babes were generally blonde, size 6 and cakephobic. It seemed that overnight Jaz Dawson, her imaginary PI and crime-fighting persona, had suddenly been joined by – *drrrrrr*, drum roll – Jazmin Dawson, Popular Feisty Redhead Babe.

Shame neither of her two alter egos could do maths though, she thought, as she dragged herself reluctantly back to the immediate present. She stared resentfully down at her maths textbook, and the page of algebraic fractions that had been set for homework. She hadn't a clue how to solve them, and she hadn't managed to get Zeb to show her how to work them out, because he had recently found some mega-tweako mates to hang with, so was not currently available for after-school tuition.

Jazmin sighed. She had eaten lunch with Zeb and his new friends today. Eww! Never again. They'd had this very earnest discussion about how, if there were four people in a room and you took seven of them away, you'd have minus three people left. But if you introduced three more people, the room would still be empty. Apparently it was a really clever maths joke. Everyone had laughed. Jazmin hadn't got it. She still didn't get it. Ho hum. Shaking her head sadly at the memory, she reached for another biscuit. Maybe tomorrow she'd hang with the Party crowd instead.

Jazmin began setting out the fractions in her workbook. If she copied them very neatly, and spread them across the page with lots of underlining, the teacher might be so impressed with her presentation that he might not notice that she hadn't actually bothered to work them out. It was worth a shot. She got out her ruler, some coloured pencils and set to work.

Sometime later, she threw her pen down with a groan, and closed her eyes. Meaningless numbers were fizzing and dancing behind her eyelids. Time to hit the kitchen. She needed a sugar boost and some strong tea. The sort of strong tea that if you turned the mug upside down, it would be a long time before anything fell out. She slammed the book shut, added it to the pile on the floor and left the room.

AT THE END OF HIS WORKING DAY, FBI AGENT CHRIS MBEKI CROSSED THE LOBBY OF HIS APARTMENT BUILDING, CHECKED HIS MAILBOX, AND HEADED FOR THE SLEEK CHROME AND PERSPEX LIFT. He was enjoying living in London. The view of the river from his balcony gave him particular pleasure, as did the simple white walls, and the uncluttered, minimalist furnishings helpfully provided by the letting agency.

He also liked living in an area of the city steeped in romance and history, where pirates and criminal gangs had once roamed. Often he lay in bed at night imagining black sails on blue, sunlit water. Big bearded men shouting salty oaths at each other. The clatter of booted feet on cobbles. Cartwheels rumbling in the depths of night.

As Mbeki approached the lift, the doors opened, and the couple who lived in the adjacent loft apartment stepped out. He greeted them with a friendly smile. "Hey, you guys, how're you doing?" The couple paused, stared at him curiously, then looked away. Putting it down to no more than traditional Brit reticence, he got into the lift and was carried swiftly upwards.

Arriving at his floor, he exited, and walked the short distance down the hallway towards his apartment. He could see there was something leaning against the door. Puzzled, he quickened his pace. He reached his front door. He stopped. Stared down. Propped against the door was a wreath. A circle of white carnations surrounded a red carnation heart, in the centre of which were three letters: RIP.

Sometime later, Mbeki sat in thoughtful solitude at the kitchen counter, eating a takeout pizza. The wreath lay on the floor just inside the front door. He stared out at the lights winking and dancing on the pewter-coloured water.

The occasional boat glided by, the sound of its engine muffled by the double-glazed window. Hey, good thing he didn't scare easily, he reflected. He closed the pizza box, slid off the counter stool, and went to stand by the window.

Of course there was another way of seeing this, Mbeki told himself, his eyes tracking the starboard light of a dredger as it chugged downstream towards Gravesend. Maybe the wreath had been delivered to the wrong address; it wasn't meant for him at all. Mistakes occurred all the time, didn't they? Somebody in the block had attended a funeral this afternoon, minus the expensive wreath they'd ordered earlier. Right. He wished. And the note left at the café? How did that fit in?

Mbeki flexed his fingers, then took a couple of deep breaths to relax his tense shoulders. He'd been doing this job for long enough to know that "mistakes" like these did not happen. *Do the maths*, he told himself. Somebody clearly knew who he was, and where he lived. It was a worrying thought.

THE HEAD OF THE ISA WAS RELAXING AT HOME AFTER A LONG DAY OF BACK-TO-BACK MEETINGS, WHEN HIS WORK MICRO RANG. HE PICKED IT UP FROM THE DINING TABLE, DELIBERATELY IGNORING THE disapproving glare of his wife, who felt strongly that work and home life should be kept totally separate at all times. The voice on the other end of the phone was that of the young American FBI agent, Chris Mbeki.

"Er...I'll just take this in my study, dear." The head of the ISA smiled apologetically. "Dinner looks lovely, by the way," he added placatingly.

He hurried out of the dining room, shutting the door behind him. Seated in his study, he listened intently to what Mbeki had to say. When the American had finished, there was a pause, while the head of the ISA thought about what had just been revealed. "I think you should run this by one of my people."

"I'd really value the chance," Mbeki said gratefully.

"The agent I'm thinking of is one of our best. I'm sure her input will be invaluable."

"It's more than generous of you, sir."

"I'll just give you the contact details." He paged down his list of staff contact numbers.

At the other end of the line, Mbeki wrote down the number, repeating it back to make sure he'd got it right. "Thanks, sir, I really appreciate this."

"No problem. We like to assist our colleagues whenever we can, eh?"

The call over, the head of the ISA got up and headed back to his dinner and the cold stare of his wife. He felt some sympathy for Mbeki. Things always got complicated when you allowed your work and your personal life to interface.

THE FOLLOWING MORNING, HALLY SKINNER ARRIVED FOR WORK BRIGHT AND EARLY. SHE WANTED TO MAKE SURE NOBODY ELSE IN THE BUILDING TOOK HER PRECIOUS WORKSPACE. TAKING THE LIFT TO the sixth floor, she powered into the office and dumped her stuff on the desk. Then she grabbed a second chair, pushed it alongside hers, and sighed happily.

Everything was working out just the way she wanted it. The rest of her department were dispersed around the building. Her boss Assia was still working from home, and today Hally was wearing a brand-new outfit, and had also treated herself to some hair extensions, expensive scent, and a flattering lipstick in what she hoped was a very kissable shade of red.

Hally started sorting through a pile of mail until Mbeki arrived. She greeted him in a carefully rehearsed how's-the-weather casual voice. At the bottom of the pile, she found a courier-delivered envelope. It was addressed to *Mr. C. Mbeki*. Her eyes widened. As far as she knew, Mbeki had not received personal mail here before. She passed it across the desk. Mbeki stared at the envelope, a puzzled expression on his face. "What the...?" he murmured. Then he slit it open, and drew out a small deckle-edged card. He stared down at it in silence.

"Something interesting?" Hally asked brightly, head on one side.

He didn't look up. "It seems to be an invitation."

"Really?" Hally grinned. "Oooh, lucky you. What's the occasion?"

Mbeki's face was unreadable. "A funeral," he said shortly.

Hally felt her face going red with embarrassment. "Omigod, I'm *so* sorry. Someone close?"

"Yeah, you could say that," he said quietly, staring straight ahead. He paused, tapping the edge of the card thoughtfully on the surface of the desk. "Look, I really need to make a private call. Do you mind?"

Hally jumped straight up out of her seat like a scared cat. "Oh, sure. I understand completely," she gabbled. "You go right ahead. I'll find someplace else to be." And grabbing her bag, she skittered towards the door.

Mbeki waited patiently until Hally was gone. When he was quite sure she was out of earshot, he took out the piece of paper containing the number the head of the ISA had given him last night. For a split second he hesitated, glancing down at it. Then, in a quick movement, he flipped up his micro and dialled the number.

JAZMIN LET HERSELF WEARILY INTO THE APARTMENT. IN COMPLETE CONTRAST TO YESTERDAY, TODAY HAD BEEN AN EXTREMELY EXHAUSTING DAY. SHE WAS STARTING TO FIND HER NEW POPULAR Feisty Redhead Babe identity rather tiring and difficult to live up to. She dumped her bag in the hall, then stuck her head round the living-room door. Her mum looked up from her laptop. "Hi, hon. Nice day?" she inquired.

"Yeah – truly fantastic!" Jazmin said in a bright never-admit-you-made-a-mistake-ever tone of voice. "How about you?"

Assia pursed her lips thoughtfully. "It's been... interesting," she murmured.

Jazmin instantly slid into the room. "Spill," she said, perching on the arm of the sofa. "Hey, don't tell me – you've been rung up by your boss, and asked to solve the crime of the century?"

"Not quite. Nothing so dramatic." Assia paused. "Although I have been rung up."

"Uh-huh," Jazmin said. "Go on."

"And asked out for a drink."

"Really? Who by?"

"Oh, well...just someone from my department," Assia said vaguely.

Jazmin eyed her mum suspiciously. "Male or female someone?"

Assia's cheeks went slightly pink. "Umm...male."

Jazmin stared. "Whoa, you have a date?" she exclaimed. "*A date*?" she repeated incredulously. "*You*?"

Assia gave her an embarrassed half-smile. "Sorry," she said. "Is it a problem?"

"Er...no. No, of course it isn't," Jazmin said, slightly too quickly. "Who is he?"

"His name is Chris Mbeki. He's an FBI agent from New

York. He's only been working in the department for a week or two. And I'm not sure it's a date in the sense you mean. He just asked me to meet him after work this evening for a drink."

"A drink after work? Sounds like a date to me," Jazmin said.

Assia shrugged. "It might just be a work-related thing," she said dismissively.

Jazmin ignored this. "Hey, my mum on a *date*! Go for it, I say."

"Right."

There was a brief pause.

"So...this *date*," Jazmin said. "Maybe you'd like some style tips?"

"Sure."

"Not the grey silk suit is my tip. Too boring."

"Uh-huh. Thanks for that."

Jazmin scrutinized her mum from top to toe. "And you'll need to accessorize properly," she added.

"Okay. Is that it?"

"And do something about your hair. And wear extra, but subtle, make-up. I'll let you know if anything else comes to mind."

"I'd appreciate that," Assia said drily. She rose from her chair. "Well, I'd better go and get ready then. I don't want to be late, do I?"

Jazmin waited until her mother had left the room. Then

she exhaled loudly. Whoa – scary stuff. Never in her wildest fantasies had she visualized her mother entering dateville. She hauled herself off the sofa. First the Seriously Popular Redhead thing, and now this! She was weirded; she needed to get cake-adjacent fast. And then she had to go and supervise her mum. Left to her own devices, she'd probably just throw on any old thing. There was no way Jazmin was going to allow her to go out dressed like that.

ASSIA PERCHED UNCOMFORTABLY ON THE HIGH CHROME BAR STOOL. SHE SIPPED HER DRY WHITE WINE, AND RESISTED THE TEMPTATION TO STUDY THE DRINKERS AROUND HER. ONE OF THE DOWNSIDES of her job was the need to constantly people-watch. There was an expression: you could read somebody's face like a book. Assia didn't read faces like books. She read faces like faces. Books had no past, no history. Faces did.

That was what had attracted her to Chris the moment her boss had introduced him to the department. His face. Open and friendly. A face that said: "trust me". She wondered what he wanted to talk about. His call had been very brief. Well, whatever the reason, she was looking forward to getting to know him better.

Glancing round the bar, Assia observed that most of the other customers were on their own too. Some were keeping an eye on the door, clearly waiting for someone to arrive. Others were staring down at the table, pretending to enjoy their night out for one. There were a few couples, enjoying a drink before going to eat in one of the many West End restaurants. Or maybe to the theatre. It was a long time since she'd been to the theatre, Assia thought wistfully. A long time since she'd sat in a bar, waiting for someone to arrive. She sipped her drink, and tried to quell the nervous fluttering inside.

Ten minutes and one empty glass later, Assia checked her watch. Must be a transport delay. The barman wiped along the counter with a cloth, refilled the little silver dishes with nuts. He'd be through that door any second, she told herself. She caught sight of her reflection in one of the bar's mirrored pillars. Her grey silk suit was exactly right, she thought, despite Jazmin's protestations. It was not too smart, not too casual. And her silver flower brooch in her lapel – a subtle touch. She caught the barman's eye and ordered a fresh drink, then decided to go check her hair and make-up in the Ladies' cloakroom.

After a while, Assia emerged from the Ladies' and returned to the bar. In her absence, her drink had arrived. But her date had not.

AN HOUR OR SO LATER, ASSIA LET HERSELF BACK INTO THE APARTMENT. IN THE LIVING ROOM SHE DISCOVERED JAZMIN AND HER FRIEND ZEB SITTING ON THE SOFA WATCHING A MOVIE together. Two empty, sauce-encrusted pizza boxes had been dumped on the coffee table, along with a maths textbook and Jazmin's workbook. Food and a superficial attempt at homework had obviously happened sometime earlier in the evening.

"Hey, Mum, how was your date?" Jazmin inquired. Then added with a frown: "You're back a bit early, aren't you?"

Assia met her daughter's puzzled stare, shook her head and sent out a brief "not now, okay" signal.

There was a moment's silence, while Jazmin received and processed the message. Then she got up. "Zeb's just leaving," she said, hauling him out of his seat.

"Oh? Am I? But I thought we were going to—"

"Sudden unexpected change of plan; we're not," Jazmin said, propelling him vigorously towards the door.

When Jazmin returned from seeing Zeb out, she found her mum in the kitchen, calmly filling the kettle. "Hot chocolate?" Assia asked.

Jazmin reached into the cupboard. "Hot chocolate, pink wafer biscuits, *and* all the full gory details," she said, perching herself on one of the units. She folded her arms and waited expectantly.

Assia grimaced. She sighed, plugged in the kettle. Then she turned round to face her daughter. "Nothing to tell," she shrugged, folding her arms. "He didn't show."

Jazmin stared at her open-mouthed. "You are joking!"

"Nuh-uh."

"He stood you up?"

"Well, I don't know whether I'd put it quite like that. I guess something more important must have happened," Assia said lamely, her eyes flicking away from Jazmin's.

"Hel-*lo*? Earth to mother – things don't just 'happen'. Did he call you?"

Assia shook her head.

"Did you call him?"

"He never gave me his number."

"Pathetic!" Jazmin exclaimed indignantly. Then, catching her mum's forlorn expression, she added more gently, "Hey, Mum, if this guy thinks he can just totally flake on you, he is obviously not worth the time of day. Right?"

"Right." Assia poured hot milk into her mug. She hesitated. "Only..."

"There is no 'only'," Jazmin cut in emphatically, "believe me, I know about these things."

Assia sighed again, feeling her shoulders sag, as she tried to bite back her disappointment.

"You'll be fine. You know what they say: men are like buses, another one always turns up," Jazmin said consolingly. She slipped off the unit, and gave her mum a brief hug. "Look, I'll run you a nice hot bath with plenty of bath oil, shall I?" she suggested. "You can relax and get all unwindy."

Assia gave her a sad little smile. "How come you're suddenly so full of wise advice?"

Jazmin tossed her head airily. "I'm a woman of the world, Mother," she told her. "And my advice is: this guy is a loser. Forget him."

IT WAS 4.00 A.M. THE YOUNG HOSPITAL DOCTOR WAS GAZING DOWN AT HIS NEWEST ADMISSION. THE ONLY SOUND COMING FROM THE BANDAGE-SWATHED BODY ON THE BED WAS THE RASP OF ITS PAIN- filled breathing. But at least he *was* breathing, the doctor reflected, which was amazing, given what he must have endured over the last few hours.

The patient had been attacked and robbed, sustaining a nearly fatal beating in the process. The young doctor winced as he ran through the checklist of the injuries: facial bruising, broken ribs. He had lost a lot of blood. Some fingers had been broken. The unknown man had been found slumped unconscious in an alleyway just off Soho by a cleaner about to go on shift. It was fortunate she had the presence of mind to realize that he wasn't just another sleeping wino, and had called for help.

The young doctor shook his head. It was a freezing cold night. Another hour, and this man would certainly have died of exposure. He was lucky. If you could call it luck, he thought grimly. He replaced the patient's notes in the folder. Then he checked the drips, wires and monitors.

"Hey, don't flatline on me," he murmured, but the only response from the Frankenstein's monster figure on the bed was the rattle of its hoarse, laboured breathing. Who was he? the doctor wondered. He must have a name, a life. It was a koan – a paradoxical riddle, he thought. Like trying to describe the sound of one hand clapping. *What do you call a man without an identity?* The young doctor shook his head. For a moment, he stood staring at the prone figure. Then he shrugged and left. He had a lot of other patients to check on. It was going to be a long night.

JAZMIN GOT OFF THE TRAIN AT CHALK FARM. IT WAS SATURDAY MORNING, AND SHE WAS ON THE TRAIL OF SOMETHING DRESSY AND SMART TO WEAR LATER ON THAT EVENING AT THE "COMMITMENT" party. Today she was dressed in black. Black jeans, black top, black scarf, and her new eight-eye black Docs. She had outlined her eyes with black kohl pencil. Her just-washed hair flamed *Titianly* in the pale winter sunshine. It was a goth-girl meets action-babe look, she thought happily, as she walked towards the bustle of Camden Market.

Reaching the market, Jazmin headed for a particular stall that she knew sold retro-vintage floral dresses. Okay, she wasn't normally a retro floral-dressy person, but she had decided that New Redhead Jazmin might be. Also retro was a shrewd choice because everybody knew it didn't have to fit perfectly. Good news for people who had not yet achieved five foot eight and size six proportions.

Arriving at the stall, she began to work her way systematically through the racks of clothes, going elbow to elbow with some other girls who seemed to be on a similar mission. Twenty minutes of selection and elimination followed. Finally she walked away triumphantly from the stall swinging a brown carrier bag. She'd got a kick dress. And she'd managed to get some money knocked off the price too. How good was that!

Jazmin picked her way through the throng of shoppers to where Tony the goth-boy had his pitch. She paused, ran her fingers through her hair, quickly checked her make-up in her pocket mirror, then strolled casually up to his stall. When she got within visual contact, however, she stopped dead in her tracks.

He was not there.

Instead, a man with a grey ponytail and matching straggly beard was running the stall. Bummer. For a second, Jazmin hesitated, undecided. Then she walked by, backed up, and approached again. She pretended to examine some necklaces. The man eyed her suspiciously. She sighed. Why did people automatically assume all teenagers were prospective kleptomaniacs? After a couple of seconds, the man edged nearer.

"Yeah?" he said pointedly. Followed immediately by, "Can I help you?"

Jazmin looked up at him innocently. She smiled brightly.

"Err...no thanks. Actually, I was looking for Tony. Is he around today?"

The man frowned. "Who?"

"Tony? The boy who was here last week. Spiky orange hair?"

The man grunted. "Oh, him. Nah, it's his weekend off." He stared at her. The corners of his mouth twitched. "Shall I tell him you dropped by?" he inquired, with heavy sarcasm. *Certainly not*, Jazmin thought to herself. She didn't want the boy to think she'd made a special effort to see him.

The man gave her a wink, followed by a knowing smirk. "Hur, hur," he chortled. Jazmin gave him a hard stare. Industrial strength. Then she spun on her heel, and walked away. *Don't waste your time*, she told herself. *Don't give Mr. Carbon-dated the satisfaction.*

She threaded her way back through the crowd, and started to walk up Chalk Farm Road in the direction of the station. What she had just experienced was yet another example of negative boyfriend karma. Exactly what she should have expected, given her track record.

She arrived at the station. Hey, maybe it was *good* that this had happened, she told herself as she got into the lift. After all, black was *such* a boring colour – unless it came with pink side-stripes, was accessorized with a well-stocked utility belt, and worn on missions of world-saveage. And to be honest, did she *really* want to hang out with somebody who had so much metal stuck through his body that he probably had to avoid standing near anything magnetic?

Jazmin made her way onto the platform. *The secret of success lies in how you emerge from failure*, she reminded herself. As a train swooshed by, she caught a glimpse of herself in the windows. Eww, what a mess! Her face was bright pink from being outside in a chill wind, and her eye make-up had started to run. Feisty Redhead Babe morphs into red panda suffering from severe cold. Unh. She was doing her best to be upbeat, but she was beginning to get that familiar two-week-old party balloon feeling. *This commitment party had better be good*, she thought. There had to be more to life than hanging around like a seagull in an updraught waiting for interesting things to happen.

THE PALE, WINTERY SUN HAD GIVEN WAY TO DARK GREY RAIN CLOUDS AS ASSIA AND JAZMIN DROVE ACROSS LONDON TO THE PARTY. JAZMIN WAS WEARING HER NEW DRESS, TOGETHER WITH her purple lace-up boots. The purple colour perfectly matched the tiny sprigs of mauve flowers on her dress. On her wrist was a silver bangle, a Christmas present from her cousin Clea. She had tried to tone down her hair by washing it several more times, but it remained resolutely and flamingly red.

Her mum's face had twitched a bit when Jazmin had entered the living room, but she hadn't said anything. Which was just as well, Jazmin thought. She shot her mum a quick sideways glance as they drove along. She was wearing a plain navy dress. Tragicistan. She really had to sort out her mum's wardrobe sometime soon. Navy was like grey, another boring blend-into-the-background colour. It said: "I'm here, but please don't notice me."

MEANWHILE, UNAWARE THAT SHE HAD BEEN TRIED AND FOUND GUILTY OF COMMITTING CRIMES AGAINST FASHION, ASSIA DROVE ALONG HAMPSTEAD LANE. SHE WAS HAVING VERY MIXED FEELINGS about the party. Working with secrecy meant she lived with secrecy. This was difficult when mixing socially with people outside her own knowledge circle. And tonight, she would definitely be mixing with such people. Not propitious omens for the evening ahead.

Also, Assia was not sure how she felt about Nerissa Cole. The reunion had been the first time they'd met in twenty-five years, and although Nerissa had gushed on about how they had all been such good friends, Assia couldn't remember it being like that. She remembered Nerissa, but as a sharp-faced, unpleasant teenager. She'd been the leader of a nasty girl gang who'd ruthlessly bullied smaller, weaker girls. Certainly not a friend. Nor was she able to recall any of the events Nerissa had talked about.

It was almost as if one of them had taken a "forget pill".

She checked in her rear-view mirror. Life was a lot like driving, she mused. To get to where you were going, you needed to keep a small, clear image of where you had come from. Maybe that was why she relied so heavily on her satnav system. She glanced down at the tiny screen. The friendly female voice told her to take the next left. She turned the car into the road where the party was taking place.

"OMIGOD, LOOK AT THIS PLACE!" JAZMIN EXCLAIMED EXCITEDLY, AS THEY PASSED THE FIRST OF THE ENORMOUS HOUSES SET BACK ON EITHER SIDE OF THE WIDE ROAD. SHE PRESSED HER FACE TO THE window, scoping out the vast gardens. Window grilles. Razor wired walls. Alarm systems. CCTV-scanned gates. Notices about security guards, attack dogs. Seriously Rich territory. The people who lived in these mansions probably bought each other small countries as "Happy Breakfast" presents, and ate off diamond plates.

"Right, we're looking for number thirty-eight," Assia said briskly, squinting at the invitation, which she had helpfully stuck on the dashboard above the satnav screen.

"There!" Jazmin pointed ahead. "That massive white house where the cars are pulling in. The one with all the gold and silver lights on the gateway. I bet that's it."

Assia slowed, peering through the windscreen. "You

know what? I think you're right." She indicated, and turned into the grand driveway.

In awed silence, they drove round to the back of the house. Assia parked the car. Then they both got out, and followed behind an elegantly dressed couple who'd just stepped out of a chauffeur-driven Rolls-Royce. Close up, the house was even bigger and whiter and fancier than it appeared from the road. A lot of architecture had happened to produce this, Jazmin thought, her boots kicking up the gravel. She wondered what on earth it must have cost. Probably zillions.

The facade of the building was awash with scroll-topped white pillars and balconies with curly white railings. On the roof were numerous little turrets with pointy conical tops and tiny arched windows. Whoever had designed this place had definitely read too many fairy tales while they were growing up, Jazmin decided, as she and her mum headed towards the brightly illuminated white front door. Either that, or they'd got a fetish about ornamental cake.

Entering the house, Jazmin and her mum stood for a moment in the wide, shiny gold chandeliered hallway. They looked around in amazement. "Whoa – it's just like Harrods," Jazmin whispered mischievously. "Which way to the Gift Department?"

Assia smiled conspiratorially, then put a cautionary finger to her lips, as a model-thin woman in an ice-pink, sequin-encrusted dress shimmered towards them on spindly silver high-heeled shoes. Diamond earrings the size of small fairy cakes sparkled in each of her ears, and her chemically enhanced blonde hair was so sleek and conditioned it looked like it had its own fitness video. Jazmin felt her mouth dropping open. The last time she'd seen something this pink and glittery, it had been in a toy shop, in a big display box with free stickers.

"Ash! How *wonderful*! Mwah, mwah!" the woman exclaimed loudly and shrilly, circling her glossy lipsticked mouth to air-kiss Assia on either side of her face.

"Hello, Nerissa," Assia murmured politely, taking a couple of steps backwards.

The glittery woman turned her attention to Jazmin. "And this must be your little girl," she gushed, her gaze travelling slowly from Jazmin's bright red hair down to her purple boots.

Little girl! Hello? And what's with the staring? Jazmin gave the woman a look so old-fashioned it could have petrified mammoths.

"Er, yes, this is my daughter Jazmin," Assia cut in quickly, before Jazmin could share her thoughts out loud. "Jazmin, this is Nerissa Cole, my old school friend."

"Jazmin? What a *cute, cute* name," Nerissa gushed. Jazmin instantly shrank back behind her mum in case Botox Barbie tried to air-kiss her as well. But Nerissa merely put a skeletally thin arm round her mum's shoulders. "You must have a drink. Have you met Cesare yet? No? Come with me then, and I'll introduce you to my *wonderful* man."

Jazmin's top lip curled in disgust. She dropped back behind Nerissa as, trailing sickly-sweet perfume, the sparkly woman propelled her mum firmly through one of the white marble archways leading off the hall.

The room Jazmin and her mum entered was even more imposing than the hallway. There were expensive-looking rugs carefully placed upon polished woodblock floor. Dark oak panelling on the walls. Groups of well-dressed people were standing around talking. They held glasses of wine, and small gold-rimmed white plates. Staff circled, carrying silver trays full of tempting nibbles. At the far end, a fire glowed in a vast black marble fireplace. Jazmin quickly scoped out the room. There was a distinct absence of other young people. Unh. She pulled a face. It was going to be one of those boring adulty evenings.

All at once, she became aware that someone was watching her. She glanced round the room, her gaze finally settling on a big, grey-haired man in his early fifties. He was standing in front of the fire, holding a brandy glass in his hand, and staring right at her. The man wore an immaculate pinstriped suit, cream silk shirt and a pink and blue patterned tie. An Armani watch adorned one wrist, a heavy gold chain the other. Looking at him, Jazmin had the uncomfortable impression that he knew exactly what she was thinking.

Meanwhile, Nerissa skimmed lightly across the room, dragging Assia with her. She came to a halt directly in front of the staring man. Jazmin hesitated, then hovered cautiously in the background trying to keep a low profile.

"Cesare, *darling*!" Nerissa cried, batting her fake eyelashes so hard they looked like two tarantulas in death throes. "I'd like you to meet Ash Dawson, my *very* best friend from school."

The man's face became more animated. "Ash – *buonasera*," he said. He bent over, and kissed her hand. Jazmin grimaced. What was with the "Ash" thing? And since when had her mum been "best friends" with Nerissa? And why all this fake kissing? She looked around the room, wanting to find somewhere to blend. Too late. The man's eyes met hers. He had very dark eyes, and they seemed to glitter in the firelight. "And this charming young lady is your daughter?" he murmured. "*Che bella!*"

Jazmin felt her face going all hot. Must be the fire.

"And what is your name, *bellissima*?" the man asked. He smiled, showing two rows of gleamy white teeth. Jazmin tried very hard not to think of wolves, even though the idea went perfectly with the man, as well as with the fairy-tale-ness of the house. She forced herself to concentrate. "Er, it's Jazmin," she told him, resisting the strong temptation to add, "and what big teeth you've got."

"*Delizioso!* So Jazmin, what do you think of our beautiful house, eh?" Cesare Frascati asked.

"Er, yeah – it's *really* great," Jazmin said politely.

Cesare Frascati stroked his chin thoughtfully with a well-manicured hand. "Ah...was it not the great Goethe who once described architecture as frozen music?" he murmured, shooting her a sly glance from under his thick black eyebrows.

"Hey, that sounds like Goethe to me," Jazmin bluffed straight back. She might not know what he was talking about, but she knew when she was being patronized.

Nerissa gave a false, tinkly little laugh. "Oh darling, you're such a *tease*!" she trilled, punching the big man playfully on his arm. "So *very* Italian!" she said, turning to Assia. Her pink-lipsticked mouth curved in a smile that didn't quite reach her eyes. Then she clicked her fingers imperiously. "Drinks here!" she commanded. A waitress glided silently over, carrying a silver tray. Assia took a glass of chilled white wine.

"There are some soft drinks on the table by the window," Nerissa said, waving an arm dismissively at Jazmin, who took the hint and moved away. She was only too glad of an excuse to wander off. She didn't like Nerissa, or her scary partner, and the hot, crowded room was making her feel slightly nauseous. There was too much gold furniture, too much ruby-red carpet. Too many dark mahogany wall panels. It was like being inside a gigantic box of chocolates. She decided to pick up a drink, and find an elsewhere to be until the desire to throw up went away.

Jazmin took her heavy crystal glass of juice out into the hallway. She leaned against one of the cool, pale-coloured walls, taking small sips. Shrill peals of fingernails-on-blackboard laughter filtered out from the main room in which the party was taking place. It sounded like Nerissa was having a fun time in there. Jazmin wondered what she should do now. Going back into that stuffy overheated place was not an option. Besides, she didn't trust the wolfy partner. He looked like he hadn't eaten for a while. On the other hand, there had to be *something* worth investigating in a freaky place like this.

Engaging lurkage mode, Jazmin began to creep along the corridor.

ASSIA WAS SERIOUSLY BEGINNING TO WONDER WHY ON EARTH SHE HAD BEEN INVITED TO THIS PARTY. THE ROOM WAS FULL OF THE SORT OF PEOPLE SHE PARTICULARLY DISLIKED: RICH AND overdressed. Their conversation seemed to be about either how much money they and their partners had made, or what posh school their spoiled kids attended.

Assia had nothing in common with any of them. She was growing tired of pretending she gave a stuff about their privileged lives, and was sorely tempted to bring them into the real world by telling them about some of the horrific things she'd encountered in the course of her work. This, alas, she knew she couldn't do.

There was also a group of sycophantic ex-school friends conducting a Nerissa-fest in one corner, but she had no intention of joining *them*. Assia glanced surreptitiously at her watch and sighed. She had only been here for forty minutes, but already it felt more like forty years.

NOT TOO FAR AWAY, JAZMIN WAS SHERLOCKING AROUND. SHE HAD DISCOVERED THE BILLIARDS ROOM, THE INDOOR SWIMMING POOL, THE PERSONAL GYM, THE SAUNA, THE EUCALYPTUS STEAM ROOM, the marble bathrooms (six and still counting). She had peered into the banqueting room, the ballroom, the chef's kitchen. She had admired the distressed-maple plank floors, the Zen massage and facial area, the Roman jacuzzi. She had even taken a sneaky peek into Nerissa's dressing area, with its wall-to-wall mirrors and computer-controlled racks of designer clothes arranged by colour and season.

Now she had made a particularly interesting discovery: she had found a library. It was in a big room overlooking the back of the house. Rounded walls of shelving were crammed with enticing books and the place was topped by a glass cupola that let in the proper amount of natural light. Many of the books were bound in leather and in series and looked untouched. Jazmin breathed in deeply; she could almost smell the stories. Hey, this was her idea of heaven.

In the centre of the room there was a huge antique globe. Rich people really liked old stuff. Maybe it was something to do with the fact that antique stuff was so expensive, thus clearly demonstrating how rich they were. The walls were hung with paintings of old sailing vessels, gold-framed and under portrait lights. At one end was a big cherry mahogany desk with a high black leather swivel chair. The chair had its back to the desk, as if somebody had recently got up out of it and left the room.

Mentally saving the desk for later (from her extensive reading of crime fiction she knew that desks always yielded rich pickings for the prospective detective), Jazmin began to make her way slowly and steadily along the shelves, checking out the books. Occasionally, she took one down, and flicked through it.

"Found what you're looking for?" a voice interrupted her.

Jazmin jumped. She turned from the bookshelf just in time to see the big leather chair slowly turning round to face her. She felt her heart lurch; an icy finger of fear ran down the length of her spine.

She had thought the room was empty; she was wrong.

BACK AT THE PARTY, ASSIA WAS STILL HAVING A HARD TIME. THERE WERE FAR TOO MANY GUESTS. TOO MUCH NOISE. THE MUSIC WAS TOO MODERN AND SPIKY. AND NERISSA WAS BEING A PAIN. SHE was showing off, laughing loudly, screaming with laughter and flirting with all the men.

Experience told Assia that the best way of dealing with a situation like this was either to get drunk enough not to care, or to leave. Currently, neither option was open to her. She had to remain sober because she was driving. And she could not leave without her daughter. Assia looked round the room. No surprise: there was a definite absence of Jazmin. Gritting her teeth, she accepted another iced mineral water from a T-shirted, white-aproned waiter and sighed. Wherever her daughter had ended up, Assia only hoped she was having a good time. *She* certainly wasn't.

THE GiRL SCOWLED AT JAZMiN. SHE HAD THiCK BLACK HAiR, AND A SMALL, DARK-SKiNNED OVAL FACE. HER BLACK EYES WERE FRiNGED WiTH LONG SOOTY LASHES. SHE WAS WEARiNG A PLAiN white top and navy skirt, giving off the rather odd impression that she'd put her school uniform on by mistake. The girl folded her arms and calmly gave Jazmin a thorough once-over.

"Has your hair always been that colour?" she inquired coolly.

Jazmin bit back a smile. She felt relieved that she was just dealing with a girl rather than an angry adult. "Recently it has," she told her.

There was a brief pause.

"I see," the girl said. "And do you have permission to be in here?" she went on.

"Uh? Excuse me?"

The girl raised her dark eyebrows. "This is a private library. You need permission from my father to be in here. You have permission?"

Aha, so that's who she was. Jazmin didn't recall her mum telling her Nerissa had a stepdaughter. "Ummm," she hesitated.

The girl stared at her. "I guess that's a 'no' then," she said. She paused. "But it's okay, I won't tell."

"Hey, thanks," Jazmin said. She smiled.

The girl did not return the smile. She continued staring at her.

"Listen," Jazmin began, "sorry, I don't know your name..."

"It's Ginevra Frascati."

"Ginevra, then. I was only looking at the books. That's all. I like reading. I wasn't going to take any of them."

Ginevra nodded. "I suppose looking is all right," she said graciously.

Jazmin slid the book she was holding back onto the shelf. "My name is Jazmin," she told the young girl. "My mum went to school with Nerissa."

At the mention of Nerissa's name, Ginevra's expression instantly changed. Hardened. Her eyes gleamed like knife blades. "Bad luck her," she muttered.

Aha, the Evil Stepmother thing, Jazmin thought delightedly. This place really *was* the stuff of fairy tales.

There was another silence.

"So what do you think of *Nerissa*?" Ginevra asked, spitting out the name as if it tasted nasty.

"Umm, she's very...sparkly," Jazmin replied tactfully.

"Yes, you're right. She is. Very sparkly. Did you know she's a big-shot psychiatrist with her own private clinic?"

"I think my mum mentioned it."

The girl pulled a face. "And she's a bully. Watch out – you need to be careful what you say when she's around," she said. She picked up a beautiful Venetian glass paperweight, and cupped it between her hands, staring down at it.

There was another awkward silence, which Jazmin did not know how to break. Eventually she asked: "So, do you live here?"

"No," the girl said. Then she closed her mouth firmly, and went on staring into the glass paperweight, her black brows contracted into a frown of concentration. There was something odd and vaguely unsettling about her behaviour. Jazmin waited a couple of seconds. Boy, this kid was hard work. "So I guess you were at the commitment ceremony," she ventured. "What was it like?"

"Rubbish," the girl said flatly, still not looking up. "They stood under a tree in the garden and said stupid things to each other: 'You are my sun: I bask in your light.

You are my moon: I have no other guide.' De-da, de-da. Nerissa wrote it all, of course."

"Uh-huh," Jazmin said, in a keep-on-talking voice. But Ginevra didn't. She lapsed into another deep, brooding silence, staring at the paperweight, and biting her bottom lip. Jazmin watched her for a couple of seconds, then turned away. She was clearly getting nowhere with this strange, moody girl. Time to exit. She was just about to tiptoe out of the room when Ginevra suddenly looked up. "Your parents – are they both here tonight?"

"Just my mum. She's in there partying the night away." Jazmin gestured towards the door.

Ginevra set down the paperweight, and got up. "Show me," she commanded abruptly.

Jazmin led the way back to the main reception room. The younger girl padded silently behind her like a small dark shadow. They stood together in the doorway, surveying the guests. "There she is," Jazmin said, pointing. "Over by the window: the woman in the boring navy dress."

Ginevra stared hard at Assia for a couple of seconds. Then remarked, "She looks nice."

"She's okay most of the time," Jazmin agreed. "Shame about the dress though. I tried to get her to wear something more party-ish, but hey, they just don't listen, do they?"

"I think she looks all right," Ginevra countered, adding, "there are too many...sparkly people here as it is."

Yeah, you're right, Jazmin thought. There were. And it was too hot. And the music was too loud. And uh-oh, here was the Evil Stepmother sparkling straight towards them.

"Ginni! Where have you been?" Nerissa exclaimed crossly, her pencilled eyebrows shooting upwards into her heavily powdered forehead.

Jazmin glanced sideways at Ginevra, waiting with interest to see her reaction. She had picked up that there was no love lost between Ginevra and her step. The younger girl froze. She stared down at the floor, clamping her mouth tight shut, as if she was attempting to drain her identity down some big black internal hole, so that the hard-faced woman standing in front of her would not notice she was there. Jazmin could almost see the hatred coming off her like dry ice.

Or could it be fear?

There was a long, jagged silence.

Then Jazmin slapped a big fake smile on her face. "Oh geez, I'm *so* sorry! It was *all* totally my fault," she gushed loudly, wondering if she was about to be killed on the spot by the God of Overacting. "Ginevra was showing me where the bathroom was because I got lost. It's such a big house, isn't it?" She turned up the wattage on the smile, and eyeballed Nerissa, daring her to get ranty in the presence of all her guests.

Nerissa paused, swallowing down her irritation with an

effort. "I see," she said stiffly. "Well, actually I think your mother has been looking for you too."

As if on cue, Assia appeared at Nerissa's side. "Ah, there you are. Ready to go, hon?" she inquired.

Jazmin nodded. Suddenly she couldn't wait to get out of the place. It looked big on the outside, but it felt stiflingly small and claustrophobic on the inside. And the weirdness between Ginevra and her step was freaking her. She gave the younger girl a sideways glance. Ginevra was still standing absolutely motionless, her face blank, refusing to look at Nerissa at all. Jazmin hunted in her bag. "Here," she muttered, handing the younger girl her micro. "Give me your number. Maybe we can stay in touch."

Ginevra took the micro, and keyed in her number while Nerissa watched her impatiently, tapping a high-heeled foot. "Hurry *up*, Ginni," she said. "Can't you see Jazmin and her mother are waiting to go home."

Her face still wiped, Ginevra thrust the micro back at Jazmin. Then, without making eye-contact with anybody, she turned and walked stiffly away.

"A very *troubled* child," Nerissa murmured quietly to Assia. "I intend to make it my top priority to see what can be done about her."

Jazmin cut Nerissa a look. The elegant blonde woman was watching her stepdaughter cross the room. Her voice sounded sympathetic, but the expression on her face was like icebergs might have worn when they passed each other in the Arctic in the middle of the night. All at once, aspects of Ginevra's odd behaviour began to make total sense. Jazmin felt very sorry for her. Having a step like that on your case had to be a one-way ticket to therapy-land.

She followed her mum into the hallway. She would contact the girl soon, she decided. Maybe work out some meetage details. She needed to Sherlock around some more. There seemed to be a lot of nasty going on.

ON MONDAY MORNING ASSIA STEPPED OUT OF THE LIFT, SKIRTED ROUND A PILE OF DUST SHEETS, A COUPLE OF TINS OF PAINT, AND A LADDER LYING ON ITS SIDE. THEN SHE PUSHED OPEN THE DOOR TO her department, and stood for a moment on the threshold, breathing in deeply. It felt good to be back at work. Even if the smell of new paint was already making her eyes water. She carried her briefcase and laptop bag across the empty room, set them down on the floor and removed the dust sheet from her desk. She hoped the decorators intended to stop by later and pick up their bits and pieces.

Assia slid into her seat, placing her things on the desk. She had deliberately arrived at work early, before the rest of her colleagues – well, specifically before *one particular* colleague, who hopefully would supply her with an explanation for standing her up on Friday night, followed by a massive apology. By arriving early, she was aiming to hold the mental high ground. Now she opened her desk drawer, and lifted out her internal phone, her picture of Jazmin and her pencil tray. She plugged the phone into the wall socket, and began sorting out the rest of her stuff.

A couple of minutes later, the head of the ISA suddenly materialized in the doorway. He gave her a brief smile. "Ah, Agent Dawson. Good to see you. Can I have a brief word in my office?"

Assia sighed. Now what? She'd only been away for five days. What could conceivably have gone wrong in such a short time? She got up, and followed her boss into his room. Like the rest of the department, the head of the ISA's office had also been newly painted. Unlike the rest of the department, however, it had acquired new window blinds, and a new carpet and furnishings.

The head of the ISA waved her towards one of the brand-new easy chairs, and made two cappuccinos with his shiny new chrome coffee-maker. He handed her one of his gold-rimmed green porcelain cups. Perks of the job. The main thing that hadn't changed was the mess. Even though he couldn't have been in his office for more than half an hour or so, the Head of the ISA had already successfully managed to restore his First Available Surface filing system.

"So," he said, perching informally on the edge of his desk. "Productive week?"

"Different," Assia admitted guardedly.

"I expect you have done your usual efficient job on those cold-case files."

Assia gave a brief nod. She hoped so too.

"But I guess you're glad to be back, eh?"

"Yes, sir."

"Uh-huh. Good. Yes. That's good."

Assia cut him a speculative glance. The head of the ISA had gone monosyllabic. Always a telling sign. It meant that she was right: something had happened. She sipped her coffee, and waited expectantly.

"I had a call from someone in the Met yesterday," he said.

Assia looked up sharply. The police would only make contact on a Sunday if it was serious.

"It was about our American colleague Chris Mbeki..."

Assia felt herself going very still.

"He was the victim of a serious assault on Friday night."

Assia stared at him.

"It appears he was beaten up, dragged into an alleyway, where he was robbed and left for dead. The police believe the incident might be racially motivated. There have been a couple of similar attacks in the West End over the past few months. They think they are all being carried out by the same group or, possibly, an individual." He exhaled, shook his head sadly. "We like to think we live in a decent, civilized society, don't we?"

Assia made a conscious effort to lower her eyes. She stared down at her hands, folded in her lap, giving her brain time to process the news. Then she glanced up again.

"I was supposed to see him for a drink on Friday night," she said. "He rang me earlier in the day. We arranged to meet at a bar. When he didn't turn up, I wondered..." Her voice tailed off.

The head of the ISA looked at her sympathetically. "Yes, I know about that meeting. He called me in the week. Said he felt he was getting out of his depth. Events beginning to run away from him. I recommended that he talked it through with you. Maybe took you on board for a bit. If you had nothing else on the horizon."

Assia nodded slowly. "I see," she said, adding, "I haven't." She paused. "So where is he?"

"Still in hospital. Because he was brought in unconscious, they had to run some tests to assess the damage. Now he's regained consciousness, they're keeping him in for further tests and observation."

"And how is he?"

"Confused and in a lot of pain. I've had a brief word with him. He can't remember what happened at all. I've arranged with his letting agent to borrow his keys. I was going to go round to his apartment after work and pick up a few personal bits and pieces for him." The head of the ISA glanced at her. "But perhaps in the circumstances..."

Assia nodded. "Of course I'll do it," she said firmly. "Leave it with me." She got up. At the door, she paused, momentarily tempted to ask what exactly Chris Mbeki was up to. And why he needed help. But the head of the ISA had his back to her, and was transferring stuff from his desk to the window sill, where it would probably stay, gathering dust, until the next departmental paint. He had also started humming tunelessly under his breath. An indication that he was no longer contactable by the real world. Assia hurried out. After all, she reasoned, she would soon find out the details for herself.

JAZMIN WAS STANDING IN LINE IN A SUPERMARKET QUEUE STOCKING UP BEFORE THE DAY GOT UNDER WAY. IN HER BASKET SHE HAD: A ROAST BEEF AND SALAD WRAP, TWO GINGER COOKIES, A BAR of chocolate, an apple and a bottle of citrus spring water. Occasionally she wondered why her genetic package had not come with moderation software. Mostly, she just ate and was grateful.

As she moved up the queue, Jazmin remembered how the gang of gate-girls led by Honi Delacy had given her such a hard time last term. Since Christmas, however, things had totally changed. Honi had found herself a brand-new, much older boyfriend. Jazmin had seen him waiting in his car to pick her up after class. He had Neanderthal shoulders and a monobrow, but Honi was boastfully ecstatic, and tormenting Jazmin had become yesterday's fun. Now the gang of girls merely nodded at her indifferently as she passed by.

Life and bullies moved on, Jazmin thought, as she finally reached the front of the queue and handed over her paycard. Maybe that was why she felt sympathy for Ginevra Frascati: she could still vividly remember that churning in the pit of her stomach. The feeling of cold anticipatory dread. Being bullied was a vile, horrible experience. But when the bully was an adult, and had just moved in with your dad? How did that work?

ASSIA WALKED OUT OF THE ISA BUILDING AND WENT TO THE NEAREST COFFEE BAR. SHE NEEDED SOME TIME OUT ON HER OWN. THE REST OF HER DEPARTMENT WERE STILL AVIDLY DISCUSSING what had happened to Mbeki, the news having managed to get round at lightning speed, in the mysterious way bad news always did. Everybody had been shocked by what had happened, but Hally, in particular, had been very upset, a reaction that had surprised Assia. She wasn't aware that Hally cared about Mbeki. As far as Assia recalled, Mbeki had mainly worked away from the building. She'd attempted to comfort her deputy as best she could.

Now, she wanted space to gather her thoughts, before going round to the letting agency to pick up the keys to Mbeki's apartment. After a brisk walk, she reached the outskirts of Holborn and entered a small café wedged between a couple of high-rise office blocks. She ordered a short black with extra shots.

Assia paid for her coffee. Then she took it over to an unoccupied table. At other tables, lawyers in pinstripes were talking together in low voices, discussing the business of the day and talking on their micros. Nobody gave her a second glance. She observed them all dispassionately.

Sometimes Assia got the distinct feeling that everyone else her age was an adult, whereas she was merely in disguise. There seemed to be no connection whatsoever between herself and these people. Or maybe Fate just threw dice to decide what she was going to be every day. Tinker, tailor, agent, spy. She stared into the small black darkness of her coffee. The world was a little bleaker and colder than it had been a couple of hours ago, she mused sadly. She finished her coffee in two quick gulps. Then she shrugged on her coat, and went to collect the keys.

EVERY MONDAY JAZMIN ALWAYS ASKED HERSELF THE SAME SILENT, DEEPLY PROBING QUESTION: WHAT AM I DOING HERE? GIVEN THAT SHE ALWAYS ASKED IT IN EXACTLY THE SAME PLACE – THE back row of the philosophy class, the question was not wholly inappropriate. In fact, it was exactly the sort of question the class loved to debate. Jazmin deeply regretted deciding to take this class. She had only signed up to it in the first place because her friend Zeb had told her it would help her cognitive thinking processes.

Yeah, right.

What he didn't tell her was that in reality, she wouldn't understand a word, and would be bored out of her skull. This was fifty per cent due to the class facilitator, an irritatingly jolly man who wore loud check shirts and badges with philosophical funnies like: "*I drink, therefore I am*" on them. He referred to his class as "people" and made philosophy jokes that she never got, but everybody else found hilarious.

The other fifty per cent of her problem lay with the rest of the students. Jazmin had absolutely nothing in common with them. In her opinion they were a bunch of angsty individuals who seemed to be constantly working through their own private childhood traumas. The afterness of a morning in philosophy class always led her to pig out in the canteen. Which in turn made her feel bloated and sleepy, and stopped her from concentrating during the afternoon. And – whoa – it was Monday, so here she was again, lurking at the back of the room, head down, getting ready to sideline herself into her usual non-participatory role for the next forty minutes.

"Okay, people," the facilitator announced happily. "Let's focus on our task today: the study of the Existence of Being. How do we know things exist? I trust we have all read the chapter on Laghenstern in our textbook?"

Jazmin groaned inwardly. She had not read the chapter on Laghenstern. Her textbook was currently serving as a doorstop. The facilitator picked up his chair, placed it on his desk. There was an instant ripple of interest. Jazmin shook her head sadly. For goodness' sake! Some of the students must have been possessed by aliens over the weekend. There was no other logical explanation for why anyone in their right mind could possibly get excited about a chair on a desk. The facilitator eyed the students archly. "So, people, who'd like to prove for us the existence of this chair? C'mon, don't be shy with me."

A forest of eager hands shot skywards. Jazmin shrunk down even lower in her seat. *Duh, Earth to boring guys: get a life!* The facilitator selected a student, who stood up and launched into the usual syllogistic "I perceive the chair, I perceive myself. I know I exist, ergo the chair must exist" construct. Other students hastened to challenge this reasoning or add their own pithy philosophical contributions.

Jazmin expelled air. *Jeez, this is about as interesting as watching paint dry.* She decided to adopt her usual disguise of staring fixedly at the whiteboard, mouth slightly ajar as if totally rapt, while letting her mind drift off into one of her fantasy daydreams. Within a nanosecond, Jazmin had mentally left the class, and magically metamorphosed into her far more interesting alter ego Jaz Dawson, who did not waste time discussing furniture, but spent her life capturing villains, saving the planet, and managing to emerge with her hair and make-up bandboxy perfect.

Time passed.

Gradually, Jazmin became aware that someone was calling her name. The voice seemed to emanate from far away, on the horizon of her consciousness. Slowly and reluctantly, she uncoupled herself from her imagination, and dragged herself wearily back to the real world. She glanced up.

Uh-oh. The facilitator was looking straight at her.

The whole class was also looking at her.

"Jazmin Dawson?" the facilitator said in his talking-to-the-hard-of-thinking voice.

"Uh?"

"Perhaps you'd like to share with us your thoughts on the existence of the chair?"

Jazmin's mouth was still playing catch-up with her brain. "What chair?"

There was a universal sucking in of breath. Followed by a shocked silence. Debate was taken very seriously in philosophy class; there were strict rules and protocols. Rudeness was not an acceptable philosophical debating tool. Students began whispering together, and staring at Jazmin, who started packing her bag in anticipation of what was about to happen.

The facilitator frowned. He gave her a long, thoughtful look. It seemed to rest for several seconds upon her hair. Then, unexpectedly, he blinked a couple of times, smiled, and clapped his hands together. "Good, *very* good," he exclaimed. "Yes, an excellent, if rather succinct, refutation of Laghenstern's Theory of Being. Well *done*, Jazmin."

Oh crud, major backspace, Jazmin thought to herself as the rest of the students joined in the applause, relieved to discover that something clever had been said after all. The Curse of the Feisty Redhead had struck again. One of her New Year's resolutions had been to get herself thrown out of this class. The facilitator'd never let her leave now.

A SHORT WHILE LATER, ASSIA WALKED UP TO THE MAIN ENTRANCE OF MBEKI'S RIVERSIDE APARTMENT BLOCK, AND LET HERSELF IN WITH THE KEYS. SHE SPOKE TO THE JANITOR MOPPING THE hallway, explained who she was, and why she was there. Then she took the lift to the top floor.

Assia unlocked Mbeki's front door. She saw red and white petals lying on the pale woodblock floor. She smelled the heavy, cloying scent of decaying flowers. Closing the door behind her, she bent down and picked up the fading, ruined wreath that had been propped up against the wall. How odd. Had Mbeki planned to attend a funeral over the weekend?

She paused for a second, tiny frown lines appearing on her forehead. Then she replaced the wreath and straightened up, crimson petals falling like drops of blood from her skirt. His private life was none of her business, she told herself firmly. She went to the bedroom, found an overnight bag in a cupboard, and began filling it with useful things.

Eventually arriving back in the main living space once more, Assia decided to check out the kitchen before she left. She might as well throw out the perishable food while she was here, as who knew when Mbeki would get out of hospital? She helped herself to a black bin bag from the roll under the waste disposal, and began sorting through the fridge.

As she placed the full black bin bag on the counter top, she suddenly noticed Mbeki's bulletin board, which was fixed to the fridge-freezer door. You could tell a lot about somebody by what they had on their bulletin board, she thought, visualizing her own messy board with its numerous scribbled "To-do" lists and threatening "Remember!!" notes to Jazmin.

She glanced up at the board.

There were two items. Firstly, a cutting from the *Los Angeles Times*. Dated December 4th, it was headlined: *Jump London! Daredevil Free-Runners Leave For England*. Under the headline there was a photograph of four young men, barely out of their teens, standing in a line on an aeroplane gantry. Assia vaguely remembered the visit taking place. Something had gone terribly wrong with it. Hadn't one of the young men died?

Under the cutting, there was a white card with black-bordered edges. It was pinned slightly askew. Assia stared at it. The card was a funeral invitation. She read the words. For a moment, she didn't get it. Then she did. The card wasn't an invitation to a funeral, it was an invitation to *his* funeral. Mbeki's. *Omigod*, she thought, and an icy comet's tail of fear suddenly brushed lightly down her spine. What was going on? A wreath of dead flowers by his door, an invitation to his own funeral. And now he was in hospital, supposedly the victim of a race-hate attack.

Assia returned to the main living area. All at once, she wanted to be as far away from this place as she could. She glanced quickly round the room, trying to find any clues that might help her get a lead on what she'd discovered, and begin joining up the dots. Mbeki's silver powerbook was sitting on the coffee table. Assia picked it up. Then, clutching the overnight bag and rubbish sack in one hand, the powerbook in the other, she hurried out of the apartment, slamming the door behind her.

THE VILLA CENERENTOLA WAS SITUATED IN THE HILLS ABOVE FLORENCE. THE ONLY ACCESS WAS VIA A SMALL, STEEPLY WINDING LANE OFF THE VIA VECCHIA. IT WAS A QUIET, PRIVATE PLACE. Eminently suitable for a late winter honeymoon.

Nerissa Cole was sitting out on the terrace. She was enjoying an espresso, a plate of ricciarelli, and the unparalleled view of the city spread out below. It was a cold, crisp afternoon; the sky was a brilliant blue, and the winter sun lit up the dome of Santa Maria del Fiore, so that it shone like a bright spider caught in the web of buildings around it.

As she ate and relaxed, Nerissa was writing in a small pink leather notebook.

A short while later, Cesare Frascati pushed wide both the doors and strode onto the terrace. His dark eyes lit up when he saw Nerissa sitting there.

"*Nerissa, amore – ecco!*" he exclaimed. "I have been looking for you everywhere."

"Oh really?" Nerissa said languidly, setting her cup back down on the table. "And now you've found me."

Cesare dropped into the seat opposite her. "So, *cara*. You have been writing?"

Nerissa carefully closed the little pink notebook. She placed the silver pen on top. Then she raised her head and stared thoughtfully at the horizon. "I have been writing. Just a few thoughts for some future research. But I have also been thinking..." she began. And paused.

"What have you been thinking?" Cesare prompted, right on cue.

Nerissa deliberately let a few seconds pass by before she replied. "I have been thinking about poor little Ginevra and her problems," she said, her voice limpid with compassion.

Cesare shifted uncomfortably in his seat. "Ah. Yes."

Nerissa let a gentle little sigh escape her. "What *are* we going to do with her, eh?" she said, fixing her large pale eyes on her partner's face.

Cesare met her gaze. He pulled a face, then looked away into the distance.

"You are quite *sure* she can't return to her old school?" Nerissa prompted gently.

Cesare shrugged, fiddling with his gold bracelet. "It is very difficult, no? I have tried to speak to the head teacher. She has not returned my call. Maybe you could...fix things," he suggested vaguely. "You know..." he went on, "her mother always used to...deal with this," he added, his voice tailing off into an awkward silence. He shrugged his shoulders and gave her a helpless little half-smile.

Nerissa studied the horizon once more, apparently deep in thought. "Well, I could certainly try," she said slowly. "If that's what you would like me to do."

Cesare looked very relieved. "That's good. Yes. You deal with it. Do whatever you think is right, *cara*. The old school, a new school. Here or in England. I'm sure you will work something out."

A little smile of satisfaction played around Nerissa's perfectly painted mouth. "Then I shall," she said nodding her head, her voice dripping sugar-sweetness. "Leave everything to me. After all, at the end of the day, we only want what's best for the *dear* little girl, don't we?"

Nerissa picked up her cup and finished sipping her

coffee. She looked across the table, and smiled brightly. "So, are you all ready to take me shopping?" she asked, leaning forward and tapping her partner playfully on his arm. "You'd better make sure you have *lots* of money with you, because I found the *most divine* little shoe shop in the Via de Cerretani, and it looks *very, very* expensive!"

CARRYING CHRIS MBEKI'S BAG AND POWERBOOK, ASSIA WALKED BRISKLY ALONG THE WHITE-PAINTED HOSPITAL CORRIDOR. SHE BREATHED IN THE ANTISEPTIC-SCENTED AIR. CHILL AND SHARP AND remote, it reminded her somewhat illogically of stars in a night sky. Eventually, she reached the small private room where Mbeki had been placed. She stood for a while outside the door, looking in through the blinds. She needed to get the shock of seeing his bandaged, bruised body out of her system before she entered. The last thing he needed right now was some overreacting visitor stressing him out. After a couple of minutes, Assia took a deep breath, knocked lightly on the glass. "Hey, if you wanted to blow me out, you only had to call," she exclaimed breezily, as she entered the room.

Mbeki turned his head slightly to face her, and attempted a lopsided smile. Then he attempted to raise himself on one elbow. A harpoon of pain juddered across his shoulder, causing him to fall back with a groan.

Assia grabbed a chair, hauled it alongside the bed and sat down, bending forward so that her face was on a level with his.

"So," she said. And waited.

"Yeah – so. Or maybe not so so," Mbeki responded. The words came out thick and slurred through his swollen mouth.

"It hurts?"

"Only when I try to live."

Assia picked up the carrier bag from the floor. "I went round to your flat and got some stuff for you."

"Thanks."

Assia placed the bag and the powerbook on top of his locker. "Can you remember anything at all?" she asked.

Mbeki scanned the bleak, windswept landscape in his head. "Nuh-uh."

"The police think you were the victim of a racial attack," Assia remarked.

There was a pause.

"Right. And you think?" Mbeki asked.

Assia shrugged. "So what's the real story then?"

Mbeki sighed gently. "How long do you have?" he asked.

"As long as it takes."

"I was going to share it with you," Mbeki said. "Ask your advice. That's why I called. Only..."

"Yes. Only."

There was a long silence. Then Mbeki lay back on the pillow and stared up at the ceiling. "Well, where to start?" he murmured.

THEY WERE JUST A GROUP OF STREET KiDS, MBEKi EXPLAiNED. GHETTO RAiSED, SCHOOL DROPOUTS. CLiCHÉS iN BAGGY CUT-OFFS AND FAKE DESiGNER HiGH-TOPS. THEiR FAMiLiES LiVED ON welfare and crime. He'd come across them through an outreach project run by a friend in the NYPD. Most of the boys were still in their early teens, but they were already street smart and wise beyond their years.

The free-running was an extension of what they did naturally every day in the streets where they hung out. Mbeki just happened to know some professionals who did it for a living. So he brought them in to help and advise. Later, he fixed it for four of the kids to go to Europe to show off their skills, and compete against other teams of free-runners. The trip of a lifetime. Most of them had never been out of their own state. They were going to have the best time. And then one of them, Blair, fell off a roof in the middle of the night and died.

Mbeki remembered getting the news. Going round to Blair's tenement to break it to his mum. The feelings of helplessness, and personal responsibility. Regret. Followed by the overwhelming desire to *do* something. To find out what had happened. That was why he'd got permission from his boss to come to London. Mbeki thought it would be simple. Ask some questions, for which there would be answers. Deal with the inevitable paperwork. Get the body released from police custody and arrange for it to be flown back to the States.

But it hadn't worked out like that.

Naturally he'd assumed the boy had been either on drugs or drunk when he died. Given his background. And the fact that all the boys had been out celebrating at a club together earlier on that evening. So it had been a shock to discover from the autopsy report that Blair had died completely clean. There were no traces of anything in his bloodstream. The coroner's report gave the cause of death as accidental.

Then he spoke to the other members of the team. They all described how happy Blair had been that night. The boys had been applauded and fêted whenever they appeared. They had just been offered the chance to turn professional. A European Tour. A bright future beckoned.

But his death told another, darker story. For as he read the police report, and looked at its grim accompanying photos, Mbeki realized that Blair couldn't have fallen from the rooftop, he must have deliberately jumped. He'd landed too far out from the building for it to have been an accident.

Mbeki was left with the baffling conclusion that a happy young man with the whole of his life ahead of him had either made a terrible error of judgement, or had decided to jump to his death. It didn't square. Clearly something must have gone terribly wrong that night, but Mbeki didn't know how to move forward. So he arranged for Blair's body to be flown back to the States, as he'd promised the grieving family he would.

Then, for a couple of days he just mooched, reread all the reports, and tried unsuccessfully to work things out for himself. He was on the point of returning to New York when, leaving the ISA building late one evening, he decided to stop off for a drink before going home to his rented apartment.

Mbeki had entered a large, busy bar near the ISA precinct and ordered a beer. Then he'd sat down at a table. Flipping open his powerbook, he was in the middle of sending an e-mail to his boss, when he was approached by a man in his mid-thirties, who asked politely if he could share his table. Barely registering the man's presence, Mbeki had murmured, "Sure."

The man sat down, nursing his drink. Mbeki had continued typing. Eventually he'd finished, looked up, and registered the man's presence. Mbeki was friendless and adrift in a foreign city. He needed to talk. Soon he was telling the stranger about life as an FBI agent – the shoot-outs, car chases and take-downs. The exciting stuff that people always enjoyed hearing about.

He missed out the long boring hours spent on stake-outs and the endless, brain-numbing admin; nobody was interested in hearing about that! He also talked about his current job in narcotics – about the kids he'd tried to rescue, the crack houses he'd raided, the dealers he'd put away and the companies he'd helped to shut down. He said that he was over here for a brief vacation. Time out from the stresses of the job. He did not mention the real reason.

The stranger had listened silently and intently. When the story had come to an end, he had sat staring into his drink for a long while without responding. Then he had looked all around him, as if checking for unseen listeners. Finally, he had asked Chris Mbeki if he'd like to meet up with him again. He too had a story. Mbeki might find it interesting, he'd said. It was about drugs, drug companies. He'd be interested in sharing it with somebody in Mbeki's line of work. The stranger gave his name as Adam Smith. Mbeki got the distinct feeling it might not be his real name.

The following evening Mbeki made his way across town to a small, quiet bar in a side street off Clerkenwell Road to meet up with Adam Smith. Mbeki's suitcase was standing ready packed by the front door of his apartment. He had nothing to do, nobody to see. He was flying out on the morning plane. A few hours spent drinking with Adam Smith was a better way of spending his last night in London than what he'd had planned: sitting on his own in the apartment getting depressed about the way he'd let Blair and his family down. So he found himself in a rather scruffy bar, on a cold and rainy night, drinking a chilled beer, listening as the man who called himself Adam Smith told his story.

Smith told Mbeki that he knew somebody who used to work for a London-based pharmaceutical company. One day, he said, this company had invented a new drug. A "wonder drug". The reason this particular "wonder drug" was such a fantastic discovery was that it seemed to have no side effects at all. This was because it consisted of chemicals already present in the human body. The drug was a fusion of serotonin, the "feelgood" neurotransmitter, and dimethyltryptamine (DMT), a psychedelic compound produced naturally in the body.

The drug was the ultimate treatment for so-called "lifestyle illnesses", a chemical cocktail that could make you feel happy, restore lost youth, and stop you from ageing all at the same time. The Elixir of Life. Achievable for the first time in one small pill. Think of the implications, Smith had said, and think of the money to be made from a drug like that.

To begin with, the drug was secretly tested on lab animals in the Far East, but as every chemist knows, it's hard to duplicate actual human conditions in animals. So they began to run human tests. Everything was carefully planned and monitored, Smith said. The trials took place in countries where people were so poor that they were willing to submit themselves as medical guinea pigs. These volunteers, who were paid, took the drug, while a control group took a placebo. The results were amazing. The company could almost smell the billions in profit. Especially as no other drug companies were working in the same field. It looked like they'd really hit pay dirt.

Then something went wrong.

The researchers discovered that in about eight per cent of the volunteers, the drug produced side effects. Alarming side effects. In this eight per cent, something changed somewhere in the brain. Their perception was altered. They thought they were immortal. They believed they could fly. They experienced an irresistible impulse to throw themselves off high places. It was as if they had entered a state of advanced hallucinogenic delusion. So the drug was pulled. The foreign clinics closed. The research papers were quietly filed somewhere and never published. A potential fortune melted away. Then, a couple of months later, strange unexplained deaths started happening all over London.

It was always the same pattern, Smith explained. People with no history of mental illness or anxiety were suddenly throwing themselves off bridges, from buildings, out of windows. No trace of any drug was found in their bodies afterwards. It was obvious that the "wonder drug" had not been destroyed. On the contrary, someone had got hold of it and was selling it to vulnerable individuals who had no idea of the harm it could potentially do to them.

At this point, Smith showed Mbeki a list of names. Mbeki scanned the list. And suddenly he recognized one of the names. Blair. Quickly hiding his shock, he asked Smith where he'd got the list. Smith shrugged, said he visited websites like anybody else, only difference was, he read in between the lines. He refused to elaborate.

Notice the age of these people? Smith continued. All young. Suggesting that someone had entered into the lucrative market for recreational and dance-floor drugs. Think about it, he said. Here you have this wonderful chemical fix. It takes you places, and leaves no footprints in your body. Unless of course you're one of the unlucky eight per cent who get taken to places they never come back from – only probably it's nearer ten per cent because the metabolism of young people reacts differently to that of adults.

However, Smith said, let's say that maybe the employee who used to work for the company was prepared to blow the whistle. Let's say maybe this person had proof of what the company had done. Let's say that maybe some lab studies "survived". There's a whole bunch of grieving families out there. And an unscrupulous individual lurking in the shadows who is getting very rich selling a highly dangerous drug to young people. If you were this ex-employee, he'd remarked, glancing across the table at Mbeki, how would you take it to the next level?

Then he had stopped speaking, and sat nursing his pint. So Mbeki had asked him point blank: this somebody, are we talking about you here? And Smith had smiled, then said cryptically that, the way he saw things, it was like riding a tiger. It was exciting, but difficult to get off. He had managed to get off, so that wasn't the problem. The problem was that the tiger knew where he lived.

Mbeki had thought hard for a bit. He desperately wanted to get his hands on those lab studies. He felt sure they were the key to unlocking the mystery of Blair's death. Maybe God had heard his prayers, and thrown him a lifeline. So he'd told Adam Smith that as an FBI agent working in narcotics, he might be able to give the "somebody" some good advice, but he'd need to read the lab studies first, so that he knew exactly what sort of drug he was dealing with. And Smith had nodded. Then he'd scribbled his number on a beer mat, got up and told Mbeki not to follow him.

Mbeki waited. Finally, he too rose, and went out into the London street. It was still raining heavily. Grey drops falling leadenly out of a cheerless night sky. He had pulled up his coat collar and walked quickly to the nearest station. Head down, deep in his thoughts.

Mbeki was familiar with aspects of the designer drug trade. He had conducted covert investigations into what were euphemistically called "research chemicals" – powerful psychedelic drugs sold over the internet. They did not have street names, but were always referred to by their abbreviated lab names. Mbeki knew them by heart: meo-DMT, 2-CT-2, nn-DMT, 2CB, MDMA, AMT. Just before he came to London, his team had conducted a dawn raid, and closed down several sites operating illegally out of New York and Manhattan Island. They had arrested the "psychonauts" behind them.

But everyone who worked in drug enforcement acknowledged they were fighting a losing battle. They were running just to keep up. There was so much money to be made from designer drugs that companies and individual chemists were always working to synthesize new ones to satisfy an insatiable worldwide customer base.

Mbeki passed a restless night.

Next morning, he had unpacked his case. He contacted his boss, explained the situation, and got official permission to stay a while longer. Then he did some digging around to see if what Adam Smith had said could possibly be true. After all, he didn't know the man from a bar of soap. He went through the police lists for the night Blair had died. He discovered several other young people had jumped, or fallen to their deaths as well. He recognized names from the list Smith had showed him. Two of them had visited the same club as Blair.

So he'd called the number Smith had given him, and arranged another meeting. The way he reasoned it, he owed it to Blair and his family, and now he owed it to the other kids who had died, and whose deaths were not being investigated. Mbeki arranged to meet him in the Savoy Grill Bar. Somewhere public, but discreet. He arrived early, waited. And waited. But Adam Smith had not showed. He wasn't answering his phone either. Not then, and not in any of the days afterwards.

Shortly after this, Mbeki realized that he was being followed.

IT WAS LAST PERIOD OF THE DAY, AND JAZMIN WAS SUPPOSED TO BE IN SCIENCE CLASS. ONLY SHE WASN'T. SHE WAS IN THE RESOURCES CENTRE INSTEAD, HIDING BEHIND A STACK OF encyclopedias. Once again, she was realizing that it was a lot less fun being the centre of attention than she had thought. She'd spent most of today hanging out with the philosophy crowd, who'd decided after her clever rebuttal in class that she was now One of Them. Yesterday, she'd hung out with the Party crowd, who'd taken one look at her hair and reached a similar conclusion. She was wondering when she'd be able to lose her "Feisty Redhead Philosopher Babe" persona, turn back into herself, and get on with the rest of her life.

Jazmin watched the pale sunlight making beams of sparkly dust that drifted around like random thoughts. Unh, mental head slap: it was better to be happy with who you were, rather than try to make yourself into somebody else. Fake popularity sucked. She wished she'd appreciated this before she'd dyed her hair.

It was also a long while since lunch, and thinking

always made her feel hungry. She reached down into her bag. The bar of chocolate she'd bought earlier was still there. She drew it out with a sigh of satisfaction. Sure, she was about to break yet another of her New Year resolutions – cut back on the snacks – but she consoled herself with the thought that Snacks Eaten When Stressed didn't count. She unwrapped the bar, and stuffed a couple of squares into her mouth. Bliss.

As she finished off the chocolate bar she glanced up, and met the cold stare of the librarian, who jabbed an angry finger at the *No Food Or Drink To Be Consumed In The Resources Centre* sign. She wondered if she should explain that chocolate was not actually a food but a therapy, or that the Aztecs used cocoa beans as currency (an interesting fact gleaned from one of the encyclopedias), but a glance at the librarian's stern face told her she'd probably be wasting her time.

MEANWHILE ACROSS LONDON, MBEKI LAY ON HIS BACK IN HIS HOSPITAL BED. THE STAFF HAD DIMMED THE LIGHTS IN THE ROOM AND PULLED DOWN THE BLIND, BUT A SLICE OF PALE LEMONY LIGHT still filtered in from under the bottom where the blind didn't quite meet the window sill. Mbeki breathed gently, feeling the sharp stab of pain from his bruised ribs. The dull stupor induced by the massive dose of painkillers he'd been given was wearing off. Outlying parts of his body had started calling in to protest vigorously. He sighed. He knew he could summon the nurse at any time, ask for more pain relief. But he wasn't going to do that. Not right now. He needed to feel pain. He wanted it to endure, to kick him awake in the long silent hours of the night. The pain was a constant reminder of what had happened. It hardened his resolve. The pain was a call to arms.

WHEN ASSIA TURNED UP AT THE HOSPITAL EARLY NEXT MORNING, MBEKI WAS WIDE AWAKE. PROPPED UP AGAINST HIS PILLOWS, HE WAS ATTEMPTING TO USE HIS POWERBOOK WITH HIS unbandaged hand.

"Hey," he growled wearily.

Assia clicked her teeth. "Should you be doing that?" she asked.

Mbeki tried to shrug. And failed.

Assia gestured towards a big bunch of flowers. "Nice."

"Yeah – they're from the guys back in NY. Good to know they haven't forgotten me!"

"So how are you today?"

"I'm doing great," Mbeki lied.

"Right." Assia nodded at him. She went to find a vase for the flowers. When she returned, Mbeki was still tapping laboriously on the keypad with his index finger. "Hey, I'll be back in business before you know it," he grunted, biting back a grimace of pain.

Assia perched on the edge of the bed. "That's good to know," she said, "especially since now you have yourself a new partner. I spoke to my boss last night, told him what you'd told me. As the drug company is located in this country, he's tasked me with helping you find it. Your crime, our patch."

Mbeki nodded in a satisfied way. "Welcome aboard," he said quietly. "He said you were the best. And I could use someone good right now. We have to crack this. Before any more kids die. And before whoever did this to me works out I'm alive and still on his case."

AS SOON AS SHE GOT BACK FROM THE HOSPITAL, ASSIA INITIATED HER INVESTIGATIONS. USING ONE OF HER CONTACTS IN THE MET SHE GOT PERMISSION FOR HALLY TO CYBERSEARCH THROUGH THE POLICE files, and pull out the names of every young person who had met with an unexpected and non-drug-related death in the past six months. She hoped that by interviewing some of the families, she might establish links or be given vital clues.

Meanwhile, she drew up a list of all the pharmaceutical companies based in and around London. Each one would be sent an e-fit image of Adam Smith as soon as it had been made up. They really needed to find out who he was. And if he was still alive. She also set up a program to webscan all sites selling drugs.

After lunch, Assia took off. She went back to Mbeki's apartment block to talk to the janitor. Somebody must have delivered the wreath. Another somebody must have either let them into the building, or taken in the wreath at the communal entrance. Here, she lucked out. The janitor had a clear memory of the wreath being delivered. After all, it wasn't the sort of thing he took in every day, he told Assia. Red roses, yeah, nice bunch of mixed flowers, sure. But a funeral wreath? Never in all the years he'd worked here. Young man'd delivered it, the janitor said, scratching the back of his head. He drove one of those fancy little runabout vans. Yellow it was. Lily something or other painted on the side. Assia thanked him and went on her way.

THE FLORIST AT LILIES OF THE FIELD BARELY REGISTERED THE WOMAN IN THE DARK BUSINESS SUIT WHO STROLLED INTO HIS SHOP MID-AFTERNOON, AND BEGAN EXAMINING THE BUNCHES OF HAND-tied flowers on display. He was far too busy taking a complicated order from one of his more demanding regulars, who was giving a big dinner party at the weekend and wanted flowers to match the colour of his table settings. The table settings were turquoise and gold. Colours that flowers didn't currently come in. It was taking a while to pick his way through that little minefield. Meanwhile, the woman approached the counter, where she stood and waited patiently until a skilfully negotiated compromise had been reached.

"Can I help you?" he asked politely.

"I hope so," Assia said. She gave him a winning smile. "I want to inquire about a wreath."

The florist instantly tuned his facial expression to deeply sympathetic. "I understand," he murmured. He reached under the counter, brought out a laminated book. "We do a wide range of most artistic and *tasteful* wreaths. Please take a look. Suitable for every sort of ceremony. Civil or religious."

"I'm sorry." Assia pulled a face. "I guess I'm not explaining this very well. I want to talk about a wreath you made a while ago."

The florist closed the laminated book. "I do hope there was nothing wrong with it?"

"No really, it was absolutely fine," Assia reassured him hastily. She hurried on, "I don't know if you remember the wreath I'm talking about: it was white carnations with a red heart in the centre and the letters RIP."

"Oh yes, *that* one," the florist said. "*Not* the sort of thing we usually do, but the customer is *always* right!" he said, his sarky tone clearly indicating that in this case they certainly weren't.

"Can you tell me about the person who ordered it?"

The florist looked at her in surprise. "It was a phone order. A man. Not young. He didn't give his name."

And I bet he paid by intercash too, Assia thought. Damn. She'd reached a dead end.

"So...why are you asking?" the florist asked curiously.

"Oh, I'm just making some inquiries. The person it was sent to wants to know who ordered it," Assia told him casually, without realizing the implication of what she had just said.

There was a stunned pause.

The florist's eyes widened in horror. "A *dead person* wants to know who sent them a funeral wreath?" he exclaimed. "Now I've heard everything!"

Inwardly, Assia cursed her sometime inability to connect mouth and brain. "Um...well, yes, thanks for your help," she said, smiling wildly. She backed away from the counter. Then she turned and bolted out of the shop at top speed, feeling the young man's eyes on her every step of the way.

LATER THAT SAME AFTERNOON, JAZMIN WAS WAITING OUTSIDE THE MALL. AFTER TEXTING GINEVRA A COUPLE OF TIMES AS SHE'D PROMISED, THEN CALLING HER FOR SOME LONGER FOLLOW-UP chats, she'd now arranged a meetage after classes finished. Her plan was: a bit of window-shopping, followed by a pizza and a nice long chat. Jazmin intended to do some detecting. She wanted to find out more about Ginevra's relationship with the slightly scary adults in her life. She was just checking the time when a glossy silver Alfa Romeo purred to a halt by the pedestrian walkway. The rear door opened, and Ginevra slid out.

"*Ciao*." She grinned cheerfully. "I'm not late, am I?"

"No, you're fine," Jazmin replied, her eyes widening in astonishment.

The last time she'd seen Ginevra, she'd been wearing a very plain white blouse, a navy skirt and flats. The Geeky Student Look. Today she was wearing a tight pink denim jacket with a black fake-fur collar, a very short pink tiered cord skirt, pink polo neck, black diamond patterned tights and black pointy lace-up boots. Her hair was piled on top of her head and secured with two big gold clips. Her eyes were black-rimmed and nocturnal, her mouth crayon-red and shiny as nails.

Eww! Fashion Deficit Disorder, Jazmin thought, trying not to let her feelings show on her face. Ginevra said a few rapid words in Italian to the driver, who nodded, circling his thumb and index finger, before pulling away from the kerb and speeding off.

"This is so great," Ginevra said excitedly. "I haven't been shopping for *days*!"

Jazmin gave the younger girl a steely look. Far be it for her to be judgy, she thought, but she'd always been told by her mum that Italians were very stylish. Not this one. Ginevra was to style what the Tooth Fairy was to cosmetic dentistry.

"Actually, I thought we might just look around for a bit and then..." Jazmin began, but Ginevra had already pushed open the big glass double doors and disappeared.

Rolling her eyes, Jazmin followed her into the mall.

"Over here!" Ginevra called, waving from a doorway. She turned and vanished inside one of the stores. Jazmin sidled reluctantly over the threshold. This was *so* not the sort of place she went into any more. She sidestepped round the carousels of cheap and brightly coloured tops and skirts. *Hello*, Planet Trashy. The store was crammed with shrieky pre-teen girls. The PA system was blasting out girl-band music. She looked around, finally spotting Ginevra at the back of the store. She was already heading for the changing area, clutching a pile of clothes. How did she do that? She'd only been in here for a couple of seconds.

"That was fun," Ginevra declared, when they finally left the shop. She was carrying a couple of carrier bags. "Now where shall we go?"

Jazmin opened her mouth to make a suggestion, but it was too late. Ginevra had already darted into another store. Gritting her teeth, Jazmin followed. Fifteen minutes later, they were back on the walkway once again. Ginevra had more bags. Jazmin had the beginnings of a headache. This was hard work, she thought to herself, as the younger girl hurried off again. And it was not how she had envisaged spending the afternoon.

It took a long, long time for Ginevra to tire, but

eventually Jazmin managed to get her out of the shops, head her off, and herd her into a coffee place. Wearily settling Ginevra and all her bags at a quiet table, Jazmin went to queue at the counter, returning shortly with two strawberry smoothies and a plate of cookies. She placed one of the smoothies in front of Ginevra, then collapsed into the opposite seat.

"Hey, I'm having the best time," Ginevra announced happily, reaching for her smoothie. "And guess what? I only spent up on two of my paycards."

"Uh-huh," Jazmin said, nodding. It felt like somebody was practising drum and bass inside her head.

Ginevra sucked noisily on her straw. "My father will be pleased. He's always saying I spend too much. Huh! As if you could ever spend too much on clothes!"

It was an opening, Jazmin thought. She was wondering how to steer the conversation *tactfully* towards Ginevra's wolfy dad. (After all, she couldn't exactly ask if Ginevra had ever noticed any bones under his bed.) "I guess it must be useful having a dad who manages a bank," she suggested craftily.

"My dad *owns* a bank," Ginevra told her loftily. "Banco Frascati – it's been in our family for centuries."

"I see. And he gets discipliny – hey, tell me about it. My mum's a real foot-putting-downer," Jazmin said, trying to draw her out a bit more.

"Poor you." Ginevra gave her a pitying glance. "Actually

my dad never gets cross with me. Never ever. He's the best. He always lets me do whatever I want. Well, he always did until *she* came along." Ginevra paused, screwed up her features and raised her voice in a quite passable imitation of Nerissa. "*Caro*, I don't think Ginni should do this... *Caro*, I don't think Ginni should wear that," she whined. She gave an exclamation of disgust: "Ugh! She makes me sick."

Jazmin nodded. "Uh-huh."

There was a pause, broken by Ginevra noisily sucking up a strawful of smoothie.

"So," Jazmin said casually, "I guess you'll be heading off back to boarding school in Italy soon."

Another pause. Ginevra stared down into her drink, as if expecting something unpleasant to rise to the surface.

"That'll be good," Jazmin continued. "You'll get away from Nerissa, see all your friends again. Bet you can't wait, eh?" She smiled encouragingly across the table.

Ginevra's small face darkened, frown lines appearing between her thick black eyebrows. Her mouth set in a thin, hard line. *Whoa – take shelter, storm clouds on the horizon,* Jazmin thought to herself.

"I shan't go back to that school ever," Ginevra said, spitting the words out like nails. "I hated it there. And I don't have any friends."

"Ooo-kay," Jazmin said placatingly, "so you're staying here in London then?"

The younger girl shrugged, made a "don't know" gesture with her head.

Another silence. Then, suddenly, Ginevra's mood seemed to change. She pushed back her chair and rose to her feet. "You know what? This is boring," she announced abruptly. "I don't want to talk about it. I don't even want to THINK about it. Let's go shopping again!"

THE SILVER ALFA ROMEO WAS WAITING FOR THEM IN A SIDE STREET. GINEVRA GOT IN, GIVING THE DRIVER DIRECTIONS TO JAZMIN'S APARTMENT. JAZMIN SLUMPED INTO THE BUTTER-SOFT leather seat, gratefully sipping the cold drink that Ginevra had passed her from the cooler. However little love there was in this family, there was certainly no shortage of money. She'd never ridden in such a posh car before. And she'd never known anyone buy so many clothes so fast. If they ever made shopping an Olympic sport, Ginevra Frascati could do it for Italy.

"You know what I'd really like now?" Ginevra remarked, breaking the shopped-out silence that had descended on them both. "A dress like the one you wore when we first met. It was neat."

"Thanks," Jazmin said.

"Where'd you get it?"

"A place called Camden Market."

Ginevra's expression brightened. "That sounds an

interesting place. Can we go there? When does it open?"

"Whoa – wait up." Jazmin smiled. "Haven't you done enough shopping for a while?"

Ginevra pouted. "You are not serious?"

"Deadly serious," Jazmin said solemnly, maintaining a straight face. "There are other things in life than shopping," she said, flexing her aching feet.

Ginevra's eyes widened. "Oh really? Are there? Such as what?"

"Oh, well – reading books."

Ginevra waved a dismissive hand. "Eww! Books are boring," she declared. "Books are for school."

Jazmin bit her lip. She was just too tired to start a major literary discussion about the merits of crime fiction.

"So, when shall we go to this Camden Market place then?" Ginevra persisted.

Jazmin paused. As she'd gone off the whole retro-goth thing, she wasn't actually planning to visit Camden Market for a while. She'd decided that for the time being she would give romance the elbow, and stick with her friend and life coach Zeb Stone. Even if his idea of a fun time was working out mathematical theories for rock-paper-scissors. But she felt sorry for Ginevra: it sounded like she was having a pretty bad time right now, and she didn't want to burst the girl's bubble by knocking her back.

"Well..." She hesitated.

"Oh *pleasepleaseplease*, Jazmin!" Ginevra said, opening

her eyes wide, and plastering a "last-puppy-in-the-pet-shop" look onto her face. "Hey, I know – Saturday! Let's go on Saturday. It's my very last day of freedom. My dad and Nerissa come back on Saturday night."

In spite of herself, Jazmin smiled. Ginevra reminded her so much of herself when she was that age. Everything was *such* a mega-trauma!

"Okay," she agreed, doing a palms-up, "you win. Saturday it is. Call for me at eleven, right?"

"You know what? You are the best friend I've ever had," Ginevra declared expansively, as the Alfa Romeo purred to a smooth halt outside Jazmin's building. She leaned across, and kissed her impulsively on both cheeks. Slightly embarrassed, Jazmin gave her a brief hug in return. Then, gathering up her one small bag, she waited for the driver to get out and open the rear door. She hoped some of the neighbourhood kids were seeing this. It was not every day that she arrived home in a posh chauffeur-driven car.

"See you on Saturday then," she said.

"*Ciao,*" Ginevra replied, waving frantically.

Jazmin stood on the pavement watching the silver car drive away. Then she turned and entered her building. It had been a worthwhile afternoon. She'd got to know Ginevra better, plus she'd learned some interesting stuff. Okay, the girl wasn't the easiest of people to hang out with, but she was certainly lively. And Jazmin'd never seen anybody shop with so much focus and determination. She was like a lapsed mall-orexic.

In theory, she ought to be envious of the girl's affluent lifestyle. But as she walked up the stairs, looking forward to a welcome from her mum, followed by a nice hot dinner and a good gossip, Jazmin knew that deep down, she wouldn't change places with Ginevra for all the paycards on the planet.

NEXT MORNING, ZEB STOOD ON THE CORNER OF THE STREET. HE WAS WAITING FOR JAZMIN TO EMERGE FROM HER BUILDING. SOMETIMES ZEB HAD TO REMIND HIMSELF THAT HE'D ONLY KNOWN Jazmin for a relatively short time because, like an annoying habit that is almost impossible to break, she seemed to have been part of his life for ever. Zeb had tried over the months of their friendship to introduce some order and structure into Jazmin's chaotic world, but it was a losing battle. Even after several weeks of philosophy class she still had the reasoning skills of an arsonist in a hayfield, he thought sadly.

He checked the time. Jazmin was running late. As usual. He sent her a quick "hurry-up" text. Zeb liked to arrive at the learning centre good and early. It gave him time to hand in all his completed assignments, then check the resources centre for any interesting textbooks that had been returned the day before.

Ten minutes later the front door opened, and Jazmin shot out, clutching a slice of buttered toast. "Jeez, Zeb," she exclaimed, hurrying towards him, "where's the fire?"

Zeb ignored the complaining. "History assignment?" he inquired briskly.

"Check."

"Maths homework?"

"Er...check."

Zeb strode on ahead, while Jazmin trailed along behind, talking loudly and animatedly about the new girl she'd recently met at a party. She frequently got animated about things. And loud. He hadn't a clue why. Girl World was unknown and scary. Terra incognita. Or *terror* incognita, more like. Entering it, Zeb always felt like he was out of his depth, and had forgotten to pack a wetsuit. He decided to fall back on his tried and trusted strategy: adopt an interested expression and murmur "M-hmm..." every few seconds.

"So *then* she got this text from her mum saying she was taking off with her new boyfriend to California, can you *believe* that?" Jazmin said, stopping on the pavement to take a breath. "Hey, Zeb, could you slow down?" she puffed. "I can't carry a heavy bag, go this speed and talk properly at the same time."

Zeb obligingly stopped. "I thought girls were good at multitasking," he observed mildly.

"Yeah, ha ha. *Fun-nee*," Jazmin cut him a look that could slice bread. "Are you listening to me?"

Zeb backtracked a bit. "Umm... You were saying something about your friend's mum's got a new boyfriend," he said vaguely, but hopefully.

"I was *talking* about my friend Ginevra. I was SAYING that her mum texted her three weeks before Christmas to say she was going to the States," Jazmin remarked. "She promised she'd send for Ginevra as soon as she had a permanent address, but guess what? Ginevra still hasn't heard from her. So she had a major mad. And the school called her dad, and there was a huge row and then she was expelled. Hello, Cruel World! How unfair is that? Just because she went a bit special forces." Jazmin paused, shifting the weight of her bag from one shoulder to the other.

"And now she lives with her father and his new partner. See – I was listening," Zeb said smugly.

"Right. Except that her father's only interested in making money. His family owns this Italian bank – Banco Frascati. And the new step is a total nightmare."

"Even so, blood is thicker than water."

Jazmin eye-rolled exasperatedly. "Unh – so is tomato soup. Your point being?"

"I'm sure it will work out okay for her. Families stick together, don't they."

"Yours might. Mine might. I wouldn't bet on hers," Jazmin muttered darkly.

They walked together in silence until they reached the learning centre entrance.

"I think it's worse for her right now, because she's only thirteen," Jazmin said, as if there had been no previous break in the conversation.

"Mhmm. Why should that make a difference?"

Jazmin clicked her teeth. "Remember being thirteen? I used to have MAJOR blues with my mum when I was thirteen. And I ran away from home." (Jazmin's mind travelled back to her childhood. She had run away an awful lot. Though only, she recalled, as far as the nearest bakery. Distracted by cake. The story of her life.) "Everything seems much worse when you're that age," she said. "C'mon, you *must* remember?"

Zeb looked thoughtful as he held the door for her. He shook his head. "I don't think I was any different then to how I am now," he remarked, as they entered the reception area.

Jazmin cut him a sidelong glance. *That's probably so true*, she reflected. She bet Zeb was the sort of kid who did sums with his wooden bricks rather than throw them out of his pram. "Well, Ginevra isn't like you," she said acidly. "Every time her step's name came up, she got this weird, twitchy look in her eye. She says she hates her, but I think she's frightened by her too," Jazmin pulled a face, "and I don't blame her. That woman's a total überwitch."

"Mhmm," Zeb said.

They stood in front of the facilitators' pigeonholes.

"I'm going to come up with a genius plan to help Ginevra. Hey, I'll let you know if I need any assistance."

Zeb winced. He'd "assisted" Jazmin once before when she was minding an elderly Russian man for her mum. The afterness still lingered. He sighed resignedly. There was probably nothing whatsoever the matter with this girl she'd befriended; it was all in Jazmin's imagination, but once she got an idea in her head, it was impossible to shift. And she refused to listen to the voice of common sense.

Zeb waited patiently while Jazmin excavated homework folders from her bag, and stuffed them into the relevant pigeonholes. Even if she came up with a so-called "genius plan", he thought, adding imaginary rabbit-eared air quotes, he bet she wouldn't consider the consequences. She never did. Jazmin was like someone who'd step off a high building saying they'd deal with the problem of the ground when it presented itself.

He was going to have to find an elsewhere to be for a while.

A LITTLE LATER THAT MORNING, HALLY SKINNER ARRIVED AT THE HOSPITAL. SHE WAS CARRYING A SMALL SQUARE ID IMAGER, THE LATEST DEVICE FOR PRODUCING 3D I-PICTURES. TODAY, MBEKI WAS going to try to replicate the face of the man known as Adam Smith. The hope was that some personnel manager at a pharmaceutical company somewhere might just recognize him, and provide them with his real name.

Hally placed the imager in front of Mbeki. "It's voice activated," she told him. "All you do is say what you saw, and it will replicate it on the screen."

Mbeki stared at the empty screen for a while. There was a brief silence while he closed his eyes, searching deep in the recesses of his mind. Trying to recall with clarity what Adam Smith had looked like. Then slowly, hesitantly, he began to describe him.

Sometime later, he leaned back. "That's the best I can do," he said. He expelled air. "Whoa, do you know how many ID i-fit sessions I've run back home for crime victims? I used to get real impatient sometimes. I wanted to yell, 'Hey, guys, it can't be that difficult to describe somebody.' Guess I never realized how hard it actually is."

Hally smiled sympathetically. "Well, you've done a really great job now," she said. She leaned forward to touch his bandaged hand gently.

"Thanks," Mbeki said. "Only hope Assia agrees with you."

At the mention of Assia's name, Hally felt her shoulders tightening.

"So where is she this morning?" Mbeki asked, blithely unaware of what Hally was thinking.

Hally sucked in her breath sharply. She really wanted to say something bitchy that would put Mbeki off

Assia. Trouble was, she knew the karmic predictability of those sort of comments. They always made their way back to the person being criticized. Usually with disastrous results.

"Uh, oh...she's probably running around after her daughter," she said eventually. Paused hopefully. "You know she has a teenage kid?"

"She told me. Jazmin – isn't that her name? I'm looking forward to meeting her. I gather she's quite a character." Mbeki grinned.

Damn! Hally gritted her teeth. "Yeah – you could say that," she said acidly. She eye-rolled. "Ah well, *teenagers*," she said, trying to pack a world of negativity into the word. "Don't you just love them, eh?"

LEGWORK. AT THE END OF THE DAY, HOWEVER EXCITING OR CHALLENGING A MISSION, IT ALWAYS CAME DOWN TO LEGWORK. ASSIA STUDIED HER LIST OF FAMILIES. THEY SEEMED TO COVER London and most of the South-East. Altogether, she had at least twenty addresses. She was going to have to pay every one a personal visit. She was not looking forward to it, knowing she was about to reopen barely-healed wounds. Meanwhile, how many more young people were going to swallow this drug and throw themselves to their deaths?

Assia started her car engine, set the coordinates on the sophisticated satnav system. Then she eased out into the busy London traffic. She had people to see, a manhunt to carry out. And many miles to cover before dark.

AFTER A LONG, PAIN-FILLED DAY, CHRIS MBEKI HAD FINALLY FALLEN ASLEEP, HIS DREAMS HAUNTED BY IMAGES OF BLAIR FALLING, FALLING IN AGONIZINGLY SLOW MOTION, WHILE HE struggled in vain to reach him before he hit the ground. He saw Blair's eyes fixed beseechingly upon his, read their message of fear and terror. But every time his hands reached out for the young man, the dream looped back to the beginning, and he was left watching helplessly as once more Blair spun and twisted through the air. And now, skimming the surface of his sleep, like a flat stone spun out across water, came the uneasy sensation that he was being watched.

Mbeki's eyes shot open. The room was dark and empty. He raised his head slightly, and caught his breath. There was somebody standing outside in the corridor. A silhouette on the blind. The head and shoulders of a man, outlined against the light. Mbeki felt his mouth go dry, his heart pound. He became aware of his own total helplessness. If "they", whoever they were, chose to attack him, there was almost nothing he could do to defend himself. The figure remained motionless. Then it disappeared. Mbeki exhaled a long painful breath.

The door to his room slowly opened.

The green-overalled hospital orderly looked concerned.

"You all right, mate?" he asked. "You look like you've just seen a ghost."

Chris Mbeki lay back, and attempted a weak smile. "Sorry," he murmured. "It was just a shock."

"Must've been. You went as..." The man paused, suddenly aware of the linguistic pitfall opening up in front of him.

"As white as a sheet?" Mbeki remarked drily, helping him out.

"Yeah. Something like that." The orderly began disengaging the brakes on Mbeki's bed. "Right, Mr. Becky."

"Mbeki."

"Yeah. You're off to see the HIT squad."

"Excuse me?"

"Holistic Intensive Therapy. Soon have you all healed up and back at work. Ready to go?"

Do I have a choice? Mbeki wondered. He nodded resignedly, then winced with pain as the orderly swung the bed round and bumped it vigorously through the door.

As his bed sped at an alarming pace down the corridor, Chris Mbeki tried to gather his fragmented thoughts. The figure outside his room: it had probably just been the orderly, he realized that now. But for a moment back then, the silent watcher had reminded him of somebody. Who? He tried to remember, forcing his mind back to the closed book of the past. And then it came to him. It was almost as if the memory had been teasing him and now, out of pity, had decided to reveal itself. One minute it wasn't there, and then it was, as it must always have been.

The stranger in the shadows. That's who he'd thought it was. The man he'd seen waiting in the shop doorway. Who'd stood watching him as he had passed by on his way to meet Assia Dawson. The man whose footsteps had followed him. Whose breath had brushed the back of his neck just as his gloved hand had reached out and gripped his shoulder.

In his mind's eye, Mbeki saw himself turn to face the unknown man, then raise his arm to protect himself from the first blow. He tried to recall the man's features, but all he saw was a dark space where his face should have been. Mbeki concentrated his mind, focusing inwards. The face remained hidden. But it was a start. He'd thought he'd forgotten what had happened. He had not.

ON SATURDAY MORNING, JAZMIN GAVE HER BEDROOM A MAJOR TIDY. USUALLY, SHE JUST EMPLOYED THE "PUT IT DOWN SOMEWHERE" METHOD, FOLLOWED BY THE QUICK "SWEEP THE ROOM with a glance" finisher. Every now and then, however, her mum got discipliny, and she had to put in the hard yards. Her mum liked rooms to be kept neat and orderly. Fair enough. Trouble was, after a major tidy, she could never find anything for days.

While she tidied, the smoke-grey sky outside her window

lightened to vanilla, and by 11 a.m., when the silver Alfa Romeo purred to a halt outside her building, there were even a few patches of milky blue struggling to be seen.

"*Ciao*, Jazmin. This is great!" Ginevra exclaimed, as Jazmin scrambled into the back of the shiny expensive car, and they headed in the direction of Chalk Farm.

"Uh-huh." Jazmin nodded. She had changed out of her tidying clothes into shopping clothes: black jeans and a black jumper, to which she'd added a stripy scarf and her purple boots. She'd also outlined her eyes with kohl and applied some deep plum lipgloss. The look was retro-goth, but with Edge.

She glanced at Ginevra, and was pleased to see that she was wearing blue jeans and a navy coat rather than the trash-o-rama stuff she'd worn last time they'd gone out together. Jazmin heaved a sigh of relief. At least she wasn't going to be embarrassed by her new friend. Now it was time to start carefully planning her strategy for the morning ahead. She would have to play it cool. Whatever the outcome, she didn't want Tony to think that she was dateless and desperate. That was not a good idea.

CAMDEN MARKET WAS BUZZING. GINEVRA'S EYES GLEAMED WITH DELIGHT AS SHE VIEWED THE STALLS, CROWDS, OPEN-AIR EATERIES, JUGGLERS AND STREET MUSICIANS. "WOW, TERRIFIC!" she exclaimed. "Where shall we start?"

Jazmin did a palms-up. "There's some nice stalls in the yard over there," she said casually, gesturing towards the area where Tony had his jewellery stall. "Want to take a look?"

Ginevra bounded off like an eager puppy on its first outing. Jazmin followed more slowly a couple of paces behind. As she'd hoped, the younger girl was drawn irresistibly to the brightly-lit jewellery stall. Jazmin stood a little way off, waiting for exactly the right moment to make her move. It came when Tony raised the lid of the glass case so that Ginevra could examine the contents more closely. As Ginevra bent absorbedly over the silver studs, Jazmin strolled innocently over.

"Found something you like?" she asked. She focused her entire attention on Ginevra, pretending she hadn't noticed the spiky-haired stallholder.

"Look at these little silver stars, Jazmin," Ginevra breathed. "Aren't they beautiful? I have to have them."

Jazmin looked hard at the studs. "Yeah, they're great," she agreed. Then she glanced up, making eye contact with the boy behind the stall.

"Hey," Tony said, grinning in recognition. "How're you doing?"

"Oh, hi," Jazmin said in mock surprise. "I'm good. Yeah."

"Jazmin, isn't it? You dyed your hair."

"Umm...yeah, I guess I did."

The boy nodded appreciatively. "Looks great. Said it would suit you, didn't I?"

"Err...did you?"

Tony glanced towards Ginevra, who was uttering little squeaks of delight as she found more nice things to look at. "Who's this? Your kid sister?"

"Nuh-uh." Jazmin shook her head. "She's just a friend."

"I'm Ginevra," Ginevra said, eyes saucer-wide as she took in the full effect of Tony's hair, studs and goth clothing.

"*Great* name," the boy said, giving Ginevra the full-on smile. "Means juniper, doesn't it? You take your time choosing, Ginevra."

Whoa – he's good at this, Jazmin thought, as Ginevra began picking up studs and placing them on a small wooden tray. Her cheeks were quite pink with pleasure.

Tony watched her for a while. Then he beckoned Jazmin closer. "So, Jazmin," he said, speaking softly. "Me and some mates, we're going out tonight. Want to come along?"

Oh boy! Jazmin did a mental count of five. "Uh, maybe," she said, acting casual. "Where are you going?"

The boy reached behind the stall, pulled out a small red and black flyer. He handed it over to her. "The Astoria," he said. "You know where that is?"

"Tottenham Court Road?"

Tony nodded. "There's a gig there. Look – good bands, aren't they?"

Jazmin glanced at the flyer. Toxic Filth, Evil Sister and Final Bloodbath were playing. Ewww. "Um, great," she lied.

"So, you on? Meet you outside at eight."

"Okay," Jazmin agreed recklessly. She knew for an absolute fact that her mum wouldn't allow her to go to a goth gig, but hey, she'd worry about that later.

"I'm ready now!" Ginevra announced from the other end of the stall.

"Coming right away, Juniper Princess," Tony said. He winked at Jazmin. "See you tonight, eh?"

"He's really, really nice," Ginevra sighed, as they walked away from the stall. "I love his hair. And all those studs and things. How great would it be to have a boyfriend like that?"

"Um. Yeah."

Ginevra looked wistful. "Do you think he might...?" she began hesitantly.

"No," Jazmin cut in quickly. "He wouldn't. Because for a start you're much too young."

"I could always make myself look older," Ginevra said hopefully.

Jazmin remembered her disastrous attempts to age up, the summer before. She shuddered. "Unh – bad idea. Seriously, don't even go there."

Ginevra's shoulders drooped. She pouted. "I guess you're right," she sighed.

"So," Jazmin went on quickly, "how about I show you

where I bought that dress you liked? Maybe they'll have one similar."

They worked their way back along the row of stalls until they came to the one selling retro clothes. "What size are you?" Jazmin asked as they began hunting through the rails together.

"A six or eight is usually fine."

Jazmin hauled a couple of flowered dresses off a rail and handed them to Ginevra. *Size six or eight.* She sighed. Mentally of course, she was a size six or eight. It was just that there were too many size fourteen snacks around. Which was why she always seemed to have slightly more hip than hooray.

Ginevra disappeared behind the changing-room curtain. There was a brief pause, then she reappeared. "Wow," she exclaimed, her huge dark eyes shining as she twirled round in front of the mirror. "Now I look just like you, Jazmin – isn't that amazing!"

Awww, Jazmin thought suddenly feeling all melty inside. Maybe playing the role of Ginevra Frascati's "best friend ever" wasn't so bad after all.

Jazmin waited while Ginevra paid for her dress. They looked around some more, then headed back to the car.

"So," Jazmin began as they walked up Haverstock Hill, "nice time?"

"Uh-huh. Nice time, thank you."

Something about Ginevra's tone of voice made Jazmin

pause. She gave her a glance. Ginevra's eyes were still bright and excity, but her face was less animated, her expression more thoughtful. She had stopped swinging her bags jauntily, too, Jazmin noted, and the nearer they got to the prearranged pick-up spot, the more she seemed to be dragging her feet. Jazmin guessed what was troubling her: she was worrying about her dad and Nerissa's return.

Maybe this was the right time to initiate the genius plan, she decided, as they crossed the main road and walked towards the Alfa Romeo. "Listen," she said, "I was thinking, why don't you ask your dad if he'd let you transfer to my learning centre? It's not that far, and I'm sure you'd soon settle in and make lots of new friends."

Ginevra nodded her head slowly. "Thanks. It's a good suggestion."

There was a significant silence.

"Go on...?"

"But I'm not living in the same house as *her*," she stated flatly.

"Right. I understand. But, remember, you'd be living with your dad as well."

"Except when he's working abroad. Which he does most of the time. Then I'd be left on my own with *her*." Ginevra shook her head emphatically. "No way," she declared. "I'd rather be dead."

Bummer, Jazmin thought. She hadn't factored in this negative reaction. "Okay, so where do you want to live?"

"With my mum, of course," Ginevra said, "but that's not going to happen, is it? She'd have sent for me by now if she wanted me. And she hasn't. So she doesn't want me, and I'm stuck with whatever *SHE* and my dad have planned."

"Oh? What do you think that'll be? More boarding school?"

Ginevra shrugged her shoulders expressively. "I don't know. But I bet *she's* made plans all right," she muttered darkly. "She doesn't want me living with her either. She hates me just as much as I hate her. Sometimes I catch her staring at me. Like there's something wrong with me, only she isn't quite sure what it is. As if I was one of her crazy patients. Except that she's the crazy one, not me!"

They reached the car. Without waiting for the chauffeur to get out and help her, Ginevra opened the rear door, and threw herself into her seat. Then she folded her arms, and stared straight ahead. The silence moved in like cloud cover. Jazmin waited for it to disperse, but it hung there, thick and heavy. A quick glance at Ginevra's closed face told her that here was somebody communing with her Inner Darkness.

Right, time to abandon the genius plan, she thought, as the Alfa Romeo sped down Avenue Road. Shame. She'd looked forward to turning into Jazmin Dawson, Teen Mentor & Support-O-Pal. And of course she'd also been looking forward to future opportunities to explore the huge fairy-tale house, and find out more about its scary occupants.

The journey passed in silence.

Finally, the silver car swooshed to a smooth halt outside Jazmin's building.

"Look, whatever happens, you can always text me," she said, as she got out.

Ginevra looked up at her. She sighed heavily. "I suppose."

"Of course you can," Jazmin said lightly. She gave the younger girl a reassuring smile. "Hey, don't worry, I'm sure everything will be just fine."

Jazmin entered the building. Sure, she felt sorry for Ginevra, and she wasn't confident she could come up with another genius plan to help her, but right now she had major issues of her own. Like how to get herself out of the house tonight without her mum suspecting anything.

She paused outside the apartment. What she needed was a trustworthy friend who could be persuaded to cover for her without asking questions. Someone who, if subjected to the maternal inquisition, would be believed implicitly. She got out her micro and called Zeb's number.

LATER THAT EVENING, ASSIA GLANCED UP FROM HER LAPTOP AS HER DAUGHTER CAME INTO THE LIVING ROOM. JAZMIN WAS WEARING HER NEW LONG WINTER COAT, BUTTONED UP TO HER CHIN, and carrying a brown paper carrier bag. "Off to Zeb's house?" Assia asked.

Jazmin nodded.

"I must say, I've never heard of a study party before."
Assia smiled.

"Yeah, that's Zeb for you," Jazmin said. "Work is the
new fun."

"So how many people are coming?"

Jazmin shrugged. "Hard to say," she said vaguely.

Assia got up and crossed the room. "Well, have a really
nice time," she said. She gave Jazmin a hug. "Love you
very much, hon," she said gently.

"Uh. Right." Jazmin extricated herself awkwardly from
her mum's embrace. "See you later," she said.

Lying has a complex molecular structure. Which was
why Jazmin walked out of the front door feeling nervous,
excited and *incredibly* guilty all at the same time.

ASSIA HEARD THE FRONT DOOR OPEN, THEN CLOSE. IN HER MIND'S
EYE, SHE PICTURED HER DAUGHTER HURRYING DOWN THE STAIRS
AND OUT INTO THE STREET. SHE SAW JAZMIN SWINGING HER BAG OF
books as she strode off in the direction of Zeb Stone's
house. She sighed gently. At least she knew where Jazmin
was going to be, and who she was going to be with.

Assia sat listening to the silence. The apartment always
felt so quiet whenever Jazmin wasn't there. She missed the
sound of her daughter's loud thumping music. The trail of
stuff that accompanied her progress from room to room.

The constant fridge-raiding. More and more she was becoming aware that Jazmin was separating from her. Making life-decisions without consulting her first. Like dyeing her hair red. That was part of her daughter's journey into selfhood. A walking away from the restraints of childhood. She guessed this was the way things were going to pan out from now on. Sadly, Jazmin was no longer a little child.

The eleventh commandment: get used to it!

Assia went into the kitchen. She knew that her part in the journey was to let her daughter go. Even if it was into a world that seemed to her to be becoming increasingly dangerous and unsafe. But that was how things went. You couldn't remain in the past. The past was not reliable. It was an old attic through which memory moved like a drunk with a torch.

She filled a bowl with mixed nuts, then opened a bottle of red wine, setting it on the counter to breathe. She took the bowl back into the living room and checked the movie channel. She was in luck: there was a good film just about to start. She returned to the kitchen, collected the wine and a long-stemmed glass. Then she settled back on the couch, the bowl of nuts at her side, the bottle and glass on the coffee table in front of her. Hey, it was Saturday night. She was home alone. She was entitled to some spoil-me time.

JAZMIN GOT OFF THE BUS AND WALKED TOWARDS THE ASTORIA. SHE WAS NO LONGER ACCOMPANIED BY THE CARRIER BAG, WHICH SHE HAD DUMPED EARLIER IN A CONVENIENT BIN. HER HAIR HAD BEEN backcombed into a fiery red mass of curls and sprayed with so much hairspray it almost clanked. Under the coat, she was wearing one of her cousin Clea's very short black dresses. She was also wearing her black Docs, matching fishnet tights, purple lipgloss, false eyelashes and a lot of black eye make-up.

The look was Retro-goth Girl Goes Out.

Approaching the Astoria, Jazmin passed small groups of older teenagers standing around, waiting for their mates to turn up. They were all dressed in black. It was like recess at a crow convention. She began scoping out the long queue that was snaking around the block.

It didn't take Jazmin long to spot Tony the retro-goth. He was leaning against a wall on the other side of the road, talking to two girls and a boy. All were dressed in dark colours, and wore garish make-up. She crossed the road and approached the little group. *Double, double toil and trouble*, she thought instinctively.

"Hey, Jazmin," Tony greeted her. "Nice to see you."

Jazmin glanced expectantly round.

"This is Jazmin," Tony said, putting a hand on her shoulder. He pointed to two girls. "Loz and Fiz," he said. He gestured to the boy. "And this is Daz. You'll be okay with them for a bit, yeah? I just have to go talk to someone.

Catch you in five." Giving her a smile and a casual wave, he disappeared into the milling crowd, leaving Jazmin and the three goths staring suspiciously at each other.

There was an awkward silence.

"So," Jazmin began brightly, "er...Loz, have you known Tony a while?"

"Who?" Loz asked. She was tall, rail-thin and wearing a very short dress made out of what looked like a dark-red damask curtain. Huge silver hoops swung crazily from her ears. Her legs were encased in black fishnet tights above knee-length black biker boots with silver stars painted up the sides. Jazmin gestured in the direction the boy had gone. "Umm...Tony?"

The group exchanged amused glances. They grinned at each other. "Oh, right, you mean *Kez*," Fiz said. She was wearing top to toe black velvet. Her long black hair hung spikily round her chalk-pale face and her deep-set eyes were ringed in kohl. *Eww, graveyard chic*, Jazmin thought.

"But I thought his name was..." she began.

"He's Kez," Fiz told her loftily. "Tony's just a name he uses sometimes. For fun," she added.

They all laughed.

"Right," Jazmin said. *I am not out of my depth here,* she told herself firmly.

There was another, longer, silence.

"So, Jazmin, go to many of these gigs?" Daz asked

eventually. He had green spiked hair, black leather trousers, and enough chains to start his own penal colony.

"Yeah, yeah all the time," Jazmin lied.

"Oh? Haven't seen you around before," Daz observed.

"Well...I..." Jazmin began.

"The doors are opening," Fiz interrupted. "C'mon, let's get moving!"

Whew, Jazmin thought as the queue surged forwards. *Saved by the doors!*

Jazmin trailed behind the three goths. She was beginning to wonder why on earth she had agreed to come. "Tony" seemed to have gone off somewhere, and she didn't fancy spending the evening with three extras from an R-rated horror movie.

Just outside the entrance, however, he turned up again. "Hey, Jazmin," he said, giving her a melty smile, "sorry about that. I heard there was some cheap tickets going." He reached inside his black leather jacket, and handed her one. "Here you go."

"Oh, right." Jazmin fumbled in her bag for her wallet.

"Hey, put your money away; it's the Tiger's treat!"

"Thanks," Jazmin said. *Except that you're not really "the Tiger", are you?* she thought as she climbed the steps, at the top of which stood the inevitable group of gum-chewing door supervisors, all wearing identical expressions, suits and earpieces. She sidled quickly past them, head averted.

Jazmin went straight to the cloakroom to check her hair and make-up. *So, what's in a name*, she mused, as she stared at her reflection in the spotty cloakroom mirror. Er, quite a lot actually. "Tony the Tiger" was dashing, exciting and retro. Whereas Kez? Unh. It was a geeky, stick-insecty kind of a name. She wondered what else he hadn't told her. And as for his creepy mates...ewww! Still, she reminded herself, she'd committed serious mendacity to be here. And she had a free ticket. And she'd never been to a goth gig. What did she have to lose? She might as well just get out there, and enjoy herself.

THE MAN STANDING IN THE SHADOW OF A SHOP DOORWAY OPPOSITE THE ASTORIA CHECKED THE TIME ON HIS BREIL WATCH. THE CROWD OUTSIDE THE VENUE WAS ALREADY THINNING, THE LAST stragglers hurrying to get in before the doors closed. An unmarked police car drove slowly by. Turning up his coat collar, the man angled his body slightly, so that he appeared to be studying the contents of the darkened window.

You like the thrill, he thought. *Stay one step ahead. Run the risk. Feel the fear, but do it anyway. You've always lived this life. Think back to when you were very young.*

He began walking away from the venue. He had sold a lot tonight. His eyes gleamed like pinpoints of light in the darkness. *What you have just experienced is a chemical experiment. One substance has been transmuted into something else by means of a catalyst. In this case, you are the catalyst. You are a modern alchemist. You have made gold out of base materials.*

Adrenaline was still pumping through his body. He laughed out loud. He felt *good*. He walked the few blocks to where he had left his car. *Darkness is your element*, he reflected, as he slid into the driving seat. *It is the only place you feel truly alive.* He started the engine. The car moved smoothly and swiftly away into the night.

HELPING HERSELF TO SOME FREE BOTTLED WATER, JAZMIN MADE HER WAY DOWN TO THE MAIN ARENA. IT WAS FILLING UP FAST WITH BLACK-CLAD GOTHS. SHE ELBOWED HER WAY THROUGH THE funereal crowd until she saw Daz, Loz, Fiz and Tony. They were doing scary poses in front of the stage. Tony looked round, and signalled to her.

"Hey, Jazmin; the first band's just coming on," he said. "Follow me." He led the way up to the balcony area. "It's better up here," he told her. "More room to dance."

The rest of his words were lost in a vast tidal wave of ear-bleeding sound as Toxic Filth launched into their first song. Everyone began cheering and dancing. Tony pulled her into an unoccupied space. "Okay?" he mouthed. Jazmin smiled bravely, circled her finger and thumb, and nodded.

Truthfully, though, she was a long way from okay. The music was unbelievably loud, the strobe lighting was cutting slices in her eyeballs, and to complete her discomfort a group of chain-encrusted boys were enjoying the music rather too close to her. They were blowing whistles, and throwing themselves into the air, so that she was constantly having to be on the alert in case one of them landed on top of her. She guessed this was what it was like at goth gigs. On the plus side, Tony was a good dancer, and she was pretty sure she'd recover her sight and her hearing. Eventually.

"Great, wasn't it?" Tony said, as soon as the band had finished their set.

Jazmin nodded. Then winced. The floor seemed to be going up and down like a ship's deck, and something in her head was still throbbing in time to the beat of the music. Tony grabbed her arm. "Let's go find the others," he said, and began pushing his way through the crowd. Reluctantly, Jazmin followed him. She had absolutely no interest whatsoever in catching up with team goth. She really wanted the two of them to have a nice "get-to-know-you" chat before the next band blasted its way onto the stage. She had prepared some choice things to say. She sighed, did a face-scrunch. This evening was not turning out quite how she'd envisaged it.

Down in the main arena, the other three were sipping water, and passing round a mirror as they tried to repair the damage done to their make-up by an hour's high-energy dancing.

"Woah – that was excellent," Loz announced.

Fiz applied black lipgloss with an expert hand.

Daz glanced swiftly over his shoulder, then felt in his pocket. "Here you are," he said, handing each of them a small transparent plastic packet. "I got us some good stuff."

Jazmin suddenly felt her insides freeze. *Omigod!* she thought. There was no way she was doing this. The other four tipped the contents of the little packets into their hands.

Jazmin thought rapidly. "Er...just going to the loo. Back in a bit," she announced. She turned and began pushing and elbowing her way through the audience, finally reaching the back of the arena and the rear exit doors just as the next band made its way onto the stage.

Hello, Planet Wacky.

She went to collect her stuff. It was time to get gone.

OUTSIDE, THE WEATHER HAD TURNED VERY MUCH COLDER. ABOVE THE FUZZY ORANGE GLOW FROM THE STREET LIGHTS, THE SKY WAS VELVET BLACK AND STAR-STUDDED. JAZMIN HUDDLED into her coat, suddenly perceiving the benefits of a warm thermal vest and thick tights. Items she was not currently wearing. She glanced at her watch. Sheesh, it was still early. Far too early to go home yet. She had told her mum she'd be staying late at Zeb's. She began walking slowly and dispiritedly down the street in the direction of the bus stop.

Ten minutes into her walk, and shivering with cold, Jazmin passed a brightly-lit chip shop. She paused, sniffing appreciatively. A bag of hot chips was exactly what she needed right now. Well salted and sprinkled with vinegar. Comfort food. She backtracked, and entered the shop. A few minutes later she emerged clutching a big, greasy, wrapped parcel. She continued down the street, pausing every now and then to pop a couple of succulent chips into her mouth, until she eventually reached the bus stop.

Jazmin leaned disconsolately against the perspex glass wall of the bus shelter. Hey, another Sad Loser Award to add to her trophy cabinet, she told herself as she waited for the bus to come. Another stupidity upgrade. And this time, the relationship hadn't even made it to the pre-romance stage. The bus arrived. She got on and went to sit upstairs.

Though maybe it wasn't *entirely* her fault, she decided, as she headed for a seat at the front. Her hair had to take some of the blame. After all, before she became Feisty Redhead Babe, she'd never have hung out with Weirds In Black, or gone to a retro-goth concert. She'd have joined the dots and run a mile. Her hair had blinded her to reality. It was Not Her Fault.

Jazmin slid into her seat. Funny how moving the blame around always made her feel better. She dug down for those juicy little crispy chips that always hid themselves right at the bottom of the bag as the bus carried her away from goth world. Hey, at least she had food, she consoled herself. Which was good, because food never let you down. Unlike boys.

ASSIA LAY IN THE DARK, LISTENING TO HER DAUGHTER TRYING TO COME IN QUIETLY. SHE HOPED JAZMIN HAD HAD A GOOD EVENING. SHE DESERVED A BREAK, AFTER ALL THE STUDYING SHE WAS doing. Assia was proud of the way Jazmin had turned her attitude around, and was now seriously applying herself to her learning. She'd stopped bunking off from the centre, too.

There was another reason she was glad Jazmin was settling down. Assia was painfully aware that ever since the summer, her daughter had somehow got caught up in her work life in a way she had never intended. Assia always scrupulously tried to keep her two lives separate. Usually she succeeded. Recently, however, it hadn't worked like that.

First there had been the Roztok mystery, where Jazmin's cousin Clea had become drawn into a sinister cult, and the ISA had tasked Jazmin with helping out. Then she had to use her daughter to befriend Dr. Ivan Kirilovitch, the elderly Russian doctor who'd gone into the ISA witness protection programme. She hadn't wanted to involve her, but there was nobody else suitable around to do it.

That was not going to happen again.

Assia heard Jazmin creeping noisily into the bathroom, the white noise of the shower starting up. She folded her arms above her head, staring up at the darkened ceiling. Yes, everything was running smoothly again, she told herself. Jazmin was on track, and as for the investigation, okay, currently it was a bit like assembling a jigsaw without any of the edges, or the lid of the box, but she'd get there eventually.

And this time, hopefully, she'd do it without her daughter's assistance!

THE WAY THE EXPRESS DRIVER TOLD IT, IT WAS 1.20 A.M., AND HE WAS AT THE END OF HIS SHIFT. HE'D LEFT BAKER STREET STATION, TRAVELLING NORTH TOWARDS WEST HAMPSTEAD. JUST approaching the end of the tunnel. And suddenly there she was. A dark silhouette standing on the bridge parapet. A figure outlined against the pale yellow street light. And then the girl was falling through the air, straight towards the track in front of him. The driver had a split second to register what had happened, to jam on the emergency brake, before the express hit with all the full force of its momentum, crushing the body under the wheels, then rolling over it, before entering the station and coming to a halt.

"She had her arms outstretched like she was trying to fly," the shaken, ashen-faced driver told the transport police later. "And I'll never forget her face as long as I live. She was staring straight at me and smiling. All the time she was falling. Smiling like she hadn't got a care in the world."

VERY EARLY ON SUNDAY MORNING, JAZMIN TIPTOED OUT OF HER ROOM. SHE CREPT DOWNSTAIRS TO THE KITCHEN, WHERE SHE CAREFULLY PREPARED A SPECIAL BREAKFAST TRAY, WHICH SHE then carried up to her mum's bedroom. She knocked gently on the door, and went in.

"Hi, hon," Assia yawned, sleepily emerging from under her duvet. She spotted the tray and her eyes lit up. "For me? This is very unexpected."

Jazmin shrugged. "Hey, it's no big."

Assia sat upright so that Jazmin could balance the tray on her lap. "Mmm – fresh orange juice, a whole cafetière, *and* hot toast and honey. What a treat. Is there any reason?"

Jazmin clicked her teeth indignantly. "Hel-*lo*? Does there have to be a reason for everything?"

Assia eyed her daughter speculatively. Then she picked up her juice, and sipped it. "No, of course not."

"Well then. Less of the suspicious. Just enjoy your breakfast."

Assia clamped her mouth firmly shut. She began meekly cutting the toast into fingers.

"I'm off for a run now," Jazmin told her. "I'll be back shortly."

Jazmin changed into her tracksuit, stuffed her hair into a hat, and hit the street. She was still feeling guilty about the night before, and the untruthy stuff that had taken place. A run would sort her out. She went into her pre-run warm-up routine, then began to jog slowly down the road. When she got back, she'd have a shower and cook herself something nice to eat. What with her stalled plans for Ginevra, and her disaster date, she had hit a temporary backspace.

When badness came knocking, it was good to steer towards the positive.

LATER, IN THE BIG WHITE FAIRY-TALE HOUSE, NERISSA COLE UNFURLED HER WHITE LINEN NAPKIN AND PLACED IT DAINTILY UPON HER KNEE. THEN SHE BROKE OPEN A WARM, BUTTERY CROISSANT and reached for the strawberry jam.

Cesare Frascati glanced up from his copy of *La Repubblica*. "Is Ginni joining us for breakfast, *cara*?" he inquired.

Nerissa shrugged her shoulders. "Who knows? I called

her ages ago. Maybe she's still packing. Or probably she hasn't got up yet."

Cesare grunted. He took a quick gulp of coffee, then glanced at his watch. Getting up from the table, he strode purposefully out into the hallway. Ginevra was just descending the wide white marble staircase, dragging a suitcase behind her. "I'm ready," she said stiffly, not looking at him.

Lugging the case across the hallway, Ginevra stood and waited by the front door.

"Have you got everything you need?" Cesare asked.

Ginevra shrugged. "Is the car here?" she asked woodenly, still keeping her face turned away from her father.

"Please – promise you'll stay in touch, Ginni?" Cesare coaxed.

Ginevra gave him a look that could have performed surgery. "No promises," she said icily, "and my name is *Ginevra*. Ginni is a little kid's name."

Cesare pulled a face, shrugged, did a palms-up. "Okay, okay," he said placatingly. "If that's what you want, *bella*. Let's go."

Ginevra pushed the door open with one shoulder, then strode out. Cesare followed, muttering in Italian. A few minutes later, a car engine revved into life. There was the noise of wheels on gravel.

In the breakfast room, Nerissa paused, listening intently until the sound of the car faded into the distance, and was gone. Then she wiped the corners of her mouth delicately with her napkin, picked up a tiny bell and rang it. The door quietly opened, and a maid entered. "Is everything all right, Dr. Cole?" she asked anxiously. "Can I get you anything?"

Nerissa glanced round. "I'd like a fresh pot of coffee," she murmured languidly. "And some more croissants. I really feel like *treating* myself this morning." She held out the empty silver serving dish, flashing the maid a two-hundred-watt smile.

MONDAY MORNING FOUND JAZMIN WALKING GLOOMILY DOWN THE ROAD. SHIVERING, SHE HUDDLED INTO HER COAT FOR WARMTH. IT WAS SLEETING, HER HAIR WAS TURNING TO RED FRIZZ, AND SHE was trudging to the learning centre without her gloves because she'd left them on the bus on Saturday night. Oh happy day. The only positive thing about the morning was that she was making the journey solo, having majorly failed once again to be ready on time to walk with Zeb.

Jazmin had spent most of Sunday micromanaging her guilt. She had done a lot of Good Daughter stuff, clocking up karmic brownie points, so that if there really was such a thing as reincarnation, she wouldn't return as something insignificant, unicellular and at the bottom of the food chain. One way or another, it had been a very weirdy weekend, she reflected.

Reaching the learning centre, she shouldered her way roughly through the gate-girls, meeting up with Zeb in the foyer.

"Hey, I see you finally made it in then," he remarked.

Jazmin gave him a lowered-eyelid look. She desperately wanted to say something cutting in reply, but her brain was too cold to sort out the relevant words, let alone arrange them in the correct order.

"So how was the gig on Saturday night?" Zeb went on, as she fumbled, icy-fingered, in her pocket for her registration card.

"Yeah, it was fine. Thanks for covering. I owe you."

Zeb shrugged. "Whatever. You know, I never associated you with that sort of music," he observed.

Jazmin's eyes widened. "Hey, Major Prejudice Attack! You should get some counselling for that attitude."

Zeb chose to ignore Jazmin's remark. "How did you go with the geography assignment?" he asked. "The one that's got to be handed over in..." he checked the time, "two minutes?"

Jazmin's brain did a fast-rewind. *Geography assignment? Hel-lo? What geography assignment?* She watched Zeb place his work neatly in the pigeonhole, on top of the big pile of already handed-in assignments. Then he stood back and waited expectantly for Jazmin to produce her folder.

"Okay, okay," Jazmin bluffed, waving her hand airily. "So I haven't actually finished it yet. But," she added, meeting Zeb's disapproving glance, "I'm working on it, right. Just a few finishing touches to add."

Zeb regarded her sternly.

"Look, you go on ahead to class. I'll catch up with you," she said.

Jazmin turned and headed for the resources centre. Honestly, she thought exasperatedly as she hustled through the glass doors, what was he like? If Zeb believed the whole world was going to come to an end because she had missed one tiny little deadline, he should try dealing with real-life issues, like deceiving her mum, bailing out on her date, and getting (briefly) drug-adjacent.

A SHORT WHILE LATER, ASSIA WAS SITTING AT HER DESK IN THE ISA BUILDING. SHE WAS STARING INTO THE MIDDLE DISTANCE, AND THINKING ABOUT JAZMIN. THERE HAD BEEN FAR TOO MUCH sweetness and cooperation over the weekend. Her suspicions had been aroused. Something had happened, or it was about to. Assia frowned, her eyes narrowing. Just because everything seemed to be running along trouble-free, she had allowed herself to be lulled into a false sense of security. She might have guessed that somewhere a big dark wave was cresting, and was shortly going to break over her head.

Assia looked up and caught Hally's eye. She gave an apologetic shrug, followed by a sheepish little smile.

"Sorry, miles away. I was just working out how to get one step ahead of my daughter."

"Uh-huh." Hally nodded sympathetically. "You know, I was only saying to Chris over the weekend when I visited, what a great job you do in spite of everything."

In spite of everything – what the hell did *that* mean? Assia breathed in sharply.

"I told him, the way you try to keep it all together," Hally continued smoothly, "the job, bringing up a kid on your own. Everything. It can't be easy for you keeping all the balls in the air at the same time."

The words "try to" hovered in the air like bricks. Assia's mouth tightened. She felt as if there were little wisps of smoke escaping from her hairline. She was just on the point of giving her patronizing deputy a piece of her mind when her intercom buzzed. It was the head of the ISA.

Still mentally fuming, Assia entered her boss's office. Over the weekend, the techies had been into the hospital and fixed up a video-conferencing facility. As she came into the room, Mbeki and her boss were talking together in low, serious voices.

The head of the ISA waved her to a chair and handed her a couple of sheets of printout. "I was just updating Chris with the latest news," he said. "According to my police source, there've been more deaths over the weekend. Same age demographic. The police aren't releasing any details until the autopsy reports are complete, but as they all died by jumping off tall structures, it looks like the wonder drug struck again."

Assia sucked in her breath. She glanced quickly at the photos, which had been taken by various police pathologists at the sites of the incidents, then looked away. "We have to stop this from happening," she said quietly.

"And we will," the head of the ISA affirmed. "How are your investigations going?"

Assia expelled air. "We've sent the i-fit picture of Adam Smith to all the London-based pharmaceutical companies. No response yet. And I've started interviewing some of the bereaved families."

"I'm sorry you have to do all the legwork," Mbeki interjected.

Assia glanced at the screen. "It's no big deal." She smiled.

"Hopefully, we'll crack this soon."

Assia nodded in response. Hopefully. An appropriate word. Now all they needed was the elusive lucky break that would turn hopefully into definitely.

After the conference call ended, Assia made her way back to her desk. In the middle of the desk was a brown paper bag and a tall lidded paper cup.

"Hey, I just thought you needed a break," Hally cooed. "I got you your usual. Pecan Danish, and a black filter coffee with extra shots."

"Did you?" Assia said stiffly. "Thanks, but you shouldn't have."

"It was no bother."

"No, I really mean you shouldn't have: I'm out of the office for the next couple of hours."

Hally raised her eyebrows. "Oh. I see," she said. "I guess you're off to the hospital now, aren't you?"

Assia groaned inwardly. *Grow up, Hally!* she thought to herself. This was like being back at school with its stupid playground politics. "Actually, I'm not," she said, trying to keep the slight irritation out of her voice, "I have a lunch appointment." She put on her coat. Then, giving Hally a brief smile, she hurried out.

NERISSA COLE ROSE GRACEFULLY TO HER FEET AS ASSIA ENTERED THE SMALL, EXPENSIVE RESTAURANT, AND SMILED EXPANSIVELY IN GREETING. SHE WAS WEARING RED HIGH-HEELED SHOES WITH GOLD buckles, Assia noted. She also had on an elegant beige wool dress, and a beautiful silk-lined fur shrug. A tiny bronze leather Bottega Veneta bag lay on the table. Assia recognized it from a photo she'd seen in a fashion magazine. She knew that the bags cost something in the region of four figures, and that there was a long waiting-list for them.

"Ash!" Nerissa exclaimed. Her red-nailed hands gripped Assia by the shoulders. "Mwah, mwah. How lovely to see you. *Sooo* glad you could spare the time from...whatever it is you do all day. But as I said when I called, I really want to discuss something important. Sit, sit."

Assia sank into a seat, draping the jacket of her well-worn navy suit on the back of it. She was not envious of Nerissa and her lifestyle, she told herself firmly. She'd rather have an interesting job than live in pampered luxury. Although she wouldn't mind trying pampered luxury for a bit. Just to make sure.

"I feel *sooo* bad you haven't been thanked for your present," Nerissa drawled. "I'm afraid we've just not got round to opening all our wonderful gifts yet."

Assia murmured something non-committal. She'd sent a card, but she had not bought Nerissa and her partner a gift. Since Christmas she was having to watch her spending carefully to make sure she didn't end up with too much month at the end of her money. Also, she resented having to buy presents for a couple whose lifestyle was so way beyond anything she could ever aspire to.

"Ah, so many lovely things," Nerissa trilled. "So many people wishing us well on our life-journey together."

Assia bit her tongue. She studied the menu. Everything looked very French and alarmingly expensive.

"Now, this is my little treat," Nerissa said, clicking her fingers to summon one of the hovering waiters.

Twenty minutes later, Assia was forking her tossed mixed salad listlessly round her plate, while at the same time trying to maintain her interested expression. Secretly though, she was getting bored of listening to Nerissa's lavish description of Florence and its wonderful shops. The designer clothes and shoes her *innamorato* had bought her. Assia had already admired the priceless gold ring which had a stone so big it could probably have supported its own planetary system.

She was also tired of the way Nerissa kept sprinkling her conversation with Italian words. It sounded artificial and affected. Rather like the woman herself. She wondered why Nerissa had invited her to lunch. They had nothing whatsoever in common. Thinking back to the past, she couldn't recall that they ever had. The two women finished their main course. The waiter discreetly cleared their plates.

Nerissa sat back in her seat and sighed deeply. "Ash, as I said earlier, lovely as it is to have lunch together, I do have a particular reason for wanting to see you."

"Really? Go on."

Nerissa paused. Her face took on a focused, worried expression. "It's to do with *mio innamorato*'s daughter Ginevra," she said. Small delicate frown lines concertinaed her alabaster forehead. "As I believe I mentioned to you last time we met, the girl is a deeply troubled child," she continued. "I am very, very concerned about her. Her behaviour over the last few months has been particularly maladaptive, volatile and unpredictable."

"Maybe she's just being a normal teenager," Assia suggested drily.

Nerissa's arched eyebrows shot up. "Excuse me?"

"I think I read somewhere that within a twenty-four-hour period, the average teenager exhibits symptoms of every known psychotic disorder in the book," Assia remarked. "I believe it's called growing up."

Nerissa laughed airily and waved a dismissive hand. "I *think* I know what I'm talking about, thank you. After all, I *am* a qualified psychiatrist, and I can assure you we are *not* talking normal teenage behaviour here. My stepdaughter, whom I have been observing in a *professional* capacity for some considerable time, displays a distinctly aberrant response to situational cues."

Poor girl, Assia thought grimly. *I bet she does.*

"Which unfortunately brings me on to what I want to discuss," Nerissa said slyly.

"Oh yes?"

Nerissa leaned across the table and patted Assia's hand. "My dear Ash, I know exactly how hard it is to bring up a child single-handedly, believe me," she said earnestly. "Most of my teenage patients come from broken homes."

Taken aback, Assia opened her mouth to protest, but was waved aside by Nerissa who went on: "So let me make it quite clear right now that I'm not in ANY way judging you..." She paused, her pale blue eyes staring coldly at Assia.

"But?" Assia got out between gritted teeth.

Nerissa expelled air. "But, indeed. Yes. You see, I gather that Ginevra spent some time in your daughter's company while her father and I were away."

"I think they went shopping once or twice," Assia said. "Jazmin sensed Ginevra was lonely, missing her friends, so she was trying to make her feel a bit more at home in London."

Without replying, Nerissa unzipped the beautiful Bottega Veneta bag. She placed a small round metal object onto the table. "I discovered *this* in my stepdaughter's bedroom on Saturday evening shortly after Cesare and I got back," she said. Then folded her arms, waiting for Assia's reaction.

"Right." Assia glanced curiously at the object. It looked pretty harmless.

"In case you don't know what it is, let me enlighten you: it's a tongue stud."

"Uh-huh. And its relation to Jazmin is?"

"Apparently Ginevra bought it at market stall. A stall owned by *your* daughter's boyfriend – who, I gather, has bright orange hair, wears make-up, body piercings, and black leather clothes with chains. Oh – and he also has several tattoos.

"My stepdaughter told me this boy sold her the...thing because he said it would *'annoy her folks'*." Nerissa's eyes hardened. "Delightful attitude, don't you think? Having found this, and subsequently extracted a *full* confession from Ginevra, I have to tell you, Ash, that Cesare was extremely upset. As was I. I never thought that your daughter could be such a malign influence. It took me a long time to calm *mio caro* down, I can tell you. Anyway, the upshot of all this is that he and I would prefer it if your daughter doesn't try to make contact with my stepdaughter again. I'm sure you understand."

Once again, for the second time that day, Assia was rendered speechless. She stood up. The expression on her face could have hammered rivets. "Let me assure you right now, Nerissa, that my daughter is not a *malign influence*," she exclaimed, every brain cell piling in to outvote tooth and claw. "How dare you even *suggest* it!" she continued, her furious voice causing other diners to glance curiously in their direction. "And I know for a fact that she does *not* currently have a boyfriend, let alone one who answers your rather bizarre description."

Nerissa's response was to sit back and regard her calmly. "No? You're absolutely sure?"

"Of course I am."

"How strange. Ginevra swears that she overheard them arranging to go to a 'gig' together on Saturday night."

"Well, she must have heard wrong," Assia spat, the words emerging like knives. "Because I can tell you categorically that on Saturday night, Jazmin was at a friend's house..." Suddenly she paused. All at once a terrible suspicion crossed her mind. Where exactly *was* Jazmin on Saturday night? Up until this moment, Assia thought she knew. But did she?

Nerissa read the doubt on Assia's face. And pounced. She smiled a pitying smile. "Maybe you should go and check with your daughter," she sneered. "It seems to me you know very little of what she gets up to. Perhaps your work–life balance needs a little restructuring too. If you don't mind me saying."

Assia was trying so hard to remain calm, she could feel herself physically shaking. She grabbed her shoulder bag, taking a couple of deep breaths to steady herself, and get control of her anger. "I have to go back to work now," she said, icicles dripping from her voice.

"Really? Must you go? So soon? But you haven't chosen a pudding!" Nerissa protested, wide-eyed with hurt innocence.

"No dessert, thank you. I'm not hungry." Her back rigid with suppressed anger, Assia spun round, and hurried out of the restaurant.

Assia hit the busy, lunchtime streets. She decided to go for a walk. She needed some time out to calm down and refocus before she returned to the office. She power walked herself round the block a couple of times. All the way, she replayed the scene in the restaurant over and over again in her mind, wishing she'd handled it differently. There were things she could have said. Should have said.

Pointless retrospection – one of her many talents.

At the end of the day, Assia caught the express home. She was still fuming. Letting herself into the apartment she noticed Jazmin's new winter coat slung carelessly on a peg. For a moment Assia stood motionless in the hallway, staring at the coat, as if hypnotized by it. Memories of Jazmin's incredibly compliant behaviour over the past twenty-four hours suddenly drifted back into her mind. Acting upon an impulse that she did not want to act upon, Assia walked across to the coat, and slipped her hands into the pockets. In one of them, she found a half-torn ticket for a gig at the Astoria. It was dated Saturday night.

In the course of her work, ISA Agent Assia Dawson had investigated, tracked and confronted some of the most devious people on the planet. Over the years, she had felt pain, anger, fear and sorrow. But all this was somehow nothing compared to how she felt as she carried the incriminating evidence into the kitchen, placed it on the table, and sat down to wait for Jazmin to come home.

JAZMIN LOOKED OUT OF HER BEDROOM WINDOW AT THE GREY SKY AND THE LEAFLESS TREES. IT WAS NOT THE GREATEST OF VIEWS, BUT SHE MIGHT AS WELL GET USED TO IT BECAUSE SHE WAS GOING to see quite a lot of it in the near future. She had just been grounded for three weeks. With extra chores. If it's not one thing, it's your mother. She opened her desk drawer, got out her bar of Emergency Chocolate and broke off a large chunk. Then she texted her friend Zeb the bad news.

Jazmin had successfully managed to keep Zeb out of the loop. When confronted with the ticket stub, she had owned up and confessed where she'd been. She had no choice. But she had told her mum that she'd made up the whole "study party" scam, and that Zeb knew absolutely nothing about it. Her mum approved of Zeb; Jazmin didn't want that opinion to change. Plus she needed a trustworthy mediator with the outside world.

Pulling a long face, Jazmin reached out for her geography textbook, and some more chocolate. She might as well get on with her schoolwork; there was certainly nothing else to do around here. Unh! Three whole weeks of no going-outness. How boring was that! She had briefly contemplated playing the "infringement of my human rights" card, but one look at her mum's face, and she had quietly reshuffled it back into the pack. Her life was slipping into a downhill spiral. She sighed, opened her book, and began filling in a rainfall chart.

Later, lying in her bed, moonlight coming in through the blinds and striping the duvet like a zebra, Jazmin thought about her mum. As far back as she could remember, her mum always dealt with her anger in the same way: she saved it up for when she needed it. Jazmin had to admit, albeit reluctantly, that her mother could have a serious mad-on with style. One day, when she was an adult running her own highly successful detective business, she intended to be just like that. (Along with being totally brilliant, elegantly dressed and universally respected, of course.)

When events had you tap dancing on quicksand, it was good to focus on the bigger picture.

NEXT MORNING, JAZMIN MADE QUITE SURE SHE GOT UP ON TIME. SHE HEADED STRAIGHT FOR THE BATHROOM, WHERE SHE STOOD UNDER THE SHOWER UNTIL HER EYES OPENED AND HER SKIN STARTED TO SHRIVEL – sure signs that she was ready to face the world. Then she dressed, and slid very quietly into the kitchen, where she found her mum sitting at the table, reading a document file and sipping strong black coffee.

Assuming an expression of pre-emptive meekness, Jazmin exchanged polite morning greetings, then inquired sweetly, "Shall I make you some fresh toast?"

"Nuh-uh." Her mum shook her head.

"More coffee?"

"I'm fine, thanks."

Jazmin sucked in some air. This downhill spiralling was uphill work.

Assia paused in her reading, and glanced up. "So have you got your books ready for today?"

"Yes, Mum."

"Done all your homework?"

"Yes, Mum."

Assia nodded. "And remember..."

"Yeah, yeah, I know: straight back home after school. Will do. Trust me."

Assia pursed her lips. "Let's hope I can," she said tartly. Jazmin sucked in some more air.

WHEN ASSIA ARRIVED AT THE HOSPITAL SHE DISCOVERED MBEKI DRESSED AND SITTING IN AN EASY CHAIR, HIS POWERBOOK OPEN ON HIS LAP.

Assia smiled at him. "You're up!"

"Yeah. And guess what? They're thinking of maybe letting me out today or tomorrow," Mbeki said cheerfully. "Good news, hey? And I have more good news. I've been eavesdropping on some pharmo-chatrooms. The story is that, yesterday, a London-based pharmaceutical company called NovaChem had all its hard drives wiped by a trojan."

Assia knew that a trojan was a computer program. It was named after the gift horse the Ancient Greeks gave to the Trojans. She also knew that they were frequently installed by disgruntled employees. The way a trojan worked was it lay dormant in the system for a while, then woke up and did its stuff. Generally a couple of months after the employee has been fired. An act of cyber-revenge.

"And you think this trojan..."

"Could have been installed by Adam Smith? He told me

his 'friend' had left some cyber-footsteps before he quit the company. So maybe. Equally, maybe not. Either way, it's worth checking out, don't you think?"

Assia nodded. *Maybe this is the lucky break we need.*

Mbeki spun the screen towards her. "Here's the company address," he said. "It's in Wembley. Perhaps you could pay them a friendly visit. But take care. If these are the guys we're looking for, they play hardball."

Assia left the hospital, and drove until she came to a quiet side street, where she parked and called the company to fix an appointment. Then she set the coordinates on satnav before heading out into the busy London traffic.

IT WAS MID-MORNING, AND JAZMIN WAS WAITING IN LINE FOR THE CANTEEN TO OPEN. WHILE SHE WAITED, SHE WAS TELLING ZEB ALL ABOUT THE GRIM WITH HER MOTHER. "AND HAVE YOU NOTICED THE way adults *always* sit on your bed whenever they want to get serious?" she finished up.

Zeb nodded. "Yes, they do, don't they?" he agreed. "It sounds as if you got off quite lightly, though," he went on. Paused. "All things considered."

"Oh really? You think so?" Jazmin gave him a hard stare. *What did he know?* Mr. I-Never-Get-Into-Trouble.

Zeb shrugged. "Okay, look on the bright side: at least you'll be able to get well ahead with your studying," he said diplomatically.

"Whoa – so I will, won't I? Oh total joy."

"That's good, isn't it?"

"Peachy," Jazmin agreed with fake enthusiasm. "Hey, you know what they say: 'staying in is the new going out'."

"Do they? Can't say I've ever heard it before."

"Duh – I'm just trying to look on the bright side!" she told him witheringly as the hatch finally opened. Jazmin selected a pink-iced Belgian bun and a carton of orange juice. As usual, Zeb eyed her food choices disapprovingly.

"Look, don't *you* give me a hard time as well," Jazmin told him. "I need a massive sugar boost to get me through the afternoon. Anyway, see: I have fruit juice."

Jazmin walked her tray over to a vacant table. Zeb followed. "Shame about your friend Ginevra," he remarked, once they'd sat down.

"Excuse me?"

"It's a bit harsh, forbidding you to contact her."

"Oh, *that*," Jazmin waved a dismissive hand, "as if I care about her demony step."

Zeb's eyes widened. "But I thought you said she said you—"

Jazmin clicked her teeth. "Like I'm going to do what that woman wants?" she said indignantly. "I don't think so. Especially as it's all her fault I've been grounded."

"Oh? I thought you were grounded because you didn't tell your mum where—"

"Hel-*lo*? Whose side are we on here?"

Zeb clamped his mouth shut.

Jazmin munched her bun.

"So, are you going to stay in touch with her?" Zeb asked after a few silent minutes had passed.

"If I want to." Jazmin tossed her head defiantly. "Huh, no hopped-up überwitch is going to order *me* about!" she added darkly.

Zeb nodded. "That sounds like a declaration of war to me," he observed.

"Yeah," Jazmin said grimly, "I guess it is."

NOVACHEM WAS LOCATED ON A NEW MODERN INDUSTRIAL ESTATE IN THE SHADOW OF WEMBLEY STADIUM. ASSIA PARKED IN A VACANT SLOT. SHE TOOK SOME TIME TO STUDY THE BUILDING, NOTING THE stylish chrome and glass frontage, and the shiny N and C interlaced with a star. This was a company clearly setting out to impress. She got out of the car, and walked quickly up to the heavy grey-tinted perspex entrance. Approaching the reception desk, she informed the immaculately dressed receptionist that she had an appointment with someone from personnel, and was politely invited to take a seat in the waiting area.

Assia sat, flicking through a company brochure to pass the time. NovaChem seemed to focus upon the lifestyle end of the pharmaceutical market. It made Serena, a drug it claimed had revolutionized the lives of time-poor "alpha achievers". The company also manufactured Excellin, a mind-boosting drug that enhanced student performance. The brochure was full of soft-focus nature photos, and glowing endorsements from various media stars and obscure members of the medical profession. Exactly the sort of company that Adam Smith had described to Mbeki.

Assia read on, her attitude becoming more sceptical with every promise. "A pill for every ill" seemed to be the company's philosophy. It was not the way she thought about life. In her experience, sometimes you just had to grit your teeth and get on with it. Eventually, the lift door opened, and a smartly suited young woman stepped out. She walked over to the waiting area, a helpful smile on her face.

"Hi, I'm Liza Shaw, Personnel Director," the woman said, holding out her hand. "Sorry to keep you waiting. We're all a bit...busy at the moment."

I bet you are, Assia thought to herself. She guessed the IT department was currently working flat out to restore and protect the computer system. She got to her feet. "It's not a problem," she said smiling smoothly, as she shook the proffered hand. "I don't know if you remember, but I sent you an ID i-fit picture a couple of days ago."

"Yes, I remember. And I meant to get back to you, only events kind of took over." The woman eyed Assia cautiously. "Sorry, what is the organization you work for?"

Assia got out her ID card. She smiled reassuringly. "I'm with the ISA. We're an international government department," she said.

It was a suitably vague reply, and had the merit of being correct, if opaque. The woman studied the card. "Oh, I see. Government funded. Well, that must be okay," she responded. "Actually, I was going to e-mail you to say that I recognized the photo – it's Dan Burrell. He used to work in Product Research and Development. I'm afraid he's no longer here though."

Yesss! Assia mentally punched the air, sending out a silent thank you to whoever had cut her the lucky break. *Dan Burrell.* She filed the name away in her mind. "Can you tell me where he's working now?" she asked.

"I don't know." The young woman frowned. "He left the company a while ago."

"Do you have a contact address?"

"Well..." The woman hesitated. "I'm not sure I should give you that sort of information."

"I *totally* understand. But it's very important I get hold of him," Assia said, maintaining her friendly expression. "As I said, I work for an official government organization. So this is by way of being an official request. Does your company have a valid reason why it cannot comply?"

The young woman's face flushed. "Oh. I see. Well, if you put it like that, I'm sure I have a contact address up in my office. Would you like to follow me?"

She led the way across the lobby.

Smiling to herself in quiet triumph, Assia followed.

TEN MINUTES LATER, A DISTINCTIVE RED DODGE VIPER WITH PERSONALIZED NUMBER PLATES PULLED SMOOTHLY INTO THE COMPANY CAR PARK. THE DRIVER SAT FOR A COUPLE OF SECONDS staring at nothing in particular. He picked a minute piece of lint from his suit jacket. Then he opened the car door, and walked swiftly towards the NovaChem building. Nodding briefly to the receptionist, he strode past the front desk and made his way towards the lift.

The man stood waiting patiently for the lift to descend. He examined his nails, the gold signet ring on his left hand. He hummed a little tune. Finally, the lift arrived. The doors opened. He moved forward, then automatically stood aside as a woman stepped out. Her face bore a preoccupied, thoughtful look, and she barely acknowledged the man's polite gesture.

The man shrugged, took a step forward. Then he paused on the threshold, his head turning to stare after the woman as she hurried purposefully across the lobby. For a moment, a puzzled expression flitted across his face. He'd seen her before. Recently. But not here. Somewhere else. He got into the lift, rode it to his third-floor office, where he picked up his phone, and made a call.

After he'd finished his call, the man stood at the

window for a while. *So*, he thought. Another beetle had come scurrying out of the woodwork. He stared down into the car park, his eyes cold and remote, like steel orbs floating in empty space. *You know how to deal with this. You put your foot firmly over the scurrying beetle and crush it. And that is the end of it.*

DR. NERISSA COLE, HEAD OF THE WELLNESS THERAPEUTIC CENTRE, A PRIVATE PSYCHIATRIC CLINIC WITH A GOOD REPUTATION IN THE FIELD OF TREATING MENTAL ILLNESS, SAT IN HER LIGHT, BRIGHT primrose-coloured office. She had just snapped shut the lid of her tiny jewel-encrusted micro. Now she rested her chin in her hands, and stared broodingly at the opposite wall. Her thoughts, which ought at this stage of the day to be centred upon writing up patient notes, were focused instead upon something else. Or rather, somebody else. She was thinking about her old school friend Assia Dawson.

Nerissa's blue eyes narrowed. Assia Dawson had always been such a self-righteous prig. She had made Nerissa's school life very difficult. She'd stopped her having what she always thought of as harmless fun, but what Assia had called bullying. Such a horrid word to use, and quite unnecessary. After all, it wasn't as if anybody got seriously hurt. Well, not often.

And there was more. Assia Dawson had reported her to the teachers on several memorable occasions. Memorable to Nerissa. Assia, on the other hand seemed to have forgotten all about them. And unlike most of their contemporaries, who'd been scared of her, Assia had never been afraid to stand up to Nerissa. And now many years later, here she was again. Interfering. On the surface, nothing had changed.

Except.

Except that this time, the pattern was not going to repeat itself. This time, *she* was going to spoil things for *Assia*. Oh yes. Her eyes glittered. Nerissa Cole wasn't the sort to just hold grudges. She gripped them tight, and used superglue to bind them to her. She smiled grimly. Right now, she wasn't sure how she was going to burst Assia's bubble but, given time, she'd think of something.

Although, realistically, she didn't have a lot of time to think, because her first priority was to keep *him* from doing anything...rash. The corner of Nerissa's left eyelid began to twitch, and something unpleasant fluttered in the pit of her stomach. There was a certain bitter irony in all this. Day in day out, Dr. Nerissa Cole dealt with mentally impaired individuals. While all the time, the most dangerous individual of them all was roaming the city streets quite freely. Nobody knew. Nobody suspected a thing.

It was her duty to make sure they never did.

WHEN JAZMIN CAME DOWNSTAIRS AFTER A GRUELLING HOMEWORK SESSION, SHE FOUND HER MOTHER CURLED UP ON THE SOFA, FAST ASLEEP. A REALITY SHOW WAS PLAYING ON THE TV. JAZMIN SLID onto the sofa arm. Assia slowly opened her eyes, stretched and sat up. She yawned. "Oh dear, I must've dropped off."

"Busy day?"

Assia nodded. "Busy, but productive."

Jazmin stared at the TV screen for a couple of seconds, then pulled a disgusted face. "Eww, should you be watching this stuff?"

Assia smiled. "Hey, don't knock it – sometimes we all need a little downtime."

"Unh. Whatever. I'd rather stick pins in my eyes." Jazmin levered herself upright. She strolled towards the living-room door. On the threshold she paused, sighed exaggeratedly. "I wonder how Ginevra's getting on," she remarked.

Assia threw her a quick glance. "You haven't been trying to contact her, have you?"

"Me?" Jazmin's eyes went wide and innocent. She did a palms-up, and shook her head vigorously. "Nuh-uh. No way."

Assia nodded. "Well done, hon. I know you tried to befriend her, but you have to comply with her parents' wishes – however unreasonable," she added.

Jazmin shrugged. "Well. So," she said. "I just came by to tell you I'm going to grab a snack before I start my maths homework. That's the homework I'm doing *after* the French and history homework that I've already done. Enjoy your programme."

Jazmin went to the kitchen, where she made herself a lemon curd and sugar sprinkle sandwich on thick white. She carried it back upstairs to her room, along with a glass of milk. She hoped her mum had got the message that she was not intending to contact Ginevra. Jazmin wasn't entirely happy about the conversation she'd just had, but sometimes circumstances forced you to be slightly economical with the truth. It was all part of the secret-agenty thing.

Back in her room, Jazmin bit into her sandwich and texted Ginevra. She'd rung several times, but all she ever got was "number unobtainable". She knew Ginevra had been forbidden to contact her too, but Jazmin secretly hoped that she might. If only to talk over the tongue-stud incident.

But that wasn't the sole reason. She really just wanted to be reassured that the girl was okay. Something didn't feel right here, she was sure of it. The Ginevra she knew was a strong-minded and very determined girl. She wouldn't think twice about disobeying her parents, especially the evil step. In fact, she'd probably go out of her way to be defiant. So the more Ginevra wasn't making contact, the more Jazmin was getting a very bad case of the suspicious.

DOWNSTAIRS, ASSIA EASED HERSELF OFF THE SOFA. SHE CROSSED THE ROOM AND LIFTED THE LID OF HER LAPTOP. SHE NEEDED TO CHECK HER INBOX. THE HEAD OF THE ISA HAD PROMISED TO SEND her the police autopsy reports on the kids who had died at the weekend. She wanted to read them, to see if there was any pattern, any connection.

Assia began scanning through the pages, her emotions torn between pity for the victims and their families, and relief that it wasn't her daughter lying on a mortuary slab, her body shattered and broken. All at once, she paused and scrolled back. Something had caught her eye. Assia rechecked the details of a seventeen-year-old girl who'd jumped from a railway bridge in the small hours of Sunday morning. She read where the girl had spent the last few hours before her death. And a cold fist slammed into the pit of her stomach.

THE NEXT DAY, ZEB STONE WAS SITTING IN THE RESOURCES CENTRE. HE WAS FEELING WORRIED. MORNING CLASS HAD COME AND GONE, AND THERE WAS A CONSPICUOUS ABSENCE OF JAZMIN. She hadn't answered the doorbell when he'd called for her earlier. She wasn't answering her micro either. Zeb was just wondering whether he should upgrade the worry, and consult somebody in authority, when the double doors swung open, and Jazmin strode in. Feeling relieved, Zeb waved, and gestured her over.

"Where have you been?" he demanded in a loud whisper. "You missed double maths."

"Really? And the bad news is?" Jazmin upended her bag, spilling books and folders onto the table.

"I copied down the homework for you," Zeb told her.

"Beauty."

There was a pause.

"I thought you were trying not to miss school any more," Zeb said reprovingly.

"So put me in jail, I broke one of my good resolutions."

Zeb eyed her curiously. He waited.

Jazmin eye-rolled. "If you MUST know, I was helping my mother with her inquiries," she muttered.

"Really – how come?"

Jazmin waved a hand dismissively. "Oh, you know," she said, "I help her out all the time." She sat down, opened her French textbook, and buried her nose in it.

Zeb watched her for a few seconds, then shrugged, and returned to his own work. Even though he was not good at the girl-empathy thing, he had learned that when Jazmin Dawson threw a moody, it was best to let her get on with it. She'd talk eventually, when she was ready.

JAZMIN STARED AT THE PAGE OF FRENCH IRREGULAR VERBS, AND STIFLED A YAWN. SHE HAD NOT SLEPT WELL THE PREVIOUS NIGHT. THE AFTERNESS OF THE TALK SHE'D HAD WITH HER MUM STAYED with her like an unpleasant taste in her mouth. The girl who died could have been Loz or Fiz. It could have been her, if she'd made different choices. After drifting off into a fitful sleep, she had awoken in the early hours of the morning. Rain was beating against her window, and unanswered questions circled around her head.

Then, as soon as she and her mum had breakfasted, Assia had driven them both straight to the ISA office, where Jazmin had met Chris Mbeki for the first time. She had carefully described the events of Saturday night to him. Everything she could recall. The bad vibage meant that she had not enjoyed her visit, even though she'd been longing to meet Mbeki ever since her mum had first told her about him. After she'd finished talking, her mum had driven her back across town, and dropped her off at the learning centre gate. It had been an uncomfortable ride. Her mum had not spoken a word, but unsaid stuff about drugs had hovered darkly.

Jazmin rubbed her eyes, and tried to concentrate on her book, but the nasty went on happening inside her head, refusing to go away.

WHEN ASSIA GOT BACK TO THE OFFICE AFTER DROPPING JAZMIN OFF, SHE DISCOVERED CHRIS MBEKI SITTING AT HER DESK. HE WAS WORKING ON HIS POWERBOOK. HALLY WAS BUSILY DOING something over on the far side of the room.

"Poor kid," Mbeki said, looking up as Assia entered the room, "is she okay?"

Assia's mouth was set in a grim line. "She'll survive."

"Main thing is she didn't take any of the drugs."

"*Tchk!* I was just saying to Chris, you never know what teenagers get up to, do you?" Hally remarked, clicking her teeth in a disapproving way.

Assia swallowed hard.

There was a difficult silence.

Mbeki cleared his throat. "Your boss has persuaded the police pathologists to check the kids who died for high levels of serotonin and dimethyltryptamine, and fax us the toxicology reports."

"Excellent."

"And while you were gone, I managed to get into NovaChem's server and find the clinical trial studies Burrell spoke about. The ones that weren't ever published." Mbeki spun his screen towards her. "Take a look."

Assia stared over his shoulder. "Interesting. I automatically assumed they'd been deleted."

Mbeki nodded. "Yeah, so did I. Then I had a hunch: I presumed when Burrell started blowing the whistle, the trial studies were deleted so that nobody else could get their hands on them. But they'd still be on the previous back-up. So then I thought that if maybe the IT guys were lazy, and didn't back-up regularly, then when the virus struck, and they restored the back-up..."

"The original studies would still be there!" Assia finished.

"Uh-huh. And guess what? There they were. Nobody seemed to have realized they needed to delete them again," Mbeki said. "I guess in all the hassle, they forgot. Easily done."

"Isn't he clever!" Hally said, smiling broadly at Mbeki.

"Yes, well done, Chris," Assia agreed, deciding in the interests of peace and harmony not to mention that she'd had exactly the same idea herself.

Mbeki shrugged. "Just lucked out, I guess," he said modestly. "I also sent an e-mail to the CEO of NovaChem – we need to talk to him urgently, put him in the picture and try to narrow down who in the company could have got their hands on the drugs."

"Have you had any response?" Assia asked.

"Not yet."

Assia held up her car keys. "So maybe before all that happens, we could go check out Dan Burrell's last address," she suggested.

Mbeki stood up. "Shall we grab a coffee on the way?"

"Sounds like a plan," Assia agreed. She needed to restore her caffeine levels. She picked up her bag and followed him to the lift.

ASSIA AND MBEKI DROVE NORTH ACROSS THE CITY UNTIL THEY REACHED FINCHLEY ROAD. ASSIA CONCENTRATED ON HER DIRECTIONS. MBEKI SIPPED HIS LATTE, AND DID SOME UPDATING ON his notebook. She navigated up Finchley Road, keeping an eye on the satnav screen.

"Here we are," she said, turning left into a side street. "Now, we're looking for 24a."

Assia slowed, peering at the house numbers. Then she pulled up, and parked in front of an old-fashioned three-storey house. It had an air of neglect. Paint was peeling off the front door and the windows were grimy with dirt. A couple of the once-elegant iron railings were missing. They got out.

"Looks like the place is divided into apartments," Mbeki observed. "I guess 24a must be the ground floor one," he went on, pointing to a hand-painted sign that directed them round the side. He opened the front gate. Assia followed him.

The entrance to 24a was located down a steep flight of crumbling concrete steps. Mbeki rapped at the door. There was no response. He lifted the letterbox and called Burrell's name a couple of times. Nobody answered.

"There's a whole bunch of mail lying on the floor in there," Mbeki said, straightening up. He looked at Assia. Then at the door. Then at Assia again.

"Okay, let's just run through why what we're about to do is illegal," Assia said. "We don't have a search warrant, do we?"

Mbeki shook his head. "Nuh-uh."

Assia pushed against the front door with her shoulder. "We're not recapturing a person who's unlawfully at large?"

Mbeki shrugged.

"And we're certainly not preventing serious damage to property."

Mbeki did a palms-up.

There was a pause.

"You're all right about this?" Assia asked.

"It's in my comfort zone."

"Right," Assia said, "then let's do it!"

She took out a tiny laser-powered lockpick, and aimed it straight at the door.

Once inside, Assia and Mbeki did a swift walk-through, their eyes taking in the books, photos, clothes and crockery piled in a heap on the floor, the door to the bedroom hanging off its hinges like a broken jaw, drawers pulled out and dumped on the bed, and the upended furniture. The detritus of a life. It looked like somebody had intended to set a fire, but had changed their mind at the last minute.

Mbeki whistled quietly. "Whew – do you think this happened before Burrell left, or after?"

Assia stared round at the chaotic mess. She shrugged, shook her head. "He hasn't made contact, has he?" she said. "And given what he said about 'the tiger', and then what happened to you recently..." Her voice tailed off into silence.

Mbeki exhaled. "And to think when I came over to London, I thought this was going to be an easy assignment," he said ruefully. "I think I have what we call mission creep."

"Yes, it certainly looks like it's getting more complicated," Assia agreed. She took another long searching look around. "Well, there's nothing useful for us here," she said. "We'd better secure the premises, and then get back to the office."

JAZMIN SPENT THE REST OF THE MORNING LURKING IN THE RESOURCES CENTRE, TOO SPOOKED TO FACE CLASS. AFTER LUNCH SHE WALKED ROUND THE RECREATION AREA ON HER OWN, TRYING to achieve mind clearage. By the end of the afternoon, she had come to the conclusion that, yeah, taking all things into consideration, currently her life was a bit of a bust.

But on the other hand, she'd been here before, many times, and the deal was always the same: get over it; move on. If she was looking for self-pity, she told herself sternly, she would find it in the dictionary. Between "no" and "way".

Self-validation. The mark of a successful crime-fighter.

By the end of the day, she was definitely feeling better.

Walking home, Jazmin found her mind returning to the other problem occupying her mental space. A week had almost passed by, but she still hadn't heard a word from Ginevra Frascati. If the younger girl had returned to school, surely she'd have texted her by now? After all, how would Nerissa and her dad ever know she'd disobeyed their orders? But Ginevra hadn't called, and the deafening silence was unsettling.

Time for a reality check, Jazmin thought to herself as she entered the door to her apartment building. Okay, she was slightly selective with the truth on occasions, and her dating life was a disaster zone, and as for her hair – hey, don't go there! BUT she had never ever wimped out on a friend, or anybody who needed her help. Or on the possibility of a mystery to solve. And whoa! Here she had all three rolled into one. Time to stop speculating, and start getting proactive. She pulled out her micro, and sent a quick text.

ZEB CLIMBED THE STAIRS TO JAZMIN'S APARTMENT AND RANG THE BELL. HE HAD BEEN IN THE LIBRARY CHECKING OUT SOME SCIENCE BOOKS WHEN HE'D GOT HER TEXT. ZEB SIGHED GENTLY AS he stood on the landing, waiting for her to answer. He wasn't sure what was lurking on the other side of the door. Right now, if he was asked to define Jazmin mathematically, he'd have said she was x, the unknown quantity. He heard the sound of footsteps approaching the door.

"Zeb!" Jazmin exclaimed, throwing open the door and greeting him with delight. "Hey, great. Thanks for calling round." She beamed at him as she showed him into the living room. "Sit down, make yourself at home. I'll just get us some snacks from the kitchen."

Oh? Zeb eyed her narrowly. It appeared that Jazmin had undergone a complete mood swing since this morning. From big black clouds to bright blue sky. Now he was really worried! He perched on the arm of a chair, and waited apprehensively until she reappeared, carrying two bowls. She slapped them down on the coffee table. "Chips and dip," she said. "Help yourself."

Zeb nodded. "Right," he said. "So you're feeling better?"

"Yeah, yeah. Don't stress," Jazmin said. She flashed him another whitey-bright smile.

Zeb looked at her. He looked at the bowls. He looked at her again. "Okay," he said. "Why don't you just come straight out with it, and tell me what you want."

"Huh!" Jazmin exclaimed indignantly. "Can't I offer a friend some hospitality without you having a bad case of the suspicious?"

Zeb did a palms-up. He helped himself to chips. He waited.

Jazmin also grabbed a handful of potato chips, and chewed energetically. The sound was reminiscent of an army marching through dead bracken.

Then, "Though...now you come to mention it," she added casually, "maybe there is something you could do for me."

Zeb sighed. "I knew it! You want to copy my homework again."

"No, no." Jazmin shook her head vigorously. "It's nothing like that."

"So what is it like?"

Jazmin frowned. "I'm concerned about my friend Ginevra," she said. "I haven't heard from her since last Saturday."

"So? Maybe she's busy." Zeb pursed his lips. "Or maybe she's just doing what her parents told her to do," he added pointedly.

Jazmin shook her head. "I don't think so," she said. "My spidey-sense is telling me something's wrong. So I need you to go round to her house."

Zeb's eyes widened. "Why?"

"I just want to know she's okay."

"But why can't you go?"

"Duh! Because somebody from the family might recognize me from the party. And anyway, I'm not supposed to contact her, remember?"

"But why me?"

Because...because Zeb had people skills. He had a totally honest face; he looked you squarely in the eye. And although she'd never experienced it, she was prepared to bet he had a handshake so firm you could moor boats to it. And he wore Clark Kenty glasses. Zeb gave off trustworthy. People really really wanted to tell him things. Hopefully.

"Listen," she coaxed, "this is dead easy. All you have to do is go round, ring the bell, smile, say you're a friend, ask some questions, pretend you need to see her about something. That's all. Nothing to it."

"What sort of questions?"

"Improvise – use your imagination."

Zeb groaned, gave her a despairing glance.

"Okay," Jazmin said. "Use my imagination. This is what I think you should do."

BY THE TIME ASSIA RETURNED FROM WORK, ZEB HAD GONE. JAZMIN WAS SITTING AT THE KITCHEN TABLE, OSTENTATIOUSLY DOING HOMEWORK. SHE'D DECIDED TO MOVE HERSELF TEMPORARILY downstairs, so that the first thing her mum saw was her beloved daughter working hard.

"Hi, hon," Assia said lightly, crossing to switch on the kettle. It was so obvious, she thought. Books open everywhere, and Jazmin doing a wonderful impression of Study Girl Does Maths.

Jazmin glanced up, assuming a suitably startled expression. "Oh wow – you're back," she exclaimed. "I was so busy, I didn't hear you come in!" She flashed her mum a high-wattage smile, then bent over her work again.

Assia dropped an Earl Grey tea bag into a cup. She stood looking at Jazmin. Twice in almost as many days she had been forced to listen while people made disparaging comments about her daughter. One a so-called specialist, the other an opinionated singleton. Women with their own agendas. It had made her feel very angry with them. But beneath the anger, lay other, more complex emotions. She did what she could, she thought, pouring boiling water into her cup. She tried to be a good mother. But she simply couldn't be on her daughter's case 24/7.

She stirred her tea, watching Jazmin pretending to be engrossed in her work. Her mind drifted back to when Jazmin was a small and mischievous child. Assia remembered how she always used to tell herself that it's the grit in the oyster that makes the pearl, whenever her daughter messed up.

She sighed gently. Hold that thought.

JAZMIN PEERED SLEEPILY AT HER BEDSIDE CLOCK. IT WAS SATURDAY MORNING, 11 A.M. PALE SUNSHINE WAS FILTERING THROUGH HER BLINDS. SHE STRETCHED HER ARMS ABOVE HER HEAD. No learning centre. Nothing planned. Bliss. She slid slowly out of bed and slouched into the kitchen in search of food. Eat. Drink. Go back to bed. That was the running order for the morning.

The kitchen was deserted. Jazmin busied herself slicing bread, assembling toppings.

"Good, you're finally up," Assia said briskly, appearing in the doorway.

Jazmin eyed her blearily. "Whaaa?"

Assia checked the time. "You'd better get moving. Chris will be arriving in the next half-hour."

"Oh?" Jazmin aimed a carton vaguely in the direction of a glass. Orange juice splashed onto the counter.

"We're going to Camden. Remember, we mentioned it to you. We want to talk to your friend Tony."

"Why?"

"I'd have thought that was obvious," Assia said drily. "So hurry up and get ready."

Jazmin blinked. "Hey, I'm not coming!" she exclaimed in horror. "You never said I had to come."

"You certainly are coming," Assia countered. "We need you to encourage him to talk to us."

Jazmin shook her head vehemently from side to side. "No. Way. Forget it."

"I don't think you're currently in a position to refuse, are you?" Assia said sweetly.

"Unh. That is so unfair!"

Assia shrugged. "Life is unfair. Get used to it."

Muttering darkly under her breath, Jazmin slapped peanut butter on some bread. She folded the bread over, and picked up her glass of juice.

"Where are you going?" Assia asked.

"To get dressed, Mother," Jazmin said coldly. "Or is walking round Camden in my PJs also part of my punishment?"

Giving Assia a look that could slice logs, Jazmin stalked out of the kitchen. *Unh, this is so majorly not happening,* she told herself. She carried her breakfast up to her bedroom. Cramming the bread into her mouth, she checked the time. Then she hurried along the landing to the bathroom. She had only a finite amount of time left to wash and get ready.

Seven minutes later, Jazmin crept quietly downstairs. She snagged her coat from its peg. See Tony again after she had walked out on him? She didn't think so! In the company of her mother? Nightmare! She let herself out of the apartment, silently closing the front door behind her.

ZEB WAS STANDING IN FRONT OF THE BIG WHITE MANSION, STARING UNBLINKINGLY THROUGH THE BARS OF THE WROUGHT IRON GATE. HE WORE A DISTANT, PREOCCUPIED EXPRESSION ON HIS FACE. The curious passer-by might well conclude Zeb was undergoing some great internal crisis.

The curious passer-by would be wrong.

The truth was even weirder. Zeb was doing sums. He was mentally working out the exact cubic capacity of each of the pillars. Zeb saw the world as a series of mathematical puzzles. (The exception to this was Jazmin Dawson. He currently saw her as a series of exclamation marks.)

Having performed his mathematical computations to his satisfaction, Zeb moved on to the next stage of the assignment. He opened the gate, crunched over the carefully raked gravel, walked up to the big white front door, and pulled the shiny brass retro bell pull a couple of times. Then he stood back and waited, mentally running through his script.

There was a loud yapping sound from inside the house. The door was flung open by a very thin woman with very blonde dyed hair and a lot of very sparkly jewellery. *The Evil Step*, Zeb thought to himself. She was accompanied by a small fluffy dog on the end of a lead. The dog was wearing a tartan coat and little black leather boots. It growled and launched itself at Zeb's ankles.

"Nice little dog," Zeb said. He bent down to pat the dog's head. "Ow!" he said, straightening up quickly. The little dog smirked. Then it sat down, and tried unsuccessfully to scratch itself behind one ear. The sparkly woman peered at Zeb suspiciously. "You're not the usual boy," she said accusingly.

"Um...possibly not," Zeb agreed.

"And you're late!"

"Late?"

The woman thrust the lead into Zeb's hands. "Not more than twenty minutes. And don't let the big dogs bully her," she ordered. And she shut the front door.

Open-mouthed, Zeb stood staring at the closed door. The small fluffy dog let out a volley of sharp barks. Zeb transferred his gaze from the door down to the dog, which had sat down on the top step. It stared back at him, its little beadlike eyes glittering. For some reason, Zeb was reminded of a recent debate in philosophy class. It had been on the existence of evil. He had argued quite forcefully that evil did not exist. Staring down into those malevolent black eyes, Zeb decided he might be prepared to change his mind. There was something very nasty lurking in there.

While Zeb and the fluffy dog were eyeballing each other on the step, the entrance gate at the end of the driveway suddenly clanged open. There was a loud barking. Zeb spun round, the spell broken. Three big dogs were throwing themselves up the drive, dragging a small cursing boy along behind them. The fluffy dog immediately got to its feet, bared its sharp little teeth, and growled in a threatening way.

"Hey!" the boy yelled, as the whole mad group got closer. "What are you doing with Princess Lotus Blossom?"

Zeb stared at him, at the circling dogs. Light dawned. "Oh, I get it," he said, relief flooding his soul. "*You* walk the dog."

"Too right, mate," the boy said, thrusting out his hand for the lead. "This is my patch. Get your own round."

Zeb handed him the lead. "I think there's been some sort of misunderstanding," he said. "I don't walk dogs." He glanced down. The fluffy dog was now conducting some sort of a stand-off with the three big ones. "Actually,

I don't really *like* dogs," he confided. "I'm only here because I'm looking for someone."

"Uh-huh." The boy shrugged indifferently. He gave the fluffy dog a sharp tug, dragging it down a couple of steps. "C'mon, furball, walkies!" he commanded.

"Hang on a minute!" Zeb said, suddenly inspired. He got out his micro. "Have you seen this girl recently?" he asked, showing the boy the picture of Ginevra that Jazmin had given him.

The boy assumed a nonchalant pose. "Maybe I have. Maybe I haven't. What's it worth?"

Zeb, a graduate of the Never-Conducted-An-Inquiry-In-My-Life school, looked at him, and frowned. "I'm sorry, could you define exactly what you mean by 'worth'?" he asked cautiously.

The boy muttered something incomprehensible under his breath. "Okay, you win, mate," he said. "I saw that girl last Sunday morning when I was walking the dogs. She was getting in the back of the big silver car. She had a suitcase with her. I haven't seen her since, right."

"Thanks," Zeb said. "Thanks very much. You've been really helpful."

The boy shrugged. "No probs." He tugged on the leads. "C'mon, fleabags. Vamoosh." As the pack of eager barking dogs headed towards the gate, Zeb saw the fluffy dog sink its teeth into one of the bigger dogs' legs. The dog yelped with pain. The small boy swore, then gave the fluffy dog a pull on the lead that lifted it off its feet. Zeb smiled in quiet satisfaction. It was good to see that evil, if in fact it existed, did not go unnoticed and unpunished.

JAZMIN LET HERSELF BACK INTO THE APARTMENT. SHE HAD SPENT THE WHOLE MORNING IN THE PUBLIC LIBRARY, HER MICRO TURNED OFF. NOW SHE STOOD IN THE HALLWAY AND LISTENED. NOT A sound. She grinned. Well, would you believe it? She'd missed Mbeki and her mum. They must have gone to Camden without her. Awww. Shame.

She sauntered into the living room and carefully placed her "Gone round to see friend, study emergency. Sorry" note on the floor under the coffee table. When challenged, she intended to adopt her "innocently bewildered" expression, and swear that she'd definitely left an explanatory note on the coffee table before she went. She carried her bag upstairs, and unloaded the contents onto her bed. Four books, all crime fiction. Jazmin always read crime fiction. She considered it was part of her professional development.

Jazmin sat on her bed, and thought about what her friend and life coach Zeb Stone had just told her. In her considered opinion, Zeb wasn't very observant. On the picking-up-cluage front, he was about as useful as a mermaid in a chorus line. Sending him to scope out the Frascati house had been an act of pragmatic desperation, so when she'd called him on her way home for a debrief, she hadn't been holding her breath. However, Zeb had really surprised her. For once he had actually managed to think outside the box. He had used his initiative, rather than his brain. She was impressed.

Sometime later, Jazmin heard the front door open, the sound of voices. She put down the book she was reading, and trekked out onto the landing. Her mum and Chris Mbeki were standing in the hallway.

"Hi, Mum," she called down.

Assia looked up sharply. "Okay, where did you get to?" she demanded, hands on hips.

Jazmin assumed an innocently bewildered expression. "Uh – sorry, didn't you see my note?"

"What note?"

"The one I left on the coffee table in the lounge. I suddenly realized that I had a major science assignment to complete by Monday, and I was missing the most important section because instead of being in science class on Friday morning, I was helping you with your inquiries." Jazmin gave her mum a look of self-righteous suffering. "So I was forced to go and borrow someone else's notes."

Assia groaned. How did she do it? Behind her, she heard Chris Mbeki laugh softly.

Jazmin came halfway down the stairs. "So, how did you get on?" she asked with fake casualness.

"We spoke to your friend."

"He isn't my friend, okay," Jazmin inputted quickly.

"Whatever." Assia shrugged.

"So?"

Assia shook her head. "Nothing useful."

Trying not to let her relief show on her face, Jazmin descended a couple more stairs.

Mbeki explained, "The way it operates is like this: there's a whole bunch of guys at the bottom of the chain. The minnows. They're the ones the kids buy from. Then there are some others higher up the chain who supply them. The larger fish. However, we're after one of the guys right at the very top. The big sharks. And they hang out in the deep water, out of sight."

"Right." There was a silence. "So, umm, shall I make us all some sandwiches?" Jazmin inquired helpfully.

Assia turned to Mbeki. "Would you like to stay for lunch?"

"Sure."

Assia gave Jazmin a long, meaningful look full of "not now, but later" stuff. Then without saying another word, she led Mbeki into the lounge. Jazmin went straight to the kitchen. She felt relieved, although there were several questions she badly wanted to ask – like, Did you mention my name? What did Tony say? – but she decided not to push her luck. Her mum's expression was sending a clear, flashing neon-lit message that right now, she wasn't Dish of the Day. She busied herself slicing bread, grating cheese and locating the pickle instead.

In the lounge, Mbeki lowered himself into an armchair. "That is one smart young lady," he said with a grin.

"Oh indeed," Assia agreed. "She certainly is smart. There's never a dull moment when she's around."

"I reckon she'll make a great secret agent when she grows up."

"If you think sheer cheek mixed with low cunning are appropriate qualities," Assia said grimly.

Mbeki did a palms-up. "It works for me every time." He laughed.

SOMETIMES BREAKTHROUGHS HAPPEN AT UNUSUAL MOMENTS. LIKE WHEN YOU WAKE UP IN THE QUIET OF THE NIGHT, WHEN EVERYBODY ELSE IS SLEEPING. THE FEELING OF PART LONELINESS, PART power. Jazmin lay on her side, staring at the street light glowing softly orange through the slats of her window blinds. Light entering the darkness.

It was four in the morning, and she had surfaced into consciousness from a vivid dream. Not with her usual sense of sleepy confusion, but with a wild, bright feeling of elation. Suddenly she knew with absolute certainty what had happened to Ginevra Frascati.

BREAKTIME THE FOLLOWING MORNING FOUND ZEB AND JAZMIN SITTING TOGETHER AT ONE OF THE CANTEEN TABLES. ZEB'S INDEX FINGER WAS TRACKING LITTLE PATHWAYS THROUGH THE CRUMBS ON his plate. "But..." he said.

"Let us consider the facts," Jazmin said, in her best Sherlock voice. "Ginevra and her step hate each other. Fact. Neither of them wants to live with the other. Fact. Ginevra confides in me that she is sure her step is making plans to get rid of her. Another fact. Then, just as we are becoming friends, Nerissa comes up with some stupid reason why we can't see each other any more. Obviously she wants to stop the friendship before I find out what she is planning to do. And now you discover that Ginevra is not living at her dad's any more. QPR as they say in science."

"That's QED," Zeb corrected her. "It means *quod erat demonstrandum*."

Jazmin waved a dismissive hand. "What. Ever."

"Maybe she's gone away to school?" Zeb suggested.

"Even if she has, and I don't think so, that still doesn't answer the question why she has never, ever contacted me since the day we went shopping in Camden," Jazmin replied. "It's just not how she'd behave, not after she said I was 'the best friend she'd ever had'," she went on, making rabbit-eared air quotes as she spoke.

"It might be," Zeb remarked. "After all, you haven't been 'best friends' for very long, have you?"

"Hey, that's how it goes." Jazmin shrugged modestly. "To know me is to love me."

Zeb smiled drily. "Okay. Point taken. Even so, it's a pretty big jump from her not living with her dad to presuming she's been locked up by her step."

"For you maybe. To me it's totally the logical conclusion. I actually got the idea from a crime novel I was reading over the weekend. It was called *The Woman in White*, and it was all about this girl who was locked up in a mental asylum because she was mad. Only she wasn't mad, and she wasn't the girl she was supposed to be, either."

"Uh-huh," Zeb ventured cautiously.

There was a brief silence.

Then he added, "Sorry, can you run that by me again; I seem to have missed an important connection."

Jazmin clicked her teeth, and eye-rolled. "Do keep up. This girl, Laura Fairlie, was put in a mental asylum. Only she was pretending to be someone else," Jazmin hesitated, "or was it the people who put her in who were pretending she was someone else, to get her money? I forget. It was a very long book, and I got kind of confused with the plot after a bit. But, don't you see, it's exactly the same: Ginevra Frascati has been locked up in her evil step's psychiatric hospital. Maybe under a different name. Just like in the story."

"Right," Zeb said. "Why?"

"Well, duh – isn't it obvious? Ginevra said her step kept looking at her as if she was one of her patients. And Nerissa told my mum how disturbed she thought Ginevra was, and how she was going to do something about it. Now she has. That also explains why I can't contact her. They've probably taken her micro away, and tapped her out on tranqs."

Zeb gave her a sceptical look.

"Listen," Jazmin asserted, "I have this spidey-sense, right? And it's saying loud and clear that's where she is."

"Your spidey-sense might be wrong."

"Nuh-uh."

"Okay," Zeb said. He paused. "Umm...I hardly dare to ask this, but what happened to the girl in the story?"

"Her friends rescued her."

"Ah. I might have guessed. Why am I suddenly getting this awful sinking feeling?"

"I don't know. Something you ate?"

There was another pause.

"Look," Zeb said, "be practical: you can't just go steaming in, demanding her step sets her free. I mean, reality check: adults don't work like that."

"Huh!"

"I'm serious. Think about it for a minute."

Jazmin sucked in some air. This was not what she wanted to hear right now. "I *was* going to ask you to help me out," she said stiffly, "but I guess that's a 'no', then."

Zeb pulled a face. "Well..." he began awkwardly.

Jazmin tossed her head. "Hey, forget about it. You did your bit. So no hards, all right?"

Zeb looked rather relieved. "I just thought of another thing," he added. "You promised your mum you would stay out of trouble, didn't you? And you're on a curfew."

Jazmin said nothing. She got up, stacking her crockery.

"Where are you going now?" Zeb asked apprehensively.

"I have assignments to hand in."

Jazmin powered through the canteen door. So it looked as if she was flying solo on this one. Which was *okay*, because some rescue missions were probably best undertaken alone. Sometimes the brilliant detective had a trusty sidekick; sometimes the trusty sidekick wimped out. But that was *fine*, because the fewer people involved the better. Jazmin slowed, then halted. She stared into the middle distance, her eyes narrowing. Oh boy, her mum'd freak if she knew what she was planning.

Lucky for both of them, Jazmin's planning didn't include telling her.

MEANWHILE, IN HIS SCRUBBED STEEL AND LIMED-OAK OFFICE ON THE THIRD FLOOR OF THE NOVACHEM BUILDING, THE MAN SAT READING SOME PRELIMINARY RESEARCH STUDIES FOR A NEW product. It was early days, but things were looking good. Not that it mattered. The product was going to be manufactured, whatever. He'd already come up with a name: Rejuve.

The man smiled. *It's a good name*, he told himself. He could envisage the press releases: ***"Rejuve" the new miraculous anti-ageing breakthrough!*** He would make sure words like "painstaking research" and "scientific discovery" appeared in the script. People liked to believe that the pill they popped in their mouth had been thoroughly tested in clinical laboratory conditions.

The man checked the time on his Breil watch. He was catching the Eurostar bullet express in a couple of hours. He was going to Paris. His hawklike eyes shone, and a smile played around the thin contours of his mouth. He had a great affection for France. It was where he'd set up his first company. But before catching the express, however, there was something important he had to do. He shut down his computer, gathered his things together.

In the outer office, his PA glanced up as he walked by her desk.

"Are you off now, sir?" she murmured.

The man nodded briefly. "I shall be out of the country for a while," he informed her. "Hold all my calls until I get back, will you."

The man made his way down to the foyer, then out into the car park. He checked the address he was going to, feeling the familiar buzz of excitement. *Dr. Jekyll and Mr. Hyde,* he thought, opening the door and climbing into the driver's seat. He started up the engine, glancing back across the car park at the NovaChem building, white and silver in the late afternoon sunshine. Something glittered in his brain.

In there, you were Dr. Jekyll.

But now it is Mr. Hyde who is coming out to play.

AT THE END OF HER WORKING DAY, ASSIA SLID HER CAR INTO AN EMPTY SLOT AND STOPPED THE ENGINE. JUST RECENTLY SHE HAD SECURED ONE OF THE COVETED RESIDENTS' PARKING PERMITS, which meant that she could now leave her car directly outside the front of the building if she chose to, rather than on the street. She slapped the permit onto the dash, got out and stretched. It had been a long day. Much of it spent stuck in traffic.

Letting herself into the apartment, she dumped her bags in the hallway. She did some neck rotations, stretching her arms above her head. Jazmin's door was closed, but her music was playing. She listened to the strange, irregular beat. More building site than music, she decided. She pulled a face. Now she knew she was getting old, she thought sadly, as she made her way to the kitchen for some herbal tea and downtime.

Assia made herself a camomile tea in her favourite china mug. She sat down at the kitchen table, breathing in the fragrant steam, and feeling the tension in her shoulders gradually easing. After she'd finished her tea she'd call Mbeki. Fill him in on her day and discover whether he'd finally got hold of the CEO of NovaChem. She closed her eyes, and was just beginning on some controlled breathing when there was a loud pounding on the apartment door.

Startled, Assia went to see who it was. Opening the door, she was astonished to see Hughie, the block cleaner and general handyman standing outside, his face white, eyes wide with disbelief.

"Uh – Ms. Dawson?" he stuttered. "You got to come and see this – somebody squashed your car!"

Wondering whether this was some kind of sick joke, Assia followed Hughie down to the residents' parking area at the front of the building, where a big crowd of residents and passers-by had gathered to gawp. She stared open-mouthed in amazement at the flattened heap of metal that only a short time ago had been her car.

"Omigod – what happened?" she gasped.

Hughie's voice shook a little with emotion as he spoke. "I was bringing up some sacks of rubbish from the basement," he said. "I just got to the front door when this truck appeared. It was a big black truck. You know, the sort with bug lights on the cab, and oversize tyres. It drove straight into the parking area really fast. Then it scrunched your car, and drove out again."

"Did you see the driver?"

Hughie shook her head. "The truck had tinted windows. I couldn't see who was driving."

"Did you get the number?" Assia inquired desperately, and without much hope.

"Nuh-uh. Sorry."

"What about the security cam on the front of the building?"

Hughie shuffled his feet and looked embarrassed. "Been meaning to see to that," he muttered, not making eye contact.

Assia took a couple of deep breaths to steady herself, and calm her beating heart. It could have been much worse, she told herself. She could have been *in* the car at the time. With Jazmin.

"So what kind of lunatic would do something like that, do you think?" Hughie wondered aloud.

"Who knows?" Assia's face was set, her eyes hard as steel.

"You want me to call the police?"

"No!" she said quickly, "I'll take it from here. Thanks, Hughie."

She turned and hurried back into the building before the other residents had time to start asking her questions. Since moving into the block, Assia had always been scrupulous about preserving her anonymity. As far as they knew, she had some boring public sector job in the city. The less other people understood what she really did, the safer she felt.

Back inside the building, Assia put her head down and sprinted across the lobby. This was no random act of lunacy. It was a deliberate targeting. From the same guy who had arranged for Chris Mbeki to be beaten up and left for dead? Go figure. Which meant only one thing: he now knew that she was part of the investigation.

Adrenaline coursing through her body like lightning, she took the stairs two at a time. There was this theory that, fundamentally, all people were the same underneath. She didn't believe it. Lots of people weren't. They weren't like everybody else. This man certainly wasn't. He came from a completely different morality. As she'd just witnessed with her own eyes. Assia powered into the apartment and grabbed her micro. She had some urgent calls to make. Then she needed to talk to Jazmin.

JAZMIN FOLDED HER ARMS AND GLARED AT HER MUM. "NO WAY!" SHE EXCLAIMED.

ASSIA MET THE GLARE HEAD ON. "THIS PERSON ISN'T JOKING around, hon," she said quietly. "They are dangerous. I can't risk anything happening to you."

Jazmin did a face-scrunch. "Unh – I am so not going to stay with cousin Clea again," she said.

"Just for a bit," Assia coaxed. "It won't be for long, I promise."

Jazmin shook her head. "Sorry, this is not how it

works," she said, recalling the philosophy class rules. "First, we discuss things rationally. After which, we come to a mutually agreed compromise."

Assia sighed deeply. "Right," she said thinly. "So let's discuss this rationally: my car has just been totally trashed. Probably by the same individual who put Chris in hospital. This person is without any conscience, completely ruthless, and prepared to stop at nothing. Hurting you wouldn't even feature on his Regret List." She paused. "Perhaps you'd like to input at this point?" she remarked drily.

Jazmin thought fast. She absolutely had to stay in London. She had an investigation of her own to pursue. "But, if you send me away, you're giving in," she suggested craftily, "you're letting him scare you. You're allowing him to call the shots."

Assia considered this for a minute.

Seizing her advantage, Jazmin allowed her train of thought to run along its rails. "Like you always say: there is nothing to fear but fear itself," she said. "Anyway, I've always got Zeb to look after me."

Assia's brain threw up a mental image of Zeb as a potential security guard. And discarded it hastily.

"Look, I could catch the underground to the learning centre if it makes you feel better," Jazmin pursued, reading her mum's expression. "Or get a cab. And, of course, I'd be extra specially vigilant all the time."

Assia's face was a study in uncertainty.

"Remember I got into all that trouble last time I stayed with Clea?" Jazmin reminded her, sensing a chink opening up in her mum's emotional armour. "And I missed out on so much education, didn't I? I've really only just begun to catch up."

Assia hesitated. Truth was, in spite of the possible danger, she'd infinitely prefer to keep her daughter near to her. She was far easier to monitor at close quarters.

"Hey, nobody will notice me, I'll just blend into the background," Jazmin said.

"With that hair?"

"Okay, I'll wear a hat and blend into the background."

"Well..." Assia hesitated.

"Hey, maybe I could carry a gun?" Jazmin suggested hopefully, sensing her mum was beginning to weaken.

"I'm not joking around," Assia said tautly.

There was a long pause.

Then Assia sighed again.

"So, I can stay? Please?"

Assia groaned. "I guess so. But I don't know how I let you talk me into this," she said.

"Must be my good looks and self-effacing charisma." Jazmin grinned. She caught the edge of her mum's expression. "Or then again, maybe not," she added meekly.

WHEN ASSIA SET OFF FOR WORK NEXT MORNING, ALL THAT REMAINED IN HER PARKING BAY WAS A SLICK OF OIL AND A FEW TWISTED SHARDS OF RED METAL. THE CAR HAD BEEN PUT ON A low-loader and taken away. She took a deep breath, biting back the feeling of regret. She'd had this particular car for a while. It had accompanied her on many missions. Its bodywork was scratched and dented, souvenirs of pursuits carried out on a surplus of adrenaline, and a shortage of common sense. It had been like a member of the team.

Assia began walking towards the train station. She kept a wary eye out for anything unusual. Somebody had sent her a warning: stay out of this. A warning she intended to ignore. A couple of minutes into her walk, an electric blue Mitzouki Cheyenne drew level with her. The driver beeped the horn, then slowed.

"Hey, lady, care for a ride to work?" he asked leaning out the window.

Assia gave the sporty little 4x4 a quick once-over. "Very nice," she said, opening the nearside door and easing into the passenger seat. "But should you be driving yet?"

Mbeki flexed his still bandaged hand. "Nope," he said, "but how else was I going to get this baby over to you?"

Assia stared at him. "I'm sorry?"

Mbeki indicated, then pulled in to the kerb. "I rented it when I arrived," he said, unbuckling the seat belt. "It's been sitting in a lock-up ever since the evening I got attacked. I thought last night after you rang, you need some wheels and I have some temporarily going spare. So I fixed it with the rental company for you to drive it too." He slid out of the driving seat and came round to her side. "Keys are in the ignition," he said, opening Assia's door. "Take it away, partner."

Assia slid over into the driver's seat. She adjusted it for her height. Meanwhile, Mbeki reached in the back for his powerbook and flipped up the lid.

"So how is it going?" Assia asked, as she familiarized herself with the gears.

"The usual: good news and not so good news."

"Tell me."

"The good news is that the tox reports are in, and they back what Burrell said: there were high levels of serotonin and DMT in all the kids who died last weekend. So now the police are beginning to take things seriously. The less good news is I've been doing some research on NovaChem. Boy, is it a piece of work!"

"Go on."

"I checked it out with the European Food and Drug Association. This company has quite a reputation. And it isn't good. Over the last couple of years, a whole bunch of so-called 'wonder drugs' have been withdrawn or delicensed after problems over safety. Seems like they do their trials offshore, because it's cheaper and less regulated. They throw a big launch for the product, pick up the money from initial worldwide sales, and quietly withdraw it once the damaging side effects start emerging."

Assia clicked her teeth.

"The company always makes big promises," Mbeki went on. "Last year, they put out a drug called RU-21. The marketing blurb said it contained an anti-ageing molecule called RNA that could give you back your youthful appearance again."

"Whoa – sorry I missed that one." Assia smiled.

"Don't worry, you weren't missing much. When they investigated it, scientists found it only contained aspirin and a few herbs. But NovaChem still pocketed millions. Nice work, huh?"

Assia negotiated the springy little jeep round a parked lorry.

"And that's only one of their many scams," Mbeki said. "These guys do seriously bad science. But they make a shedload of money out of it. And they don't return my calls!"

Assia dropped Chris Mbeki outside the ISA building. Then she parked up for a while to gather her thoughts and prioritize her tasks. First, she needed to call Jazmin and make sure she had arrived at the learning centre safely. Then she had people to interview south of the river.

JAZMIN FLIPPED DOWN THE LID OF HER MICRO. SHE HAD JUST REASSURED HER MUM THAT, YES, SHE AND ZEB HAD ARRIVED AT THE LEARNING CENTRE ON TIME AND, NO, THEY'D SEEN NOTHING suspicious on the way. Now she dropped the micro into her coat pocket and stuffed her bag into her locker, slamming the door shut. Then she walked straight out of the building by a back entrance. She had told her mother the truth: that she'd arrived at the learning centre. She hadn't told her that she had no intention of staying there.

Last night, after persuading her mum to let her stay in London, Jazmin had gone on the Net and checked out the Wellness Therapeutic Centre, the psychiatric hospital run by Nerissa Cole, where she believed Ginevra Frascati was locked up. She worked out how to get there. Now it was time to initiate her rescue mission. And nobody was going to stand in her way.

THE WELLNESS THERAPEUTIC CENTRE CONSISTED OF A LINKED SERIES OF MODERN TWO-STOREY BUILDINGS SURROUNDED BY BEAUTIFULLY LANDSCAPED GARDENS. FROM EVERY WINDOW, visitors and patients (who were always referred to in the glossy brochure as "guests") could feast their eyes upon green lawns and flower beds rioting with bright blooms. This was quite deliberate. Exposure to nature was an important part of the holistic healing treatments employed at the centre.

The focus upon nature also carried on into the centre itself. Miniature bay trees in white ceramic tubs flanked the front entrance. Huge glass bowls of freshly cut flowers adorned the foyer, and every room had its allocation of flowers and plants. The centre was painted in restful natural colours – soft greens, rose pinks, pale yellows and apricot.

At the touch of a button, guests could project holograms of woodlands, seascapes and snowy mountain ranges onto the walls of their rooms. Flower and herb scents filled the air. All the woodwork was white birch, contributing to the harmonious effect of light and space. As the brochure proudly announced: *At the Wellness Therapeutic Centre, we bring the outside world in, while seeking at the same time to draw the inside world out.*

Jazmin sat in the visitors' reception area, puzzling over this statement. She finally decided that, like many other mission statements she'd read or seen, it sounded impressive while meaning absolutely nothing. There were other things puzzling her too. Like why the staff she saw walking to and fro on their way to do therapeutic things with the guests were not wearing white coats. She had expected them to look slightly more *hospitally*. Two further things were also currently jostling for mental space. Firstly: where was Ginevra Frascati being kept? And the biggie: how exactly was she going to get past the eagle-eyed receptionist so that she could find her?

To pass the time while she was waiting for solutions to materialize, Jazmin got up and went over to the snack bar. She helped herself to a second lemon-iced fairy cake. Her cognitive skills always improved when she was snacking. *(Jazmin Dawson, mission statement: I think, therefore I eat.)* And right now, it looked like she definitely had a two-cake problem on her hands.

ON THE OTHER SIDE OF LONDON, THE HEAD OF THE ISA POURED COFFEE FROM HIS NEW CAFETIÈRE. HE HANDED A CUP TO CHRIS MBEKI. "MILK? SUGAR?" HE ASKED.

"Sure. Thanks." Mbeki helped himself to milk, spooned sugar into his cup. He had been warned by numerous members of staff that the head of the ISA liked to bond with his department. Especially if he didn't have much to do. Mbeki glanced surreptitiously at his watch, hoping this bonding session wasn't going to take long. He was busy. Things were happening. He needed to be there to monitor them.

The head of the ISA settled back comfortably in his chair, folding his arms behind his head. "So, how are you finding it working with us 'Brits'?" he inquired.

"Fine," Mbeki said. "You have a great bunch of guys here."

The head of the ISA nodded in a satisfied way. "I like to think so," he agreed complacently.

There was a pause. Mbeki drank some coffee, and wondered whether he could suddenly invent some dire emergency that required his immediate attention. *Dear Lord*, he prayed. *Help me out here. I really need a miracle. Please. Just a small one.*

"Good," the head of the ISA said, filling the empty verbal space.

There was a further pause. The space opened up again.

"Well," Mbeki said, placing his cup deliberately on the desk. "I have some cyber-checking to do."

The head of the ISA groaned. "Computers! Don't talk to me about computers!" He leaned his elbows on the desk, steepling his fingers.

Mbeki smiled politely. He had a sinking feeling that he knew what was coming next.

"You won't believe what my oldest son did with his laptop over the weekend!"

Mbeki made polite listening noises. He remembered being warned about the head's "amusing" family anecdotes by some of the staff. Run, they'd said. He wanted to get on with his investigation, but guessed he'd have stay to listen to the story. Ah well, it was the least he could do, he thought to himself resignedly. The guy had given him office space, and had loaned him a member of his staff. Mbeki sat forward in his seat, trying to fake genuine interest.

"Well," the head of the ISA began, "he'd just finished a

college assignment – a two thousand word essay on something or other. Took him weeks. Anyway, next minute the stupid boy accidentally—"

There was a sudden series of urgent beeps from Mbeki's pager. "Uh, excuse me," he said, checking the message. Then he looked up. "Sir, I have to go," he said. "Something urgent has just come up." He rose to his feet, trying to keep the look of relief off his face. "Geez, it was good to visit with you. Great cup of coffee too, thanks," he said, and he hustled out of the office.

Hally grinned as Chris Mbeki re-entered the workplace. "I thought you might need rescuing," she said.

"You thought right," Mbeki said. "Thanks for paging me. He's a nice guy, but..."

"But," Hally echoed, smiling. "Don't worry, we've all been there."

Mbeki strode over to his workspace. "Anything I should know about?" he asked.

"Oh, nothing in particular," Hally said. "Assia's called in to report on her first interview."

Mbeki eased into his seat. "Good. I need to contact her," he said.

"Oh yes?" Hally stiffened, but managed to keep her voice neutral. "Has there been a development?"

"I managed to sneak a look at NovaChem's company accounts," Mbeki said.

Hally's eyes widened. "How did you do that?" she

queried. "No bank will normally divulge such information. Even to another bank."

"Unless it's an STR."

"I'm sorry?"

"A Suspicious Transfer Report. Like if they suspect it's money used for drug-trafficking or terrorism. Then the account will be tagged. Electronic transfers can be tracked. There are ways of doing it, even with strong encryption. It's strictly non-legal, of course. Nobody will admit to doing it."

"But you just happened to find somebody who would."

Mbeki shrugged. "Put it this way: I got friends at the Bank of America who kind of owe me," he replied. "So I called in the favour. Information is currency. But the way I see it, currency is also information. I told them the company was under investigation and the FBI needed access to its accounts. The rest was history. Or rather, geography. You wouldn't believe how many offshore and foreign deposit accounts this company has. The CEO must be a multibillionaire and then some. And it's all stashed away in tax-free multi-havens. Nice work, eh?"

Hally gave him an admiring look. *My hero*, the look said.

Mbeki got out his micro. "I'll just leave a message on Assia's voicemail," he said, flipping up the lid and beginning to dial.

Hally retreated to her side of the room. She bent over her

keyboard, feigning busyness. In reality, she was straining her ears listening to the tone of Mbeki's voice as he spoke, trying to work out whether he and her boss had progressed from a professional relationship to a personal one.

BACK AT THE WELLNESS THERAPEUTIC CENTRE, JAZMIN WAS WALKING ALONG A CORRIDOR, FOLLOWING SIGNS TO THE ADOLESCENT UNIT. GETTING PAST THE RECEPTIONIST HAD BEEN easy. Practically a piece of cake, she thought to herself happily. As soon as she'd spotted the delivery van arriving, she'd known exactly what to do. Slipping out of the main entrance, she had waited patiently until the driver had opened up the rear doors. Then, smiling sweetly, she'd offered to help him unload, indicating with a vague wave of her hand that her mum was working somewhere in the centre.

Walking close behind the delivery man, and keeping her eyes fixed firmly forwards, she had carried a couple of small cardboard boxes past the front desk, and through to the pharmacy, where she'd stacked them on the floor. Then she had simply walked off down the nearest corridor. It had been that easy. And now here she was, striding purposefully towards the birch framed glass door that led to the adolescent unit. It always paid to stride purposefully. It stopped people in authority questioning where you were going, and why.

Approaching the door, Jazmin paused. There was a male nurse coming towards her on the other side. She waited while he produced a card from his pocket, and swiped the lock on his side to open the door. Then she scurried through before it closed. The male nurse eyed her curiously, but didn't say anything. Jazmin went on walking along the corridor in a determined Girl-on-a-Mission way, looking straight ahead and concentrating upon giving off the impression that she had every right to be there.

She failed to notice the tiny CCTV camera that had started tracking her every movement.

IN HER OFFICE, NERISSA COLE WAS STARING AT THE IMAGE OF JAZMIN DAWSON HEADING TOWARDS THE ADOLESCENT UNIT. SHE LEANED IN TO THE COMPUTER SCREEN TO OBSERVE MORE CLOSELY, her pale blue eyes sparking dangerously.

Standing on the other side of the desk was the male nurse who had passed Jazmin in the corridor earlier. He was studying Nerissa's face with interest.

"Do you recognize her?" he asked.

Nerissa nodded slowly. "Oh yes," she murmured, "I know who she is."

The nurse's eyebrows raised. "Really? What's she doing here?"

Nerissa gave a small lift of her shoulders, indicating that

either she hadn't got a clue, or if she had, she wasn't going to tell him.

"Do you want me to deal with her?" the nurse asked.

"No," Nerissa said shortly. "I want you to do nothing at all. Just keep an eye on her. Let's give our visitor all the rope she needs," she said. She gave the nurse a brief, dismissive wave. "Please excuse me now, would you, I have some work to do," she said without looking up.

The nurse left the office. For a long time after he'd gone, Nerissa sat very still, staring at the small image on the screen. The look on her face could have bored holes through titanium. Eventually, she seemed to reach some sort of a decision. Without taking her eyes from the screen, she reached out a hand, and pressed a red buzzer on her desk.

THE YOUNG WAITRESS IN THE MOTORWAY SERVICE STATION FLICKED A DAMP CLOTH OVER A NEWLY VACATED TABLE, MENTALLY NOTING THAT THE WOMAN CUSTOMER IN THE CORNER WAS STILL STARING vacantly into space. There was an untouched cheese salad baguette, an apple and a bottle of mineral water on the table in front of her. The woman had been sitting like that for ten minutes, and it was beginning to creep the waitress out.

Moving swiftly to the next table, the waitress piled crockery onto a tray, deliberately clattering the cups and plates as loudly as she could. She glanced across to the woman's table. Again, no reaction. Maybe she suffered from some weird catatonic illness, the waitress thought. It certainly couldn't be the food's fault – she hadn't eaten a bite since she sat down.

The waitress studied the woman. She had seen all sorts here: noisy families, exhausted business people, silent couples, sad singles. All humanity passed through the service station restaurant. What was different about this customer was the depth of her stillness. It was as if her whole being was focused inwards. Like she was staring into some fathomless well deep within her soul.

The waitress stood, cloth in hand, temporarily mesmerized. She didn't think the woman had even *blinked* for the last thirty seconds. Then, as she continued to stare, the woman customer suddenly seemed to come out of her trance. She glanced quickly up at the restaurant clock, and seemed surprised at what time it was. Picking up the apple and the drink, and wrapping her baguette in a serviette, she hurried out.

Odd, the waitress thought, her eyes following the woman as she left the restaurant. *Very odd. I wonder what's going on in your head.*

OUT IN THE CAR PARK, ASSIA WALKED QUICKLY TO THE JEEP AND GOT IN. THEN SHE GROANED OUT LOUD, THUNKED HER FOREHEAD WITH THE HEEL OF HER HAND. STUPID! STUPID! STUPID!! EVER SINCE she had read through the glossy NovaChem booklet, something had been trying to draw attention to itself, but she'd been so preoccupied that she had failed to make mental space for it. She shook her head, amazed at her own lack of perception. For a few seconds she sat motionless, staring out of the windscreen, her face blank. After a while she took out her micro and made a call. Then she started the engine and headed for the main motorway.

THE YOUNG WAITRESS GOT ON WITH CLEARING TABLES AND CLEANING SURFACES. AND WHEN SHE HEARD THE SIRENS OF THE EMERGENCY SERVICES SCREAMING PAST A WHILE LATER, SHE never even looked up from her work. There were accidents on this stretch of the motorway almost every day. You got used to it.

JAZMIN HAD SPENT AN INTERESTING TIME TALKING TO SOME OF THE PATIENTS IN THE WELLNESS CENTRE. THOUGH "INTERESTING" WASN'T EXACTLY THE RIGHT WORD. STRANGE, BIZARRE, AND freaky were probably better words to describe her interface with the reality-challenged individuals she'd encountered over the last few hours.

Deciding to work her way systematically round the adolescent unit on her search for Ginevra, Jazmin had started by spending time in the communal area, where she had some conversations with a couple of kids whose worlds appeared to be connected to hers only by their fingertips. Then she had gone on to visit some of the rooms, still looking for Ginevra. Everyone had been okay for her to visit with them, except one girl, who remained curled up in a ball on her bed, her face turned to the wall, and didn't utter a single word, even though Jazmin tried to coax her to speak for ages.

In the course of her investigation, Jazmin had been informed on numerous occasions that everybody's parents were evil, the food was total crap, and the psychiatrists were so mad they should be locked up. She had learned a whole heap of fascinating, and at times seriously flaky stuff. Except she hadn't learned where Ginevra was. Nobody seemed to know her, or to have seen her. Jazmin had finally decided that Ginevra must be locked up in some isolated part of the complex. Which made sense. Nerissa wouldn't want it getting out that she'd falsely imprisoned her own stepdaughter in a psychiatric hospital, would she?

Now it was afternoon, and she was wondering what she should do next. Her mum'd be home late tonight – she had a lot of travelling, and a twilight meeting to attend when she got back. So she had a couple of hours detecting time left. After a brief stop-off at the canteen for a top-up, Jazmin decided to revisit the main building, and snoop around. Somebody somewhere must know where Ginevra was being kept. It was only a matter of time before she located her, and liberated her from this place.

NERISSA COLE HAD SPENT THE AFTERNOON WRITING PATIENT REPORTS, WHILE TRACKING JAZMIN'S PROGRESS ROUND THE ADOLESCENT UNIT WITH GROWING INTEREST. NOW SHE WAS speaking to her senior clinician, a thin, nervous man who'd worked with her for many years. While she spoke, Nerissa kept her eyes fixed once again upon the tiny CCTV screen. When she'd finished giving her instructions, the clinician hesitated. He was used to Dr. Cole's occasionally unorthodox methods. Even so...

"But..." he began, biting his lower lip.

Nerissa looked up sharply. "But what?"

The clinician pulled a face. Dr. Cole's nasty temper was legendary amongst the staff. "Er...is this absolutely necessary, do you think?"

"I think it is," Nerissa said crisply. "Why? Are you questioning my judgement?"

The senior clinician swallowed. "No, of course not. I was just wondering: if she fails to return home this evening, what about her family?" he ventured bravely. "Won't they be worried?"

Nerissa smiled viperishly. "Oh yes, I certainly hope so," she said.

JAZMIN TURNED A CORNER, AND RAN STRAIGHT INTO A BIG, BURLY MAN IN A BLUE SHIRT WITH "STAFF NURSE" ON THE BREAST POCKET. NO PROBS, SHE THOUGHT. SHE FLASHED HIM A WIDE INNOCENT smile. To her astonishment, however, instead of standing aside to let her go by him, the man reached out and grabbed her by the elbow.

Jazmin struggled to free herself. "Hey, let go!" she cried.

The man tightened his grip. "Oh dear, oh dear, what are you doing out of your room after curfew?" he demanded.

"Huh?"

The man clicked his teeth disapprovingly. "Five-thirty. Lockdown time. You should be in your room."

"But I'm not a patient."

"Yes, right." The man laughed. Then he began hauling Jazmin back along the corridor towards the adolescent unit.

"Hello? Did you hear what I said?" Jazmin exclaimed, trying unsuccessfully to wrench her arm free while digging her feet into the floor at the same time.

The nurse continued walking. "Yeah, yeah I heard. You're not a patient. And I'm not a nurse. And this isn't a psychiatric clinic, and we're all living on Planet Mars."

"*What?*"

The man peered into one of the rooms, grunted, then swiped the lock with his keycard. The door swung open. "Here you are, back in your nice safe little room," he said, pushing her in front of him.

Jazmin glanced around. The room was almost Zenlike in its simplicity. There was a bed, a table, a built-in wardrobe and a pod-like chair in red perspex. "You're making a big mistake!" she exclaimed.

"Uh-huh. Right. They all say that."

"You can't lock me up; I have rights!"

"Not in here you don't," the man said.

"Also, I have a gun," Jazmin lied recklessly.

The man was finding it hard to suppress his laughter. "Oh wow – I'm really scared! Can I see?" he said, miming scared.

Jazmin eye-rolled and muttered.

"No trying to escape this time, okay?" the man said. He paused. "Micro?" he said, holding out his hand.

"Excuse me?"

"Give me your micro."

Jazmin clutched her bag closer. "No way."

The man continued to hold out his hand. "Stop messing around," he said. "You know you can't have a micro in here. It interferes with the medical equipment."

Jazmin looked around the room. "What medical equipment?"

The man sighed in a long-suffering way. "Micro," he repeated. "Now. Or do I have to get it off you myself?" he added menacingly, taking a step towards her.

Jazmin swallowed. Fear moved within her, a small writhing wormy thing. Silently, she dug into her bag and handed over her micro.

"That's better," the man said, pocketing it.

Jazmin glared at him. "You're so going to be in trouble when they find out what you've done," she added defiantly.

"We'll see," the man sneered. "All right now, sweet dreams. Watch out for that gun, eh!" And he left, closing the door behind him with a click.

Shaking her head in disbelief, Jazmin sat down on the bed. Now what? She sat for a bit, then got up, and went over to examine the door. It was very solid and very locked. She banged on it for a while. Nothing happened. She kicked the door. More nothing happened. She yelled at the top of her voice. No one came. Jazmin went on yelling and kicking the door for some time. There was no response. Finally, reality dawned. They weren't going to do anything.

Cursing under her breath, Jazmin sat back down on the bed, and began looking around for escape routes. The door was locked from the outside. The window was high up and flush with the wall. She got to her feet, and went to explore the built-in wardrobe. Opening the door, she peered inside. Unh. There were no fur coats, so clearly there was not going to be a snowy forest with a lamp post at the centre of it. No escape route there, then. *Another cherished childhood belief bites the dust*, she reflected sadly.

Jazmin closed the wardrobe door, picked up the red perspex chair, carried it across the room, and stood on it to look out of the window. It was beginning to get dark outside. The sky was pewter coloured, filling up fast with ominous black clouds. Sheesh, even the weather had gone metaphory on her. Returning to the bed, she threw herself down, and lay staring at the ceiling. After a while, she checked the time. It was getting late. And dark. And she was a long way from breakfast.

Any minute now, Jazmin thought to herself hopefully, her mind would start flying in supplies of common sense to construct a huge anchor in sanity. Then she'd be able to convince herself that what had just happened to her hadn't really happened, and if it had happened, hadn't happened much.

She remembered reading somewhere that Tibetan monks were made to sit in graveyards at night to stop them feeling afraid. She wished she'd had some Tibetan monk training. It would certainly come in handy right now.

IT WAS VERY LATE WHEN ASSIA FINALLY GOT HOME. SHE WAS UTTERLY EXHAUSTED – SURPRISING, REALLY, WHEN ALL SHE'D DONE WAS SIT IN A LINE OF CARS ON A MOTORWAY. SHE EASED OFF her shoes, flexed her aching feet, and tiptoed into the kitchen to make herself a hot drink. The apartment was dark and silent. Jazmin must have gone to bed ages ago. She'd catch up with her over breakfast.

Assia carried her drink quietly upstairs. She moved softly along the landing, past Jazmin's closed bedroom door, trying not to wake her. Entering her own bedroom, she was suddenly overcome by weariness, and lay down on top of the bed. She ought to get up and take a shower, she thought, trying to stifle a yawn. And finish her drink. She also needed to think about the conversation she'd had earlier in the day with her twin brother Ian and, finally, she had to work out a strategy for what she was going to do tomorrow. As she reflected about tomorrow, she felt a ball of something tighten within her chest. Not fear, she decided. It was more like a feeling of tension, longing to be released.

Assia felt her body relax, her mind hovering over the darkness. She tried to fight against it, but the craving for sleep was too strong. Her eyes closed, and she drifted away.

JAZMIN OPENED HER EYES. IT WAS MORNING. THE CONTOURS OF THE ROOM WERE UNFAMILIAR, SO THAT FOR A COUPLE OF PANICKY SECONDS, SHE WASN'T SURE WHERE SHE WAS. THEN THE snowball of consciousness turned into the avalanche of memory. Swinging her legs off the bed, she stood up, and headed for the tiny en suite to freshen up. Today she was going to have good escaping karma, and she was getting out of this place, she told herself firmly.

Returning to the main room, she shrugged on her clothes. Then she sat on the red perspex chair, waiting for something interesting to happen. After a while, she heard the sound of a trolley making its way slowly along the corridor. *This had better be breakfast*, she thought grimly. *And there'd better be a lot of it.*

SUNLIGHT POURED THROUGH THE FRENCH BLINDS. ASSIA SAT UP AND CHECKED HER BEDSIDE ALARM. OH NO – IT WAS AFTER 9 A.M. SHE HAD OVERSLEPT BADLY. AND SHE WAS STILL WEARING THE CLOTHES she'd worn yesterday. How embarrassing! Hastily, she undressed, hanging her creased suit in the wardrobe. She wrapped her dressing gown round her and hurried downstairs to the kitchen to make herself a large strong cup of coffee.

Switching on the coffee maker, Assia observed how nice and tidy her daughter had left everything. She'd even put her dishes back in the cupboard after drying them up. *Bless,* Assia thought to herself, feeling a warm glow inside as she surveyed the immaculate kitchen. The message had finally got through: Jazmin was clearly making an effort to be helpful.

Returning upstairs to shower and dress, Assia pushed open Jazmin's door. The room bore its customary HURRICANE HITS TEENAGE BEDROOM! appearance. Oh well, you couldn't have everything. She guessed Jazmin must have checked on her, then sneaked out quietly so as not to wake her up. They'd do something special together just as soon as this assignment was over. She headed for the shower, mentally reminding herself to send her daughter a text before she left for work.

While she dressed, Assia played over the events of the day before. She spent some time thinking about the people she'd talked to. From her interviews, she had learned that the drug, which had been bought at various venues and over the internet, had been marketed as completely non-addictive and totally safe. Over and over again she had been told that the tabs consisted of "natural proteins" that worked on hormones already present in the body to produce the biggest brain surge; the ultimate high. One young girl described it as "like dancing with angels on top of the world".

The more she had learned, the angrier Assia had become. The seductive simplicity and flawed logic with which this dangerous product had been promoted defied belief. She'd also been told it was easy to buy other similar drugs over the internet. She'd been given the names of several websites, all of which seemed to have mysteriously disappeared when she'd checked them out. She didn't need a degree in rocket science to work out that their demise had to be linked to the current investigation. Meaning that the companies were probably owned by the same person.

It had been while she was lunching in the motorway service station yesterday that the gentle whisper of unease had finally stood up and shouted at her. And suddenly she had made the connection. Later, after sitting for a long time at the table, Assia had returned to the electric blue

Cheyenne, the pounding in her head so bad it felt almost audible. She remembered noticing at the time that the sky had been very clear and blue. She had looked at it for a while. Then she had pulled out her micro, and called her twin brother Ian.

IAN DAWSON LIVED IN ONE OF THE NEW VERTICAL COMMUNITIES THAT HAD SPRUNG UP ALL ACROSS THE COUNTRY. HIS SO-CALLED SKY CITY WAS LOCATED JUST A SHORT DISTANCE FROM THE PICTURESQUE old city of York. Ian worked hard, running a successful cyber company. He was rich, his family enjoying an affluent lifestyle. Assia didn't envy him, though. She would rather earn less, but get to watch her daughter grow up. Her brother lived a 24/7 work life. He was rarely at home.

Assia was lucky: Ian was on a break between meetings when she called. They spent a couple of minutes playing catch-up on family news. Then Assia had said, "I don't know if the name means anything to you, but I recently met with an old school friend, Nerissa Cole."

"Uh-huh. Are we talking about the Nerissa Cole who told lies, spread rumours and broke up friendships. Or am I thinking of someone else?" Ian replied.

"No, that's the one," Assia told him.

"So what's good old Nerissa up to?" Ian asked.

"Oh – living the high life," Assia said. "Lovely house, beautiful clothes, rich new partner."

"Poor you. Bet she's enjoying rubbing your nose in it."

"Uh-huh," Assia agreed. She paused. "She had a brother, didn't she?" she went on. "He was slightly younger. I think he went to your school. Can you remember his name?"

(For the first eleven years of their lives, Assia and Ian had done the twin-thing. When they reached secondary school age, they had decided to untwin, and had gone to separate learning centres.)

There was a brief silence at the other end of the phone. Then Ian Dawson had laughed softly. "Nicholas Cole – now there's a ghost from the past. Chemical Nic we used to call him."

Assia did a swift indrawing breath. "Interesting nickname. Why?"

"He was always messing around in the science lab. Doing experiments, playing about with chemicals, inventing stuff. To begin with, the facilitators loved him – he was a real boff. The rest of us, we tended to avoid him. He used to get this look in his eyes when anyone tried to stop him doing what he wanted. Sort of mad professor on acid. It was scary."

"Go on."

"Remember the burn marks on my arm? That was Nic. He lost his temper about something or other, and chucked a lighted Bunsen burner at me. Just missed my face. I was lucky: another boy got acid thrown at him."

"Sounds like he was a little crazy."

"Understatement of the century, sis. He was always getting suspended. As I recall, the centre ended up expelling him altogether. Hey, I wonder what happened to him."

"He got a PhD in chemistry. Currently he's the CEO of his own pharmaceutical business."

Ian whistled. "That's a surprise. I always speculated one day he'd lose it, and end up in prison for murder. Still, Nic Cole was very bright, very focused. If he wanted to do something, he'd do it. I'd be interested to see the vapour trail, though. He was one seriously dangerous guy." He paused. Then added slightly more cheerfully: "But hey, who knows, maybe he's changed, huh?"

Assia had made some non-committal noises. She knew individuals like Nic Cole, who had what were called sociopathic personalities, often made good captains of industry. They were ruthless and utterly determined. Cole hadn't changed. He was still seriously dangerous. Assia had chatted with her brother for a bit longer, but her thoughts were elsewhere. As soon as the call ended, she had started the jeep and headed for the motorway. Adrenalin was circulating through her, bright as mercury. She needed to get back to London to share what she'd learned with Mbeki. She wasn't to know, she told herself, that even as she was driving the jeep as fast as she could along the outside lane of the motorway, twenty miles further ahead a lorry had overturned and burst into flames. She couldn't have guessed that she'd spend the next five hours stuck in a giant tailback.

BACK IN THE PRESENT, ASSIA FINISHED DRESSING FOR WORK. DECIDING SHE'D GET HERSELF SOME PROPER BREAKFAST ON THE RUN, SHE GRABBED HER BRIEFCASE AND HER KEYS, and hustled out of the apartment.

Assia took the lift down to the ground floor. Then she made her way to the quiet side street where she'd parked the jeep. She checked under the jeep with a mirror, felt along the tops of the wheels. Just in case. Satisfied that the vehicle had not been tampered with overnight, she got in, throwing her bag onto the back seat. As she headed for the inner-city commercial area, where the ISA headquarters were located, she felt a ripple of anticipation. She had important information to communicate to Mbeki. The net was finally closing; it was going to be an interesting day.

JAZMIN HAD FINISHED HER BREAKFAST. HER TRAY HAD BEEN COLLECTED. SHE HAD BEEN SMILEY-POLITE TO THE HOSPITAL ORDERLY COLLECTING IT, BUT HE HAD TOTALLY BLANKED HER. NOW she had been left alone once more. She scoped out the room again, just in case there was some escape route she'd missed. There wasn't. She called out. Nobody came. Unh! She did some mental knuckle crunching as she felt her lower jaw muscles tighten. Therapy-land was starting to get to her.

Jazmin breathed out sharply. She was fed up with this. The inside of her head was beginning to resemble her bedroom at home. She was in acute danger of going down with a severe case of lack-of-perspective syndrome. It was no use, she was just going to have to throw an attack of the bipolars. She stepped back, took a run at the door, and landed a heavy kick on it.

Almost immediately, she heard footsteps in the corridor. A voice shouted, "Quit it!"

Jazmin ignored the command and carried on kicking. There was a burst of swearing, then the door was unlocked by the same male nurse who'd locked her in the previous evening.

"What?" he snapped.

Jazmin rolled her eyes, and gave him a mad grin. "I need a toothbrush," she said.

Giving her a look so frozen she could have skied on it, the man withdrew, locking the door once more. A couple of minutes later, he was back with a packeted toothbrush and a tube of toothpaste. "Here," he grunted, thrusting them at her through a crack in the door. "Happy now?"

Jazmin waited until he'd gone. Then she took another run at the door. So they thought she was just going to sit here quietly? They were so wrong. Until she got out of this dump, she was going to make everybody's life as difficult as possible. Starting. Right. Now.

ASSIA WAS RUNNING LATE. LITERALLY. SHE PUSHED OPEN THE OFFICE DOOR, AND POWERED ACROSS THE ROOM TO HER WORKSPACE, TRYING TO WRESTLE OFF HER COAT AT THE SAME time. Hally looked up from her screen, her lips curving into a malicious grin. "Morning, boss," she sang out. Paused. "Just," she added.

Assia winced. She could rise above this, she told herself. She gave Hally a fake smile. "Yeah, yeah – I hold my hands up: I overslept," she admitted. *Think happy thoughts*, she commanded herself as she dumped her briefcase on her desk. "Where's Chris?" she asked.

"Out," said Hally unhelpfully.

"Okay. Will he be back soon?"

Hally shrugged. *If you'd been here on time*, the shrug implied, *you wouldn't have to ask.*

Assia exhaled sharply, feeling her shoulders tense. Another reason she wanted an end to this assignment: the situation between her and her deputy was bugging her. To take her mind off things, she turned on her laptop, and started reading through her notes. Before Mbeki's arrival, there had always been a certain chemistry between her and Hally, she thought to herself. That's what made things run so smoothly. There had to be a way to get that back.

Twenty minutes of screen-studying, carried out in a silence so thick Assia could have cut it and served it in slices, ended when the door opened and Chris Mbeki entered.

He crossed straight over to Assia's desk, and perched on the edge. "Hi. I see you made it in," he remarked.

"Uh-huh."

"Guess Hally's been filling you in with all the latest details."

"Not as yet."

Mbeki's eyebrows shot up. He shot Hally a questioning look. Hally winced and went bright red. "Oh...umm...I was just going to," she stuttered.

Assia glanced at her flustered deputy and shrugged. *If you'd spoken up earlier*, the shrug implied, *you wouldn't be lying through your teeth now.*

"Okay, no problem," Mbeki said quickly. He turned to Hally. "How about you go get us some coffee, and I'll bring Assia up to date with the developments, huh?"

Hally nodded. "Of course, Chris," she said, smiling at him. "Your usual – skinny vanilla latte and a raspberry glazed doughnut?"

Mbeki gave her a thumbs-up. "You got it."

"I'll have my usual too," Assia said.

There was a small pause. Hally waited, looking at her quizzically. Assia sucked in her breath. "Coffee. Just get me a black coffee, extra shots," she muttered between gritted teeth.

Hally picked up her purse and left the office. Seemingly oblivious to the flak going on around him, Mbeki turned to Assia. "You got back okay last night?"

Assia nodded. "Yeah, eventually," she told him.

"Well, I heard from NovaChem late yesterday," Mbeki said, flipping up the lid of his silver powerbook. "Cole's PA finally contacted me: he's out of the country right now. She doesn't know when he'll be back."

"Look, about Cole: I think I worked out –" Assia began, when she was interrupted by the door to the office swinging open. Hally entered, carrying two brown paper bags and three cups. She carefully handed over Mbeki's cup and paper bag as if she was parting with the crown jewels. Then she dumped Assia's coffee casually down on her desk so that the lid slipped slightly, slopping coffee all over a pile of documents.

Assia pretended she hadn't noticed. She got out her micro, punched in a number, then plugged it into her laptop. "This is the recording of a conversation I had yesterday with my brother Ian," she said to Mbeki. "I think you should take a listen."

STAFF NURSE KARN UNLOCKED THE DOOR OF JAZMIN'S ROOM. "COME ALONG, YOU. DR. COLE WANTS TO TALK TO YOU RIGHT AWAY," HE ANNOUNCED ABRUPTLY.

"Oh really? What does Dr. Cole want to talk to me about?" Jazmin asked, deliberately not moving from her chair.

The staff nurse cut her a withering glance. "I don't know. You're so clever, aren't you? What do you think?"

Jazmin shrugged. "Maybe Dr. Cole wants to talk about kidnapping. Or unlawful imprisonment," she said, regarding him levelly.

Karn gritted his teeth. He had taken an instant dislike to the new patient from the moment he first met her, and nothing she'd said or done since had changed his mind.

"Right, are you coming with me? Or do I have to summon assistance?" Karn growled.

"Oooh, hard call – let me think about it," Jazmin said. She assumed the look of resentful perplexity of someone confronted by an intellectually challenging problem. She pretended to consider the two options. Her lips moved silently. She frowned, studied her nails, the backs of her hands, sighed softly.

Meanwhile, Staff Nurse Karn waited in the doorway, his frustration, antipathy and impatience growing by the nanosecond. Jazmin watched him from under half-closed eyelids. Annoying bossy adults was something she'd practised to perfection. Eventually, just as he approached boiling point, she glanced back up at him. "Er...sorry, what were the choices again?" she asked, with a look of innocent bewilderment.

Giving her a glare that could strip paint, Karn gestured towards the door. "Get out here right now," he commanded, "before I make you!"

Grinning, Jazmin rose to her feet. She followed the staff nurse along the corridor. Whoa – she was *good,* she thought to herself happily. Years of successfully irritating the facilitators at her learning centre had refined her technique to cutting edge. If they ever made it an Olympic sport, she could Wind Up Adults for England. And she'd be right up there on the winner's rostrum.

Jazmin glanced at the back of Karn's thick neck. She began plotting her next move.

ASSIA WAS STARING AT HER COMPUTER SCREEN, TRYING TO IGNORE THE COFFEE-STAINED DOCUMENT FOLDERS BY HER ELBOW, AND THE ICE CHASM THAT HAD OPENED UP BETWEEN HER DESK AND THE ONE opposite, where Hally was fiddling around with stuff in her in tray. Assia knew she was only pretending to be busy. In reality, Hally was listening avidly to everything that was going on.

Mbeki stood deep in concentration, silently absorbing Assia's and her brother's recorded conversation. When it ended, he tossed the remainder of his doughnut into the bin. "So," he remarked quietly, "you think Cole is our man?"

"I'm beginning to. Everything points his way." Assia nodded grimly. "He has the type of personality, and easy access to the drugs."

Mbeki digested this. "And you went to school with his sister? Whew – that is some coincidence. Excuse me for saying so, but she doesn't sound like a very nice person."

"She isn't," Assia stated flatly. "I'd say she has the same sociopathic personality as her brother has. But wherever he is, and whatever he's been up to, I bet she'll know about it."

"Do you think she'll talk to us?"

Assia's mouth formed a straight line. "Who knows?" she said thinly. "But it beats sitting around here doing nothing."

Mbeki caught the grim undertone in her voice. "Maybe you and this Nerissa have some unfinished business from the past to settle," he remarked quietly.

Maybe, Assia thought. She recalled Nerissa's hurtful remarks about Jazmin. *And some from the present as well.*

"Okay," Mbeki went on, "no time like the present. Shall we phone first and make an appointment?"

Assia held a quick mental debate with herself. "No, let's not," she said. "We'll just turn up and let things happen."

Mbeki nodded. "It's your call."

Assia picked up the coffee-splashed pile of documents from her desk. Holding them at arms' length, she transferred them to Hally's desk. "These need sorting and filing, please," she said, "preferably after you've dried them all off carefully." Then she snagged her bag from the back of her chair. "Do you mind if we stop off at my apartment on the way?" she asked Mbeki. "There's something I need to pick up before we go."

"Sure," Mbeki agreed. Closing down his powerbook, he followed her out of the room.

A SHORT TiME LATER, THE PiLOT OF THE PiPER NAVAHO WAS RUNNiNG THROUGH HIS PRE-TAKE-OFF CHECKS WiTH AiR TRAFFiC CONTROL AT CHARLES DE GAULLE. NOT THE EASiEST OF THiNGS TO do, as the controller's French accent was like something out of a bad retro-movie.

"Charles de Gaulle Tower," the pilot said, "this is Golf Bravo Whisky Hotel Tango, request start-up and I have Information Delta."

There was a crackle at the other end. Then the heavily accented voice said: "Golf Bravo Whisky Hotel Tango start-up approved, report ready for taxi. Roger Information Delta, confirm QNH 1012."

The pilot decoded this. "Golf Hotel Tango, will depart ready for taxi," he said. He turned to his sole passenger. "Seat belt on now, sir."

The passenger, a middle-aged businessman in an expensive charcoal-grey suit, folded his paper, then fastened his seat belt. He checked the time on his Breil watch. The pilot taxied the plane towards the runway. He'd flown this man before. Many times. Always between London City Airport and Charles de Gaulle. Odd sort of chap, the pilot thought. Never said a word, but exuded a kind of aggressive silence. If such a quality could be said to exist.

The Piper Navaho sped down the runway, its 325 h.p. twin engines screaming. The pilot pulled back on the control stick, feeling the plane's nose rise up in response. The rumble of the runway disappeared, and he heard the whirr of the wheels coming in, the doors closing with a reassuring clunk.

The plane settled into a climb, quickly entering the cloud bank. The pilot shot a searching glance at his passenger. He knew some people didn't like this ascent into milky blindness. It made them feel nervous. The man, however, just stared silently out of the window. But at the back of the cold grey eyes, the pilot thought he saw something unpleasant flicker momentarily. Only one hour to London City Airport, he reminded himself as the plane rose out of the clouds and into the bright sunshine above.

AS HER OFFICE DOOR OPENED, DR. NERISSA COLE GLANCED UP, GAVE A BRIEF HALF-SMILE AND GESTURED SILENTLY TO A CHAIR. JAZMIN SAT DOWN. NERISSA STARED AT HER, RAISED ONE eyebrow, and pretended to look puzzled.

"Oh, give me a break, you know perfectly well who I am," Jazmin said.

Nerissa looked down at her notes. "But the question is: do you, eh?" There was a brief pause. "I gather that you told the staff nurse your name was 'Hyacinth Potts'," she murmured, her voice soft and purring, but with claws in it. "Why did you do that?"

"I just made it up on the spur of the moment, all right? There were some hyacinths in a flowerpot on the table. Joke."

"Really? Why?"

Jazmin shrugged.

"Mmm-hmm, I see. *No particular reason,*" Nerissa murmured again, making notes on a piece of paper.

"Why are you writing that down?" Jazmin asked. She craned forward, trying to see what else had been written about her.

Nerissa shielded the paper with her left hand. "Just something for a piece of research I'm conducting," she said. She finished writing. "Did you know," she remarked casually, "that statistically, one in three people suffer from some sort of mental disorder?"

"Good thing there's only two of us here then, isn't it?"

There was another long silence. Nerissa stared hard at Jazmin, who stared hard back. Nerissa was the first to blink. "So," she said, "here you are."

"Uh-huh. Here I am."

"And the reason for your rather unexpected visit is...?"

"I've come to find Ginevra," Jazmin stated, "and I don't intend to leave until I know exactly what you've done with her. So you might as well tell me where she is."

Nerissa's eyes glinted with secret amusement. She sat

back in her chair. "Ginevra is in California," she said. She folded her arms, and waited for Jazmin's reaction.

Jazmin's jaw dropped open. "But...I thought..."

"Yes? What did you think? That something *bad* had happened to her? Oh really!" Nerissa scoffed. "You teenagers, you're always *so* melodramatic!" She leaned forward, her eyes hardening. "Ginevra Frascati is a spoiled, rich little Daddy's girl. If she doesn't get what she desires, she sulks and throws a tantrum. From the moment I met her, she has tried her hardest to mess things up between me and her father."

Jazmin gave a little shrug. Privately, she thought if any messing up had been done, it was Nerissa who'd messed things up for Ginevra.

"If you want to know what happened," Nerissa continued, "after a lot of ringing round, I'd finally found a suitable boarding school for Ginevra, one which focused upon hard work and strict discipline. She was all packed and ready to leave when, out of the blue, her mother rang from the States saying she'd arranged a flight over for her. So that was that. Instead of leaving for her new school, Ginevra was driven straight to the airport – not a word of thanks to me for all the effort I'd put in on her behalf, I may add. Now she is living with her mother in some exclusive beach community in Santa Barbara. Sun, sea and shopping. It must be every spoiled teenager's dream. She's probably having the time of her life. My guess is she'll have forgotten all about you. I doubt if she even remembers your name."

Jazmin went on staring at her in amazement.

"Ah, I *understand*," Nerissa continued in a talking-to-the-hard-of-thinking voice. "You thought Ginevra was *here*. You came to *get* her! Aww...gallant Jazmin Dawson riding to rescue poor little Ginni, kept prisoner by her wicked stepmother." Nerissa's voice dripped honey. "How terribly, terribly sweet. It's just like something out of an old fairy tale."

"How do I know you're telling the truth?" Jazmin demanded.

Nerissa got out a tiny pink leather organizer. "Here's Ginni's number in California. Feel free to call it," she said airily, pushing the phone across the desk. "Oh, and here's a current list of all my patients. Do study it carefully. As you can see, there is no Ginevra Frascati. So it looks very much like you had a wasted journey, doesn't it? What a shame." Nerissa threw Jazmin a bright smile. It was the sort of smile you wanted to back away from very fast.

Jazmin stared at the list of patients. This was not what she'd been expecting.

Nerissa watched her.

"You could easily be lying," Jazmin said. "She could be here under another name. Or not be on the list at all."

Nerissa lifted her shoulders in a tiny, nonchalant shrug. "I thought you checked out the whole complex very thoroughly yesterday," she said. "I was following you on the CCTV and I don't think you missed a single room. Of course, you didn't check all the cupboards. Or the drug store. Or the laundry room. Maybe you'd like to go and search those?"

Jazmin took a couple of deep breaths. "Okay," she conceded reluctantly, "perhaps you are telling me the truth: Ginevra isn't here."

"Such a pity you never got to say goodbye," Nerissa murmured. "Still, perhaps it's all for the best, eh? *Mi caro sposo* is very protective of his little princess. I'm sure you understand."

Jazmin stood up. "Right, I'm out of here," she said briskly. "Oh – can I have my micro back, please? I need to contact my mum. She'll be worried sick about me."

Nerissa appeared not to have heard her. She shrugged, then busied herself writing up her notes again. Jazmin stood and waited. When nothing happened, she raised her voice and said, "Hello? Did you hear what I said? I want my micro back. One of your nurses took it yesterday. Oh, and you might like to have a major word with him. I think there are laws about manhandling people and locking them up."

There was a nanosecond's pause.

Then Nerissa looked up, and gestured towards the chair again. "I think you'd better sit down, Jazmin," she said. "I see there are some things I need to make clear to you."

LEAVING THE ISA BUILDING, ASSIA LED THE WAY TO THE UNDERGROUND CAR PARK WHERE SHE HAD LEFT THE BLUE JEEP. THEN SHE DROVE MBEKI ACROSS LONDON TO HER APARTMENT. She kept the conversation minimal. Mentally, she was preparing herself for her meeting with Nerissa Cole. Her hands steady on the wheel, Assia stared straight ahead, lost in her own private thoughts. Since the conversation with her brother, more events from the past had begun to filter back into her mind.

She had started to recall just how really evil Nerissa Cole had been. How she had bullied and intimidated other students. Bad memories that she must have wiped from her mind over the years had returned, like long-drowned bodies bobbing to the surface again. There was what Jazmin would probably call "a lot of nasty" still between them.

Reaching her block, Assia parked the Cheyenne in the residents' bay. Then, leaving Mbeki to guard the jeep, she got out and hurried inside. Entering her apartment, Assia went straight to her bedroom and opened her wardrobe. She lifted out a white cardboard box. If she was going to go one on one with Nerissa Cole, she thought grimly, she needed to make sure she went suitably equipped.

JAZMIN SAT IN SILENCE, STARING AT HER CLASPED HANDS. NERISSA WATCHED HER, A SUPERCILIOUS LITTLE SMILE PLAYING UPON HER PINK-LIPSTICKED MOUTH.

"Do you think I didn't *know* you were here all the time?" she said scornfully. "You must believe I'm very stupid! Let me enlighten you, Jazmin. For your information, every step you have taken has been monitored from the moment you arrived. Every conversation. Everything that has happened to you has occurred because I allowed it. I could have let you leave at any time over the last twenty-four hours. I could even have had you thrown out. But I didn't."

Jazmin lifted her eyes from her hands and looked at Nerissa.

Nerissa leaned across the desk. "And I'm not going to let you leave now," she said softly.

"But you can't stop me. My mum—"

"Will probably be out of her mind with worry," Nerissa cut in. "Of *course* she will. Once she realizes you've gone – which, given her rather inadequate work–life balance, might be some time. Out of her mind with worry," she repeated slowly and with great relish. "And that's exactly what I want her to be."

Jazmin stared at her. "Excuse me?"

"It's very simple, Jazmin. You see, this is all about payback," Nerissa continued smoothly. "You probably don't realize it, but the assignment your mother is working on right now is upsetting somebody very close to me. A member of my family, in actual fact. And when people in your family get hurt, you have to hurt back, don't you?"

Jazmin swallowed uneasily. "Um...when you say 'hurt'...?"

Nerissa waved a dismissive hand. "'Oh, don't worry, I don't mean it *literally*." She paused. "Yet," she added.

"Uh. Right."

"And there's another reason why I'm not going to let you go," Nerissa went on. "Your mother and I, we also have – how shall I put it diplomatically – *history*. Between you and me and these four walls – and it gives me no pleasure to say this to you – when we were at school together, your mother was very cruel to me. She was a bully, and she made my life totally miserable. Now it's my turn to repay her for everything she did to me."

A bully? I seriously doubt it, Jazmin thought grimly. *If there was any bullying in the past, I bet I know who did it.*

"So you see, you coming here has given me a golden opportunity," Nerissa said brightly, fixing her cold blue eyes on Jazmin's face. "Quite irresistible, in fact. I have several scores to settle. And here you are to help me do it. It must be kismet, Fate."

Jazmin felt her insides going into freefall. "You are making a very bad mistake," she said to Nerissa, trying to keep the tremor out of her voice. "My mum will guess exactly where I am."

"I'm sure she will. Eventually. But it will take her several days. Maybe longer. After all, this is not the most obvious place to look for you, is it? And until she works it out, she will go through a very bad time indeed. I can't imagine what it must be like to discover that your only daughter has vanished into thin air without trace. It will be most interesting to watch her suffer. I'm really going to enjoy it."

Jazmin opened her mouth to protest.

"Oh, I know *exactly* what you're going to say," Nerissa smirked. "You're going to say: *you won't get away with it!* Or some other silly cliché. Sadly for both you and your stupid mother, I probably will."

"But you can't keep me here," Jazmin exclaimed, "I have rights!"

Nerissa waved a dismissive hand. "Oh, you teenagers and your so-called *rights*. It's all I ever hear about." She laughed lightly. "Rights, rights, and more rights. As I always say: forget about your 'rights' for a while. Just be grateful you have landed up somewhere that can deal with your problems."

"Excuse me? What 'problems'? I don't have any problems."

Nerissa smiled. Then she opened her eyes wide. Delicate frown lines cracked her porcelain-white forehead. "Oh Jazmin, Jazmin, Jazmin, where do I start?" she said, shaking her head slowly from side to side. "Or should I call you Hyacinth? You clearly have a split personality. Possibly borderline schizophrenia. Then there's your deluded belief that my stepdaughter is imprisoned here.

And your rather bizarre gun fantasy. Tut, tut." Nerissa clicked her teeth. "And, finally, let's not forget the rather serious matter of self-referring to a private psychiatric unit without completing the necessary paperwork – extremely aberrant behaviour." She cut Jazmin a sly glance. "You know what? The more I think about it, the more I'm convinced that, even in the unlikely event of your mother turning up in the next few hours, you're still going to have to stay here until we get to the root of what's wrong with you. However long that takes."

Time stood still for several heartbeats.

Then Jazmin jumped to her feet and ran for the door.

Nerissa pressed a button under her desk. "Escape is impossible," she said silkily. "There is an extremely good security system in operation throughout the complex. Anyway, according to the 2012 Mental Health Act, I am legally permitted to section you, and treat you with or without your consent."

Two hospital orderlies entered the office so quickly that they must have been lurking just outside the door. "Take this patient back to her room," Nerissa ordered coldly. "And make sure she doesn't associate with any of the others. I want her kept on strict twenty-four-hour lockdown until further notice."

The orderlies grabbed Jazmin's arms and began dragging her out of the room. She tried to resist their efforts, kicking and struggling as hard as she could. Meanwhile, Nerissa sat back in the chair, calmly watching her unsuccessful attempt to escape. "Ah, Fate plays such amusing games, Jazmin Dawson," she laughed, "and just like me, she doesn't always stick to the rules."

ASSIA AND MBEKI DROVE THROUGH THE GATES OF THE WELLNESS THERAPEUTIC CENTRE. ASSIA SLUNG THE JEEP INTO ONE OF THE SLOTS LABELLED "RESERVED FOR MEDICAL STAFF ONLY". THEN SHE turned off the engine and spun round to face Mbeki.

"If you don't mind, I'd rather do this on my own."

"Sure thing. I'll wait here for you."

Assia got out her micro. "I'll call your number as soon as I meet up with Nerissa. Keep your phone on. That way you'll hear everything that happens," she said. She handed him a tiny recording device. "If you plug this into your micro and your dashboard charger, you'll be able to record the conversation. We might be able to use something she says as evidence against Nic Cole."

Mbeki gave her a swift glance. "You carrying?"

Assia smiled briefly at him without replying. Then she opened the driver's door and stepped out.

Mbeki watched her go up the steps. Even his trained eye couldn't spot the telltale bulge of a gun. On the top step, Assia turned and glanced back at him. Mbeki gave her a brief thumbs-up. She nodded, then disappeared through the double doors.

Assia waited at the front desk while the receptionist paged Nerissa. A lot of her time at the moment seemed to be spent hanging around in reception areas. Perhaps it was a metaphor for her life. After ten minutes, the glass door leading to the main part of the centre swung open and Nerissa appeared. She was wearing a smart pink silk suit – probably handmade by some exclusive Italian designer, Assia thought. Round her neck was a dainty seed pearl necklace, and she wore tiny matching pearl earrings.

"Ash!" Nerissa exclaimed loudly, raising her eyebrows in surprise. "How lovely. What a completely *unexpected* surprise!"

As Nerissa advanced towards her, arms outstretched, Assia found herself automatically taking a couple of steps backwards. Her occupational reflexes kicking in.

"Do come through to my office; we can talk there," Nerissa cooed, aiming a couple of loud air kisses vaguely in the direction of Assia's face. She turned, led the way along a vanilla-scented corridor and through a set of double doors, which she swiped open with a keycard. Her high-heeled pink shoes clacked rhythmically on the woodblock floor. Eventually, she stopped outside a door labelled *Dr. N. Cole, Director*. "In here," she said, ushering Assia into a bright, modern, primrose-coloured room. She waved her to a seat. "Tea? Coffee? Iced water?"

Assia shook her head. "Nothing, thanks."

Nerissa perched herself on the edge of the desk, crossing

her legs elegantly. "I'm *so* glad you came to see me," she said. "I felt we parted on rather awkward terms last time we met, but I'm sure you now understand, I was only doing what *mio caro sposo* told me to. You know how *demanding* Italian men are," she went on, giggling girlishly. "Anything my Cesare wants, he has to have, and *pronto*!"

"Does he really," Assia said drily.

"Anyway, I think it was all for the best," Nerissa continued, waving her hand in the air. She paused. "And how is Jazmin getting on? I do hope she didn't give you a hard time about the secret boyfriend. Believe me, I know *exactly* how difficult it is to discipline wayward teenagers. I do it every working day."

Assia felt her jaw muscles beginning to tighten. Somewhere in her youth, Nerissa Cole must have undergone a total tactectomy. She glanced quickly at her face, but could detect nothing under the deceptively bland smile. She had to stop being oversensitive where Jazmin was concerned, Assia told herself firmly. She took some deep breaths and tried to relax her shoulders.

"So what is your daughter up to today?" Nerissa cooed.

"She's not 'up to' anything," Assia said. "She's studying hard at her learning centre."

"Ah, I see. Yes, of course," Nerissa said, her eyes twinkling starrily. "You must feel rather relieved to know exactly where she is right now, eh?"

Assia consciously uncurled her fingers one at a time. She placed her hands, palm-side down in her lap, and took a couple more deep breaths, reminding herself firmly that she was not here to discuss Jazmin and her whereabouts. Or to allow Nerissa Cole to pull her emotional strings and jerk her around. She was here in her official capacity as a senior ISA agent, to ask Nerissa some searching questions about her brother. It was time to stop the social chit-chat, and start asking them.

JAZMIN HAD FINISHED EATING HER COOKED LUNCH: STEAK PIE, CHIPS AND CREAMED CORN, BUT SHE'D BEEN FAR TOO ANGRY TO ENJOY IT. NOW SHE SAT ON THE BED, GOING THROUGH HER LACK OF options. She really needed to pull a Houdini as fast as possible, because things were getting way out of hand. It was patently clear that Nerissa Cole's mind was so twisty you could stick a handle on it and use it as a corkscrew. Also, she urgently had to contact her mum, and warn her about the revenge thing. She glanced desperately round the room, but the miraculous escape route went on failing to materialize.

Jazmin sighed. Jaz Dawson, her über-diva alter ego would have a utility belt stuffed full of useful equipment for just such an occasion as this. There'd be a couple of sticks of explosives, a laser gun that could take out a wall, and a fast getaway vehicle with state-of-the-art Global

Positioning System parked out front. Whereas all she had was a set of plastic cutlery and a stupid dinner plate.

A dinner plate.

Jazmin picked up the white china plate, weighing it thoughtfully in one hand. Then she set it down on the tray again. Slowly, her face cleared. The tense expression faded away, to be replaced by one of steely determination. She got to her feet, paused, took a deep breath, then headed towards the door at high speed. Somebody was about to discover Fineberg's Theory of Unintended Consequences. She really hoped they weren't going to enjoy it.

THE RED DODGE VIPER SPED ALONG THE FIVE-LANE LONDON ORBITAL ROAD, DIVING IN AND OUT OF THE TWO FAST OUTER LANES. INSIDE THE CAR, PROFESSOR NIC COLE'S KNUCKLES WERE BLUE-white; his hands were gripping the steering wheel so tightly they seemed to be trying to strangle it. His thin lips were set in a snarling rictus of fury.

You were having a good time in Paris, he told himself. *Enjoying the nightclubs, the casinos and the fine restaurants. You were having fun. And then she rang. And she went on and on about some stupid girl she had got hold of, and how you had messed up big time, and how she was going to have to get you out of trouble again. On and on and on, spoiling your fun. Just like she always spoils everything.*

And now, the big SUV in front of him was refusing to move over. He sounded his horn loudly. The driver flicked him a contemptuous V-sign. Cole deliberately moved up close behind the SUV so that the Viper was practically butt kissing its shiny steel bumper, forcing the driver to swerve dangerously across into the middle lane. Cole grinned. He mashed the accelerator to the floor, glancing in his rear mirror as he sped by, gratified to see the SUV driver's face, chalk-white and terrified as he struggled to regain control of his vehicle.

It's time you deal with her once and for all. Time you took control, and show her you're not going to be bullied and bossed around any more. She needs to be taught a lesson. A lesson she'll never forget. After all, you are no longer a child. Are you?

STAFF NURSE KARN WAS NOT A HAPPY MAN. UP UNTIL TODAY HE COULD HONESTLY SAY, HAND ON HEART, THAT HE ENJOYED HIS JOB. HE LIKED BEING IN CHARGE OF THE ADOLESCENT UNIT, THROWING his weight around when the occasion demanded, but all this kindergarten cop stuff was getting him down. He was fed up with Hyacinth Potts's attention-seeking games. He strongly suspected there was nothing much wrong with Hyacinth Potts that exposure to some good old-fashioned slap-round-the-head therapy wouldn't solve.

Karn was also increasingly fed up with the stupid

invitations issued every time he unlocked her door to "stop and have an interesting discussion". The last time he'd gone to see what she wanted, the little snot had placed her chair in the middle of the room, and asked him to prove it existed using Laghenstern's Theory of Being (at least that's what he *thought* she'd said). He was pretty sure that somewhere along the line, he was being laughed at.

Staff Nurse Karn's lip curled. He did shouting, he did dishing out pills, he did restraint. What he didn't do was mind mouthy little brats whose sole purpose and enjoyment in life seemed to be winding him up. In the distance, he heard once again the unmistakable sound of somebody kicking a door.

"Right, this is the last time!" he snarled at his colleagues, who were standing with him around the water cooler on their break. "Listen up: from now on, nobody – and I mean *nobody* – is to take any notice of that new kid. Okay? She can kick at that door until her freaking legs drop off!"

Gritting his teeth, Staff Nurse Karn went to see what the little pain wanted.

"Sooo..." NERISSA COLE DRAWLED, "I GUESS WE'RE ALL TALKED OUT ON BADLY BEHAVED TEENAGERS, EH?" SHE SMILED AT ASSIA, WHO SUDDENLY REALIZED WHY NERISSA HAD CHOSEN TO SIT ON THE desk rather than behind it. It meant she could look down on her and pretend to be superior. Just like she used to do when they were both at school together. Unh – pity she hadn't cottoned on before. Assia glanced around the room, but short of leaning against the door, which would look a little odd, there was nowhere else to position herself. Gritting her teeth, she mentally resigned herself to remaining in her lowly seat.

Nerissa flicked a quick glance at her tiny white leather Fendi watch, subtly suggesting that her time was limited and Assia was currently approaching its borderline. "Well, it was lovely to see you again, Ash," she said, in a crisp I'm-very-busy-and-important voice, "and of course I *entirely* understand why you had to run out on me when we last met for lunch. Believe me I *totally* sympathize." She held up a hand. "No need to apologize – let's just put the whole thing behind us and move on, shall we?"

I wasn't going to apologize, Assia thought grimly. A sudden vision flashed onto her mental screen of a small girl, her back pressed against some playground wall, being forced to say "sorry" to Nerissa Cole for something she didn't know she'd done wrong. It was the same old technique. That was how Nerissa had always exerted power. She pretended to be the victim. In reality, she made other people her victims. *But not now,* her subconscious told her firmly. This wasn't the playground, and she was not that child.

Assia sat a little more upright in her seat. "Actually,

Nerissa, I didn't come here to talk about our last meeting," she said briskly. She reached into her pocket and drew out her ID card. "I'm here in my official capacity as a senior officer working for the International Security Agency. My team is currently conducting a high-level investigation. I need to locate your brother, Professor Nicholas Cole, and ask him a few questions."

Nerissa stared at her. "My *brother*?" she exclaimed in astonishment, her eyes widening. "Questions about what?"

Assia maintained her official pose. "It's nothing for you to be concerned about," she said calmly. "Just some routine matters we need to clear up. Can you tell me where he is right now? It's important we talk to him and eliminate him from our inquiries."

Nerissa's expression hardened. She shook her head. "No, I certainly can't tell you where he is."

"So you don't know?"

"Yes, of course I know, but it's none of your damn business," Nerissa said, her voice rising with annoyance. "Honestly, Assia Dawson, who do you think you are? I invite you to my party; I take you out for lunch; I make a *huge* effort to forget all the *terribly hurtful* things you did to me in the past. But it just isn't good enough for you, is it? You have to come pushing your way into my private office making wild accusations against my brother – one of the most reputed scientists of his generation, in case you weren't aware."

"I don't recollect making any 'wild accusations', as you call it," Assia countered. "I merely asked you to tell me where your brother is right now."

"Well tough, I'm not going to tell you anything," Nerissa said coolly. She folded her arms and stared defiantly down at Assia. "And there's nothing you can do to make me."

STAFF NURSE KARN UNLOCKED JAZMIN'S DOOR. HE ENTERED THE ROOM, TELLING HIMSELF FIRMLY THAT HE WAS THE ADULT, SHE WAS THE CHILD. IT WAS A CONCEPT HE WAS INCREASINGLY HAVING to remind himself of as the day wore on and his sense of normality trickled away like bath water down a plughole.

"Yes, what is it now?" he snapped.

Jazmin's eyes lit up at the sight of him. She flashed him a wide, joyful smile. "Hello, Mr. Nurse," she said happily. "It's you! Hooray. Would you like to see a trick? I've got a really good one. Shall I show it to you?"

Staff Nurse Karn rolled his eyes skywards.

"Did you know I'm a Twelfth Dan Ninja," Jazmin said, innocence hanging from her words like loops of toffee.

Karn grinned sardonically. "Oh really?"

"Yes. And that means I can split this plate in two with my bare hands."

"Yeah? Somehow I don't think so," Karn sneered.

Jazmin picked up the dinner plate and beckoned him over. "Want to see me do it?"

"Some other time. I'm busy right now, okay," Karn snapped, but his eyes were reluctantly pulled to the plate in spite of himself.

"Aw, you can spare a couple of minutes," Jazmin coaxed. "Are you ready?" she asked, watching his face intently.

Karn gave in. The prospect of the trouble Hyacinth Potts would be in for deliberately breaking canteen property was suddenly irresistible. "Yeah, yeah. Whatever. Do your stupid little trick," he growled.

"Come a bit nearer, you'll see it better." Jazmin raised her left hand and held the plate out in front of her. "Watch my left hand," she commanded.

Staff Nurse Karn fixed his eyes on her hand, trying to look as if he couldn't care less.

"Are you watching my left hand?" Jazmin asked.

Karn nodded. Jazmin kicked him hard in the groin, then, as he doubled up, she smashed the plate over his head. "Pity. You should really have been watching my foot instead," she said reprovingly.

As Karn crumpled to the floor, clutching himself and groaning in agony, Jazmin bent down and calmly helped herself to his keycard and his personal alarm. Then she ran out of the room, slamming the door shut behind her.

Staff Nurse Karn waited for everything to stop revolving. Then he got groggily to his feet and, holding his crotch, limped painfully to the door. It was locked. He fumbled in his belt for his alarm to summon assistance. And found that it wasn't there. Cursing, Karn banged on the door with his fist. Nothing happened. He banged on the door some more. No response.

Puzzled, Karn stood back from the door. Why was no one coming? Then he remembered. Nobody was coming to his assistance because he'd told them not to respond, hadn't he? Staff Nurse Karn cursed his unbelievable bad luck. He'd been tricked by a stupid girl. Now he was locked in. And he was going to have to stay locked in either until he broke the door down, or he figured out some other way to get out.

JAZMIN SPRINTED ALONG A CORRIDOR, TOOK A SHARP RIGHT, BARRELLED THROUGH A SIDE DOOR, AND FOUND HERSELF UNEXPECTEDLY IN THE KITCHEN, WHERE A COUPLE OF STARTLED cooks were washing up the lunch plates. Waving a cheery greeting, she dodged past them, then out the door at the back of the kitchen, almost colliding with a couple of big dustbins. Her directional antenna finally kicking in, she scurried round the side of the building, heading for the front gate and freedom. A small blue jeep was parked out front in one of the staff bays. As Jazmin ran by, the driver's window slid back and a head leaned out. "Hey," the driver called. "Jazmin? Wait up!"

Jazmin skidded to a halt. She cut the man a lightning glance. Huh? It was Chris Mbeki, the man her mum was helping. Why was he here? On the other hand, why was she wasting time asking herself? She sprinted to the car. Mbeki leaned across and opened the passenger door. Jazmin slid in, slamming the door behind her. "Okay, *drive*!" she commanded.

There was a pause while nothing happened.

"You're not driving!" Jazmin exclaimed accusingly.

"Sorry, ma'am," the man said. He shrugged, giving her an amused glance. "Guess you picked the wrong day for a getaway. I'm kind of riding shotgun with your mum right now."

Way to go, Mum! Jazmin thought. She might have guessed her mum'd work out where she was and come straight to her rescue. So much for Nerissa's dire predictions!

"So where is she?" she asked, looking round.

Mbeki nodded towards the building. "In there talking to Dr. Cole."

"How did she find out?"

"Your uncle."

"What?"

"He told her about the brother. The rest kind of fell into place."

Jazmin stared at him. This was way too cryptic. But hey, at least she was with an adult she knew and trusted, she reassured herself. Even if he wasn't making much sense.

"Okay," she said, taking a deep breath. "Right." She gave him a quick glance. "Did you say 'shotgun'? Are you...armed?"

Chris Mbeki nodded. "I always carry a modulated taser," he told her. "Shoots a six-fifty megahertz dart that delivers a five millisecond jolt. *Woomph*. Down you go. Only lasts a few minutes though."

"I thought guns were for killing people."

Chris Mbeki shook his head. "Nuh-uh. People think that, but they're not. On the contrary, they're so you *don't* have to kill people. Most weapons are for having. They're for being seen. For a warning."

"Right." This was interesting. Jazmin was rapidly beginning to lose sight of the fact that she was meant to be On the Run and Fleeing for her Life. She had just opened her mouth to ask Mbeki some more questions about the ethics of weaponry when a red Dodge Viper with tinted windows and a personalized number plate screamed in through the gates and drove up to the main entrance, its wheels crunching on the gravel. The driver slid into a vacant slot, braked sharply, and cut the engine.

Mbeki stilled. He sucked in his breath. "Uh-uh," he murmured. "Look who's just arrived."

"Who?" Jazmin asked, craning round to see.

"Professor Nic Cole. The man we badly want to interview. He's supposed to be out of the country, but it looks like he's unexpectedly back in town."

The man got out of the car, stretching his arms wearily above his head. Then he began walking purposefully towards the main entrance. Mbeki opened the door, a grim set to his mouth. "Stay where you are; he is dangerous!" he ordered Jazmin. He leaped out and began following the man.

Jazmin leaned out of the passenger window. The man turned and saw Mbeki. His expression changed. He gave a sudden cry of recognition, swore loudly and broke into a run. At the base of the steps he paused, his hand groping for something in his jacket pocket. Without breaking stride, Mbeki pulled out the taser and brought it up to shoulder height.

There was a crackling sound. The man screamed and fell backwards.

INSIDE THE WELLNESS THERAPEUTIC CENTRE, NERISSA COLE WAS RIDING THE CREST OF HER ANGER. SHE SLID OFF THE DESK AND STOOD TOWERING MENACINGLY OVER ASSIA, HER ARMS FOLDED IN a threatening manner.

"So you think you can waltz in here, waving your stupid little ID card and get me to talk?" Nerissa raged, two spots of anger flaming in her cheeks, her pale blue eyes sparking daggers. "Huh! I'd like to see you try!"

Assia sat motionless, her calm expression masking her inner thoughts, which were currently running on the lines of, *Question: what's the difference between a psychiatrist and a four year old? Answer: very little.*

Nerissa glared down at her. "What are your threat lines, *Ash*?" she spat. "What are you going to do? Report me to the teacher? I don't think so. Maybe you have a gun hidden on your person?" She swept Assia a sneering head-to-toe glance. "Nuh-uh, I think not. So I don't believe I will talk to you any more." Nerissa stopped to draw breath. "This meeting is terminated," she said, her voice dripping icicles. "Please leave my premises at once. Or I will have to summon a couple of my staff and have you thrown out!"

Assia's response was to rise swiftly from her chair. She made a sudden darting forwards movement. There was a small crunching noise. Then Nerissa gave a gasp, and the colour drained out of her face. She looked down in horror. Assia smiled sweetly at her. "What is currently sticking into your foot," she murmured, "is the eight-centimetre steel-and-rosewood spike heel of an extremely expensive Goody Two-Shoes leather boot. They were a Christmas present from my generous brother, in case you're wondering. Though I guess you aren't. What you're probably wondering is: *could she actually push it all the way to the floor?* and you know, I'm not sure. But it would be *very* interesting to try, wouldn't it?"

Assia exerted some more pressure. Nerissa's complexion turned mushroom coloured.

"I've always liked the thought of owning a pair of killer

heels," Assia murmured thoughtfully, in a voice that made honey look like gravel. "Rather an unexpected choice of weaponry, don't you think?" She paused. "So, Nerissa, are you ready to talk to me now?"

Nerissa swallowed, opened and closed her mouth a couple of times...

...just as the crack of the single gunshot ricocheted in from outside.

OUTSIDE, JAZMIN WAS STANDING NEXT TO CHRIS MBEKI. BOTH WERE GAZING DOWN AT THE PRONE BODY OF PROFESSOR NIC COLE. JAZMIN FELT A BRIGHT SLICK OF ADRENALINE CIRCULATING through her. So this was what it was like to be a real fearless crime-fighter. "Whoa, did you see that?" he said proudly, looking sideways at Jazmin.

The man on the ground made a low moaning noise and began to twitch.

"Stay back!" Mbeki ordered Jazmin. "He may kick out as he comes round. I'm going to cuff him. Here, hold this for me for a second, would you," he said, handing her the taser as he fumbled in his utility belt for some handcuffs.

THE TWO WOMEN RUSHED ALONG THE CORRIDOR. ARRIVING ON THE FRONT STEPS, ASSIA SAW NERISSA STOP DEAD AND STARE DOWN AT THE TWITCHING BODY OF A MIDDLE-AGED MAN LYING ON THE

gravel, with Chris Mbeki bending over him. Her face went chalk white under its make-up. Then she gasped in horror. "Nic? Nic, what's happened? Are you all right?" She clattered down the steps, and ran towards him. "Let him go, you bastard!" she yelled, and began punching Mbeki with her clenched fists.

Assia remained on the top step. She watched Mbeki brush Nerissa off as if she were a bothersome fly. She watched him haul the groaning, dazed Professor Nic Cole to his feet, and begin to manhandle him roughly towards the jeep. Then all at once, she spotted Jazmin standing a few metres away, staring wide eyed at the unfolding drama. She hurried towards her. "Hon? What are you doing here?" she queried, frowning. "Shouldn't you be at the learning centre?"

Jazmin dragged her gaze away from the developing situation and fixed them on her mum's face. Assia's eyes travelled downwards. Her body stiffened. Suddenly Jazmin realized she was still holding Mbeki's weapon. Hot damn. She tried to hide it behind her back. Too late. Assia paused, her eyes hardening and locking in. She pointed at Jazmin's hand. "*Jazmin Dawson! What on earth are you doing with that taser?*" she exclaimed.

Jazmin caught Mbeki's eye. They exchanged a guilty look.

Uh-oh.

SOMETIME LATER, JAZMIN WAS DAWDLING SLOWLY ALONG THE PAVEMENT. SHE WAS HEADING IN THE DIRECTION OF THE LEARNING CENTRE. THE WEATHER WAS TRYING TO RAIN, BUT HAD ONLY GOT AS far as producing a spitty grey drizzle which was more like fog with a weight problem. Just as well, because she hadn't got an umbrella.

As she walked, Jazmin got out her pocket mirror and checked her appearance. Ewww, Captivity Pallor was not a good look. And her hair seemed to have recently undergone some electroconvulsive therapy. On the plus side, however, she was free, so a little temporary discomfort was no big.

Lines of cars slurred by, windscreen wipers arcing hypnotically to and fro drawing manic eyebrows on the wet glass. If some aliens looked at London, they'd probably conclude that the car was the dominant life form, she thought. In a sense, they would be quite right. She decided to cheer herself up by mentally going over yet again what had taken place in the car park of the Wellness Therapeutic Centre.

As soon as Nerissa had realized her brother was being taken into ISA custody for questioning, she had gone absolutely rampageous. First she had turned on Jazmin's mum, screaming incoherently at her like a crazed animal. Then she'd launched a tirade of abuse at her brother, to which he'd responded with equal savagery. Jazmin had listened in horrified fascination as the Cole family skeletons had all come trouping out of the cupboard, like children on their way to a Christmas party. After a bit, Mbeki and her mum had made "enough already" signs at each other, and bundled Nerissa and her brother into the rear of the blue jeep. Then they'd slammed the doors on them.

At this point, Jazmin had stepped forward. She wanted to tell her mum where she'd been, and what had happened to her over the past twenty-four hours. She hoped this would get Nerissa into even more trouble. And it might stop her mum freaking about the taser. But her mum was far too busy with the take-down to pay her any attention. Jazmin had tried explaining things, but her mum had merely waved her away, saying they'd talk later after work. Then she had told Jazmin to get back to the learning centre quick smart. After that, she and Mbeki had leaped into the front of the jeep and driven off at high speed, leaving Jazmin standing in the driveway, staring after them with a look of bewildered astonishment.

Still, the expression on Nerissa Cole's face had definitely made up for being ignored and abandoned, Jazmin thought, her lips curving into a smile. Nerissa's perfectly plucked eyebrows had practically disappeared into her bleach-blonde hairline when she'd spotted Jazmin standing innocently by the jeep. Her mouth had opened and closed like a stranded cod. It had been a shining moment! Jazmin simply couldn't resist giving her a jaunty little finger-wave as the blue jeep roared out of the gate, spitting gravel in its wake.

But that was then, and now here she was, damp and hungry, and approaching the hated learning centre. Bummer. Jazmin checked her watch. Well, unh – would you look at the time? There were only twenty minutes of class left. Was it really worth going in? She wasn't going to learn anything much. And now she came to think of it, she was feeling rather dizzy, because she hadn't eaten for ages, so she probably wouldn't be able to concentrate anyway. She decided to head for home. Home: the place where her fridge was. Another missed school day could always be put down to her chronic Attendance Deficit Disorder.

Head averted, Jazmin walked quickly past the learning centre. She wished she'd got her micro with her, but it was still locked away somewhere in the Wellness Centre. She missed her micro. Without it, she felt almost naked. If she had got her micro, she could text Zeb and tell him what had been happening to her. Jazmin couldn't imagine how he'd react to her news. Although, actually, thinking about it, she *could* guess pretty well how he'd react. "You've missed biology," he'd say. Closely followed by: "Luckily, I copied down the homework for you."

Jazmin sighed. Duh – what was with everybody? She had been locked up and threatened. Then she'd applied her philosophical knowledge to make a brilliantly spectacular escape (who'd have ever thought that boring class would come in useful after all?) and ended up helping to apprehend a nasty villain. She had actually lived out her fantasy, morphing into Jaz Dawson, the brave superheroine of her imagination. But at the end of the day, what was the point of achieving superheroineness, she thought gloomily, if there was nobody around to bask in her glory?

A COUPLE OF HOURS LATER, ASSIA WAS HURRYING BACK TO THE APARTMENT. SHE HAD LEFT MBEKI TO CONTINUE QUESTIONING THE COLES ON HIS OWN. AFTER ALL, AT THE END OF THE DAY, IT WAS his case. She had something even more important to deal with. In all the excitement of the past few hours, Jazmin had somehow got pushed to the back of her mind. However, words like "kidnapped" and "locked up" kept floating to the surface of her subconscious. Now, Assia felt an overwhelming urge to be with her daughter, and find out exactly what had been happening to her.

IT WAS THE FOLLOWING EVENING. THE LOCATION: A SMART ITALIAN RESTAURANT IN SOHO. CANDLES FLICKERED IN SMALL GLASS BOWLS, THEIR SOFT LIGHT REFLECTING OFF THE SHINY SILVERWARE. Jazmin finished her drink. A waiter glided over and discreetly refilled her glass. She glanced across the restaurant table at her two dining companions. "This is really good," she remarked.

"Glad you're enjoying it," Mbeki said.

Jazmin placed her knife and fork together on her empty plate. The waiter hovering at her shoulder quietly removed it. "You know what? I can't get my head around that Professor Cole selling drugs! What a total creep."

"That's certainly one way of describing him," Assia said drily. "The police have raided a lock-up he rented, and found boxes of tablets all neatly stacked up waiting to be sold on the streets, so the evidence against him is incontrovertible. Interestingly, it was his sister who told us about it. In the end, she was quite happy to betray him. Similarly, he was only too eager to tell us all about her. So much for family loyalty. But that wasn't all we found out," she went on.

"That's right," Mbeki took up the story, "it's like this: everything has a front and a back. Normally, they're of equal size. With NovaChem, however, the back was much bigger than the front. Once the Coles started talking, it rapidly became clear what they were up to. NovaChem was a middle-sized company selling into the lucrative "lifestyle drug" market. But behind that, brother and sister were running a huge counterfeit drug business. Cole was copying tablets and pills, and storing them in an annexe at the clinic. His sister then arranged for the copies to be sold to clinics in the developing world and over the internet. They were making millions."

"Wow," Jazmin breathed. "And Cole was the man who attacked you?"

Mbeki nodded. "He tried to deny it at first, but the fact that he recognized me in the car park was a bit of a giveaway."

"Hey, good thing I was there to help you out," Jazmin said.

Her mum cut her a look.

"The police also found a black Hummer H6 in Cole's lock-up," Mbeki said, "so we think he was the person who trashed your mum's car."

"So what's going to happen to the Coles now?" Jazmin asked.

"That's for the police to decide," Assia said. "They're taking over the investigation now. And hopefully, some of the relatives of those who took the drug will consider bringing a class action against NovaChem, and put it out of business."

"Nice one."

Two waiters approached their table, wheeling a trolley laden with desserts. Jazmin's face lit up. "Whoa, I think I could get used to this," she sighed rapturously.

"I hope not," Assia muttered under her breath.

Mbeki smiled. "Enjoy yourself, Jazmin. It's my treat," he said. "I owe you both so much. I'd never have found out how Blair died without your help."

"Hey, anytime, no problem," Jazmin told him.

Mbeki laughed and exchanged a quick complicit glance across the table with Assia.

Assia rolled her eyes skywards.

Jazmin turned her attention back to the dessert trolley. "Yum, it all looks so good. I can't make up my mind between the cheesecake or the profiteroles."

"Why not have both?" Mbeki advised. "After everything you've been through, I guess you deserve it."

Jazmin grinned. "You know what? I think you are right," she said. And she signalled to the waiter to fill her plate.

NEXT MORNING, JAZMIN WOKE EARLY. SUNLIGHT FLOODED THROUGH HER BEDROOM WINDOW. SHE STRETCHED LUXURIOUSLY. THERE WAS NOTHING TO BEAT THAT "END-OF-A-SUCCESSFUL-MISSION" feeling. It was like being bathed in sunshine on the inside.

She rolled back the duvet and got up. Today she and her mum were taking Mbeki to the airport. She was looking forward to it. Okay, not the "goodbye" part: goodbyes were always sad, but airports were great places to scope out – so many strangers, so many mysteries. She showered, dressed and went in search of breakfast.

Entering the kitchen, Jazmin spotted a small parcel by her plate. She eyed it curiously.

"What's that?"

"It's something for you; it came via a courier this morning," Assia said, as Jazmin picked up the parcel and shook it gently to see if it rattled.

Jazmin tore off the brown outer wrapping. Inside, a blue and white bead-braided friendship bracelet lay on a bed of pale-pink tissue paper. Underneath the bracelet was an address card and a folded note. She opened the note and read:

Hi Jazmin,

I guess you've heard that I'm living with my mum now. It's so the best thing that has ever happened to me!! Sorry for not contacting you before I left London – I threw my micro at Nerissa and it broke! Anyway, all that's history. I've started at junior high school here and made some new friends already. Nobody as kind as you, though. I'm sending you a present to say thank you for being there for me. I'll never forget you. Let's stay in touch, shall we?

Ginevra X

P.S. Hope the date went well. Lucky you!

"Everything all right?" her mum asked, placing some hot toast on Jazmin's plate.

Jazmin slipped the bead bracelet onto her wrist. "Everything's just peachy," she said, smiling as she picked up her knife and reached for the butter.

SOMETIME LATER, JAZMIN STOOD BY THE AIRPORT BOOK STALL. SHE FLICKED THROUGH THE LATEST BIG BLOCKBUSTER NOVEL, PRETENDING TO BE ENGROSSED IN IT. IN REALITY, SHE WAS GIVING her mum and Chris Mbeki a last chance to get couply before he flew back to the States. She peered round the carousel. Unh. They were still sitting drinking coffee and talking. How boring was that?

A voice on the tannoy announced the final call for the flight to JFK. Jazmin put down the book and strolled across the concourse.

"There you are, hon," Assia said, looking up at her brightly.

"Yup, here I am," Jazmin agreed.

Mbeki rose, and began collecting his hand luggage. "Hey, good timing," he told her. "I couldn't leave without saying goodbye to a future top secret agent!"

"Really?" Jazmin beamed. "You reckon?"

Mbeki gave her a hug. "I reckon," he said.

Jazmin watched Chris Mbeki striding purposefully towards the departure gate. At the barrier, he turned to look back at them. She waved. Mbeki blew her a kiss. He gave Assia a heart-melting smile. Then he walked through the barrier, and was gone.

Jazmin sighed. "Whoa, I really liked him," she said.

Assia nodded. "Me too."

Jazmin shot her a sly glance. "Do you think you two might have a future?"

Assia smiled. "Nice idea, hon, but there are... complications," she said diplomatically. Then, seeing Jazmin's crestfallen expression, she added, "And anyway, right now, the future's so far in the future that I can't visualize it."

They lingered in the departure lounge, waiting until the flight number disappeared from the board. When it had gone, Assia turned and looked at her daughter. "Well, that's that," she said. "What would you like to do now?"

Jazmin thought hard for a bit. "How about if we go and buy me a new micro?" she suggested. "It might help me recover from the terrible trauma I've been through," she added, lowering her voice for suitably dramatic effect.

Assia's mouth twitched. "Yes, we could do that."

"A red one would be nice."

"Right. Red it is."

"And then, why don't we drive back home, and make ourselves a special lunch."

"Anything in mind?"

"Lasagne, with a mixed salad and blue-cheese dressing. Followed by double-crust apple pie and organic vanilla ice cream for dessert."

Assia laughed. "That sounds very good to me," she said. Linking her arm through her daughter's, they began to walk towards the exit. "And later, maybe we ought to go through my wardrobe together. I think it's high time I had a complete makeover, don't you?"

"Hey, no more boring colours?"

"Boring colours are history."

Jazmin expelled air. "It looks like we've got a lot to do."

Assia pushed open the heavy glass door that led to the outside world. "We'd better get on with it then," she said.

ABOUT THE AUTHOR

Carol Hedges is the successful author of several books for children and teenagers. Her writing has received much critical acclaim and her novel, *Jigsaw*, was shortlisted for the Angus Book Award and longlisted for the Carnegie Medal.

Carol has one grown-up daughter and lives in Hertfordshire with her husband, two cats and a lot of fish.

The Dark Side of Midnight

Jazmin Dawson is a super-cool secret agent with hi-tech kit and a hi-octane life of crime-busting...in her dreams! In reality, Jazmin is a schoolgirl with a serious snack habit, whose biggest battles are with her maths homework.

But then everything changes. Jazmin's mum, who *is* a spy, goes missing and Jazmin is sent to rescue her. Stepping off the plane in Prague, Jazmin finds herself at the centre of an international mystery, and with a dangerous mission to infiltrate a rogue scientific institute.

"An action-packed page-turner with a heart."

Books For Keeps

ISBN 9780746067505

Out of the Shadows

Smart-talking, super-stylish crime fighter Jazmin Dawson is back to save the world from evil... Well, one day maybe. Right now, Jazmin's toughest challenges are dealing with the girl gang at school and fighting her way to the cookie counter.

Then her secret-agent mum sets her a mission, and Jazmin ditches her homework to befriend a crucial witness in a case of international identity theft. But when the witness vanishes, Jazmin is pitted against powerful enemies in the race to find him.

"The secret agent with attitude!" *Mizz*

ISBN 9780746070833

Dead Man Talking

Jazmin Dawson, Spy Girl, is back – just in time to save the world, again. Well, not quite. But Jazmin does have a two-cookie problem on her hands, what with looking after the new weird twins at her learning centre, and the fact she's Enemy Number One with the class bully.

Jazmin's secret-agent mum, Assia, also has problems, trying to identify a murdered man. When the trail leads to a long-buried secret, Assia is forced to confront a man more evil than she could ever imagine. The trouble is, Jazmin has got there first.

"Top stuff that is not afraid to talk intelligently to its readership."   *Telegraph*

ISBN 9780746078341

For more thrilling reads check out
www.usborne.com/fiction

Paula Rawsthorne

The Truth About Celia Frost

CELIA FROST IS A FREAK.

At least that's what everyone thinks. Her life is ruled by a rare disorder that means she could bleed to death from the slightest cut, confining her to a gloomy bubble of "safety". No friends. No fun. No life.

But when a knife attack on Celia has unexpected consequences, her mum reacts strangely – and suddenly they're on the run. Why is her mum so scared? Someone out there knows. And when they find Celia, she's going to wish the truth was a lie...

A buried secret, a gripping manhunt, a dangerous deceit... What is the truth about Celia Frost?

"Nail-biting and thought-provoking." *The Bookseller*

ISBN: 9781409531098
EPUB: 9781409537663 / KINDLE: 9781409531098

Paula Rawsthorne

Blood Tracks

GINA WILSON IS ON THE EDGE...

Her dad died in mysterious consequences, and she is the only one convinced that something isn't right. As she struggles to find the truth, Gina is plunged into a world far removed from the one she has known – a world of lies, crime and betrayal.

A world she can't run from...

A dark and dangerous thriller with a harrowing secret at its heart, from the author of the award-winning The Truth About Celia Frost.

"A psychological thriller, packed with mystery."
Lovereading4kids.co.uk

ISBN: 9781409532156
EPUB: 9781409541752 / KINDLE: 9781409541769

Jack Heath

Money Run

WHAT WOULD YOU DO FOR $200 MILLION?

Would you break into a billionaire businessman's
top-security skyscraper?

Would you drive a priceless sports car off the roof?

Would you fly a helicopter with only a handbook
to guide you?

Would you take on an unstoppable hitman intent
on your destruction?

For teen thieves Ash and Benjamin, it's a no-brainer...

**MONEY RUN is a high-octane thriller, starring two
unlikely heroes with a dangerous appetite for
adventure...and big stacks of cash.**

ISBN: 9781409531081
EPUB: 9781409538523 / KINDLE: 9781409538530

Tim Wynne-Jones

The Boy in the Burning House

Jim doesn't want to believe that his missing father has been murdered but Ruth Rose is determined to help him root out the truth – no matter how painful or dangerous it is.

"This classy teenage thriller really gets the heart pumping... Phew – it's hot!" *The Funday Times*

Shortlisted for the Guardian Children's Fiction Prize 2005

9780746064818

The Survival Game

When Burl runs away into the Canadian wilderness, he must find a way to survive and escape his bullying father's dangerous games for good.

"Just about everything you could possibly want from a book." *Publishing News*

Winner of the Canada Council Governor General's Literary Award

9780746068410

Jack Heath

Hit List

HOW DO YOU BEAT THE DEADLIEST ASSASSIN IN THE WORLD?

And a gang of murderous mercenaires...

And a thief who can walk through walls...

And a detective with a grudge...

...when they all want to destroy you?

Teen thieves Ash and Benjamin are suddenly top of everyone's hit list. And when you're about to break into the largest intelligence agency in the world to rescue a mysterious stranger, that's a seriously dangerous place to be.

"Gripping to the final page. Perfect for fans of Anthony Horowitz." *The Sun Herald*

ISBN: 9781409531104

EPUB: 9781409541714 / KINDLE: 9781409541721